John Torrey Morse

John Adams

John Torrey Morse

John Adams

ISBN/EAN: 9783337400620

Printed in Europe, USA, Canada, Australia, Japan

Cover: Foto ©Andreas Hilbeck / pixelio.de

More available books at **www.hansebooks.com**

American Statesmen

JOHN ADAMS

BY

JOHN T. MORSE, JR.

BOSTON AND NEW YORK
HOUGHTON, MIFFLIN AND COMPANY
The Riverside Press, Cambridge
M DCCC XCVIII

EDITOR'S INTRODUCTION

FOLLOWING the Revolutionary Period of our history came what may be designated as the Constructive Period. The second group of biographies in the present series deals with that epoch, and includes John Adams, Alexander Hamilton, Gouverneur Morris, John Jay, and John Marshall.

On the 19th day of October, 1781, Lord Cornwallis surrendered. As a consequence, Great Britain, after fifteen months of delay and much unworthy caviling, brought herself to admit explicitly in a treaty of peace the independence of her ex-colonies. Yet though warfare was over, this was by no means the reaching of an end on the part of the emancipated States; on the contrary, they had not even made a beginning; they had rendered it possible, but as yet this was all. It was on September 3, 1783, that our commissioners set their signatures to the definitive treaty. It was not until the autumn of 1788 that the Constitution, which really created the national unit, the United States, was adopted. It was not until the end of March, 1789, that Washington took the oath of office, and it was already April when enough delegates had at last come together to admit the organization of Congress. The intervening years, filled with anxious and bitter experiences, have never formed an attractive subject of study. No great name is connected with them, and they are always hastily passed over in order to come to the Constitutional Convention. That the Constitution was framed and accepted is among the wonders of the world's history. The convention *adopted*, but never *agreed;* and when the instrument was referred to the several States, many delegates in the state conventions gave yea votes without faith. One would fancy a Destiny at work to bring such a result out of such conditions. Able men were in the ranks of the opponents of ratification, but the end of the business left them with the character of obstructionists. Therefore with them this series has no concern, save only so far as Patrick Henry had previously earned his place in our list. That patriot seems unfortunately, in these days of a new crisis, to have lost the clear foresight, the prophetic instinct of his earlier years, and he led the fight in Virginia against ratification with a vehement ardor that was very dangerous.

The men who first devised the Constitution and then made it operative, — who invented our governmental machine, and who then set it at work and ran it successfully until it ceased to be regarded as a dubious experiment, — these are the subjects of the second group of biographies in this series. Washington was chosen to preside over the convention. He had lately proved, though the fact is only of late becoming fully appreciated, that he was a great military genius. He was now about to show a not less distinguished ability in civil government. It has been a serious misfortune for Washington that he possessed so high a character, that he was endowed with such various capacities, and that he had such a power to succeed, and always honorably. Much namby-pamby moralizing, much pompous laudation, have tempted cheap wit, in reaction, to hack clumsily on his memory. Twaddle and jesting concerning him are offenses which certain classes of persons can never be prevented from committing. But his reputation cannot be seriously affected by either of these forms of misfortune, and he is sure to take permanent rank among the grandest and noblest of the heroes of all mankind. In the position of president of the convention he joined little in debate, but he exerted a great influence towards agreement.   Franklin also brought to the discussions the wisdom of his many years; and it is singular that the aged man espoused the most advanced theories of government; he was so much a believer in a decentralized government and in control by the mass of the people, that there can be no doubt that a little later on he would have stood among the Jeffersonians.   Hamilton is commonly supposed to have exerted a powerful influence on the other side.   But his scheme, which would have created a strong centralized government, was rejected. Gouverneur Morris was the chief spokesman of this school, constantly on his feet, and arguing in a very forcible style.   Madison, however, always has been, and probably always will be, regarded as coming nearer than any other member to the position of leader and creator.   It is noteworthy that John Adams, who had made a thorough study of theories of government, and Jefferson, who had a natural taste and capacity for such speculation, were both in Europe at this time.   Neither was Jay a member of the convention, though afterward he aided Hamilton and Madison in writing those famous papers of "The Federalist," which undoubtedly induced the acceptance of the great national charter.

Washington, of course, was the first President, hardly less essential now than he had been in the Revolution. He had the advantage, never afterward possible, of being not only the choice of the people, but properly the chief magistrate of the nation as a political unit. No parties were yet formed; for the opponents of the Constitution were no longer a party after the Constitution had been adopted. The first President, therefore, had an opportunity such as could never come to any successor, in that he was free to form a cabinet of men who differed widely in their intellectual tendencies and their political faiths. The hope was that such a body might tend to harmonize and unite the leaders of opposing schools of political thought; but when the opposition was based on the fundamental moral and mental make-up of the men, it was idle to expect such a result, and the failure was soon apparent. It seems droll, not to say absurd, now to think of Hamilton and Jefferson as coadjutors. None the less the experiment was entered upon with much sincerity of hope in its success. Of course it never had the slightest chance; the two men never collaborated heartily, never liked or trusted each other, and could not long work in an even ostensible harmony. It was very simple-minded, or, we may say, politically unsophisticated ever to have anticipated a different result, for the practical questions of government inevitably evoked opposing opinions from men who differed by their implanted natures. Thus it came about at last that Washington, much to his disappointment, was obliged to give up his effort to hold together men who were preordained to disagree and in common honesty were obliged to quarrel. In the clashing which ensued, and which of course soon created partisanship, Washington would never admit that he was a party man. Yet it is clear that he became so in fact, though refusing the name. The Federalist measures generally seemed to him right; the broad Federalist policy he undoubtedly esteemed sound; the Federalist statesmen had his sympathetic confidence.

Of these Federalist statesmen, Hamilton was always the chief. An unusually large proportion of the men prominent in this party possessed great capacity for public affairs, yet they all deferred to him; they submitted to his control and accepted his policy without a serious question or a murmur loud enough to be audible. The impress of strength which he left upon the government has ever since remained. Indeed, if it had not remained, it may be doubted whether the government itself could have survived. As secretary of the treasury he showed extraordinary ability in rehabilitating the embarrassed nation, and no list of the great financiers of the world can be made so short that his name does not stand in it, and in a high place too. But there was more than financial purpose in his arrangement of the national debt and the state debts and in his general organization of the national revenue and money matters. There was the policy so to construe the new Constitution, as yet unconstrued, that upon it there could be based a powerful centralized government. Jefferson saw, appreciated, and opposed; but in vain. For Washington leaned towards Hamiltonian views, and that turned the scale for eight years. After that time it was too late to go back to the starting point for the purpose of moving along another road.

Hamilton was to the Federalist party what the brain is to the body. But he was absolutely unavailable as a candidate for the presidency. It is odd to see how generally, though tacitly, this fact was acknowledged. With him out of the competition, it was natural that John Adams should succeed Washington. If Adams's character had been as well understood by contemporaries as it is by later generations, it would also have been seen to be certain that no Federalist would succeed him. He had a genius for embroilment. All his life long, wherever he was, there were anger and fighting and personal enmities. Accordingly it came to pass that, as president, he soon had the Federalist party by the ears, and at the end of his four years he left it a disintegrated aggregation of discordant individuals, utterly incapable of political cohesion or personal loyalty. I have said, in my Life of him, that in my opinion he was right in the most important act of his administration, and in that which wrecked his party. But if so, he was, at least for his party and for himself with it, fatally right. One of his last acts, however, made up for the earlier blows which he had dealt to Federalism, and turned out to be of far-reaching importance. This was the appointment of John Marshall to be chief justice of the United States. Presidents and cabinet ministers might inaugurate policies, congressional leaders might carry bills to enactment, but ultimately the Supreme Court gave or refused the seal of constitutionality. The commanding influence of Marshall meant that Federalist theories were to be the accepted basis of judicial decisions. This appointment therefore insured the permanence of the Federalist work. Twelve years had seen the task of national construction very thoroughly accomplished; Marshall was now left in charge of it, to see that it should take no detriment from those who had regarded it with jealous disfavor, and who were now about to come into power.

JOHN T. MORSE, JR.

September, 1898.

PREFACE

THE liberality with which the Adams family
has emptied for the public use its abundant
stores of manuscripts would make it unreason-
able to hope that they have yet more to give
out concerning John Adams. Indeed, the latest
ransackings in many private hoards throughout
the country have probably been nearly or quite
exhaustive of all contemporary documents of
substantial value relating to the Revolution and
the three first presidencies. If this is the case,
biographical writing for that period must in
future consist simply of new portraits of the
several personages; and the memoirist will no
longer be able to promise to unfold facts which
have lain unknown until he has the privilege of
disclosing them. The usefulness and the interest of his work will therefore consist in the
faithfulness and skill with which he reproduces
the traits of his hero.

Such was already the condition of things when
this Life of Adams was written. Nothing has
since found its way into print which adds to the

facts which were then known, or which places
those facts in a fresh light, or makes them links
in any new chain of historical or political argument. In re-reading my presentation of Mr.
Adams's character, I see no change which I
wish to make therein. I think of him now as
I thought of him then. But there is one chapter some parts of which, not directly relating to
Mr. Adams, no longer seem to me altogether
satisfactory. The strictures which I have made
upon Franklin during the period of his stay in
France, especially while Mr. Adams was with
him, are unjust in their severity, and give a
false idea of the true usefulness of that able
diplomatist at that time. I have become convinced of this error upon my part by subsequent
much more careful and thorough study than I
had made, at the time of writing this volume,
concerning the facts of Franklin's mission. At
first, in making this revision, my impulse was to
correct the defect by alterations; but I soon
found that nothing short of a complete re-writ-
ing would suffice, and to this course there were
objections. It was not my business to introduce
a new book into the series. Moreover, there is
sound reason for letting the matter stand as it
was first written, though I no longer wholly
approve of it; for it is a fair presentation of

the view held by John Adams himself, and
which was often and vigorously expressed by
him.   The only fault that he would find with it
would be that it is altogether too mild in its
fault-finding.   Adams was a contemporary and
competent witness, and the trouble about his
testimony lies not in his lack of knowledge, but
in his own temperament.   This, indeed, made
his deposition very untrustworthy.   Yet in a
Life of him his opinions and beliefs ought to
find expression ; there is a *possibility*, however
remote, that they were well founded.   He would
rebel, in his grave, if his biographer should dare
to vindicate Franklin's career in France; and
really it would hardly be fair to use this volume
for that purpose.   So I am content only to file
this *caveat*, the more so, because the antidote
for the errors is close at hand, in the Life of
Franklin, in this series.

JOHN T. MORSE, JR.

January, 1898.

CONTENTS

ILLUSTRATIONS

The figures from the left of the picture to the right are Jay, Adams, Franklin, Laurens, and Franklin's grandson, William Temple Franklin. Richard Oswald, who died in 1784, was to have been included in the group.

From a painting by Gilbert Stuart, in the collection of Charles Francis Adams, Lincoln, Mass.

Autograph from a letter in possession of Winslow Warren, written from Quincy, July 16, 1773, to Mrs. Mercy Warren of Plymouth.

JOHN ADAMS

CHAPTER I

YOUTH

In the first charter of the colony of Massachusetts Bay, granted by Charles I. and dated March 4, 1629, the name of Thomas Adams appears as one of the grantees. But he never crossed the Atlantic, and Henry Adams, possibly though not certainly his younger brother, first bore the name on this side of the water. In 1636 this Henry was one of the grantees of sundry parcels of land at Mount Wollaston, soon afterward made the town of Braintree, in which neighborhood descendants from him have continued to have dwellings and to own extensive tracts of land to the present day. The John Adams with whom we have to do was of the fourth generation in descent from Henry, and was born at Braintree, October 19, 1735. His father was also named John Adams; his mother was Susanna Boylston, daughter of Peter Boylston, of the neighboring town of Brookline.

The founder of the American family apparently could do little better for himself than simply to hold his own in the desperate struggle for existence amid sterile hills and hostile Indians. At his death he left, as his whole estate, a small bit of land, of which there was no dearth on the new continent, a house of three rooms, and a barn: in the house there were three beds, some kitchen utensils, a silver spoon, and a few old books; in the barn were a cow and calf, pigs, and a little fodder. The whole property was valued at £75 13*s*. Little by little, however, the sturdy workers in successive years wrenched increased belongings from the reluctant soil; so that the inventory of the estate of our John Adams's father, who died in 1760, shows £1,330 9*s*. 8*d*.

A man so well-to-do as this could afford to give one son a good education, and John Adams, being the eldest, had the advantage of going through Harvard College. Such was the privilege, the only privilege, with which primogeniture was invested by the custom of the family. Indeed, our John Adams's grandfather, who also had educated his eldest son at college, afterward divided his property among his other children, thinking that thus he made matters as nearly equal and fair between them all as was possible. John Adams was graduated in the class of 1755, which, as his son tells us, "in proportion to its numbers contained as many men afterwards eminent in the civil and ecclesiastical departments as any class that ever was graduated at that institution." He was reputed to be a very good scholar, but cannot be accurately compared with his comrades, since rank was not then given for scholarship. The students took precedence according to the social standing of their parents, and upon such a scale the Adams family were a trifle nearer to the bottom than to the top. In a class of twenty-four members John was fourteenth, and even for this modest station "he was probably indebted rather to the standing of his maternal family than to that of his father." John Quincy Adams very frankly says that in those days "the effect of a college education was to introduce a youth of the condition of John Adams into a different class of familiar acquaintance from that of his father." Later in life John Adams became noted as an aristocrat, and incurred not a little ridicule and animosity through his proclivities and personal pretensions of this kind. In fact, he was that peculiar production of American domestic manufacture which may perhaps be properly described as a self-made aristocrat, — a character familiar enough on this side of the Atlantic, but which

Lord Thurlow almost alone could bring within the comprehension of Englishmen. Fortunately, in Adams's individual case, his ability to maintain the position prevented his passion from appearing so comical as the like feeling so often does with inferior men. Nor indeed was he always and altogether devoid of sound sense in this respect; he wrote in 1791 that, if he could ever suppose family pride to be any way excusable, he should "think a descent from a line of virtuous, independent New England farmers for a hundred and sixty years was a better foundation for it than a descent from regal or noble scoundrels ever since the flood." The truth is that a proper pride in one's own descent, if it can be sustained, is neither an unamiable nor a mischief-working trait; Adams had it in the true American shape, and was influenced by it only in the direction of good. He was at once gratified and satisfied with having a lineage simply respectable.

The boyhood and youth of John Adams are incumbered with none of those tedious apocrypha which constitute a prophetic atmosphere in the initial chapter of most biographies. No one ever dreamed that he was to be a great man until he was well advanced in middle age, and even then, in the estimation of all persons save himself, he had many peers and perhaps a very few superiors.   As " the fourth Harry, our King " philosophically remarked, upon hearing of " Lord Perse's " death at Otterburn,

"I have a hondrith captains in Inglande, he sayd,
    As good as ever was hee ; "

though, probably enough, Percy's valuation of himself was different.   Pretty much the first authentic knowledge which we get of John Adams comes from his own pen.   On November 15, 1755, just after his twentieth birthday, he began a diary.   Intermittently, suffering many serious breaks provokingly to diminish its just value, he continued it until November 21, 1777. Only a few years more elapsed before the famous diary of his son, John Quincy Adams, was begun, which ran through its remarkable course until 1848 ; and it is said that a similar work has been done in the third generation. If this be so, much more than one hundred years of American annals will be illuminated by the memorials of this one family in a manner unprecedented in history and equally useful and agreeable.   So portentous a habit of diary-writing is an odd form for the development of heredity.   But at least it enables historical students to observe the descent of traits of mind and character more naturally transmissible than such a taste.   The Adams blood was strong blood, — too strong to be seriously modified by alien strains introduced by marriage. It was not a picturesque stream, but it was vigorous, it cut its way without much loitering or meandering, and when strange rivulets united with it they had to take its color as well as its course. John Quincy Adams, whose story has been told before that of his father in this series, was a veritable chip from the old block, a sturdy, close-fibred old block, well adapted for making just such solid, slightly cross-grained chips. Only the son was more civilized, or rather more self-restrained and conventional, than the father; the ruggedness of the earlier fighter and self-made man was rubbed smoother in the offspring, inheriting greatness and growing up amid more polishing forces.

In youth John Adams was an admirable specimen of the New England Puritan of his generation, not excessively strait-laced in matters of doctrine, but religious by habit and by instinct, rigid in every point of morals, conscientious, upright, pure-minded, industrious. The real truth about that singular community is that they mingled theology with loose morals in a proportion not correctly appreciated by their descendants; for historians have dwelt upon the one ingredient of this mixture, and have ignored the other, so that the truth has become obscured. Certain it is that long ser-

mons and much polemical controversy were offset by a great deal of hard drinking and not a
little indulgence in carnal sins. John Adams,
like the better men of the day, reversed the proportions, and instead of subordinating morality
to religion, he gave to morals a decided preponderance. In his diary he grumbles not only at
others, but also very freely at himself, partly
because it was then his nature always to grum-
ble a good deal about everything and everybody, partly to fulfill the acknowledged Christian duty of self-abasement. He had an early
tendency to censoriousness, not to be compared
in degree to that development of this failing
which disfigured his son, but furnishing a strong
germ for the later growth. While passing
through periods of discontent, which occasionally beset his opening manhood, his deprecia-
tory habit was too strong to be checked even
in his own case, and he constantly falls his
own victim, beneath his passion for uncharita-
ble criticism. Also like his son, though more
intermittently and in a less degree, he is possessed of the devil of suspiciousness, constantly
conceiving himself to be the object of limitless
envy, malice, hostility, and of the most ignoble
undermining processes. As a young man he
often imagined that his neighbors and acquaint-
ances were resolved that he should not get on

in the world, though it does not appear that he encountered any peculiar or exceptional obstacles of this kind. But to his credit it may be noted that in his early years he had a knowledge of these weaknesses of his disposition. He wishes that he could conquer his "natural pride and self-conceit; expect no more deference from my fellows than I deserve; acquire meekness and humility," etc. He acknowledges having been too ready with "ill-natured remarks upon the intellectuals, manners, practice, etc., of other people." He wisely resolves, "for the future, never to say an ill-natured thing concerning ministers or the ministerial profession; never to say an envious thing concerning governors, judges, clerks, sheriffs, lawyers, or any other honorable or lucrative offices or officers; never to show my own importance or superiority by remarking the foibles, vices, or inferiority of others. But I now resolve, as far as lies in me, to take notice chiefly of the amiable qualities of other people; to put the most favorable construction upon the weaknesses, bigotry, and errors of others, etc.; and to labor more for an inoffensive and amiable than for a shining and invidious character," — most wise communings, showing an admirable introspection, yet resolves which could not at present be consistently carried out by their maker. Adams's nature, both in its good and in its ill traits, was far too strong to be greatly re-shaped by any efforts which he could make. The elements of his powerful character were immutable, and underwent no substantial and permanent modifications either through voluntary effort or by the pressure of circumstances; in all important points he was the same from the cradle to the grave, with perhaps a brief exception during the earlier period of his service in the Revolutionary Congress, when we shall see him rising superior to all his foibles, and presenting a wonderfully noble appearance. The overweening vanity, which became a ridiculous disfigurement after he had climbed high upon the ladder of distinction, was not yet excessive while he still lingered upon the first rounds. Indeed, he is shrewd enough to say: " Vanity, I am sensible, is my cardinal vice and cardinal folly; " and he even has occasional fits of genuine diffidence of his own powers, and distrust as to his prospects of moderate success. Only when that success actually came did all chance of curing himself of the fault disappear. As a young man he cherished no lofty ambition, or at least he kept it modestly in the background. He does not at all resemble his rival of later years, Alexander Hamilton; he is conscious of no extraordinary ability, and longs for no remarkable career, nor asserts any fitness for it. His anticipations, even his hopes, seem limited to achieving that measure of prosperity, good repute, and influence which attend upon the more prominent men of any neighborhood. A circuit of forty miles around Boston is a large enough sphere, beyond which his dreams of the future do not wander.

A youth who had received a collegiate education, at a cost of not inconsiderable sacrifice on the part of his parents, lay in those days under a sort of moral obligation to adopt a profession. Between law, divinity, and medicine, therefore, Adams had to make his choice. Further, while contemplating the subject and preparing himself for one of these pursuits he ought to support himself. To this end he obtained the position of master of the grammar school at Worcester, whither he repaired in the summer of 1755. His first tendency was to become a clergyman, not so much, apparently, by reason of any strong fancy for the clerical calling as because there seems to have been a sort of understanding on the part of his family and friends that he should make this selection, and he was willing enough to gratify them. It was not altogether so singular and foolish a notion as at first it strikes us. The New England clergy still retained much of the prestige and influence which they had enjoyed in the earlier colonial days, when they had exercised a civil authority often overshadowing that of the nominal officers of government. Men of great ability and strong character still found room for their aspirations in the ministry. They were a set to be respected, obeyed, even to some extent to be feared, but hardly to be loved, and vastly unlike the Christian minister of the present day. They were not required to be sweet-tempered, nor addicted to loving-kindness, nor to be charitably disposed towards one another, or indeed towards anybody. On the contrary, they were a dictatorial, militant, polemical, not to say a quarrelsome and harsh-tongued race. They were permitted, and even encouraged, to display much vigor in speech and action. Nevertheless the figure of impetuous, dogmatic, combative, opinionated, energetic, practical, and withal liberal John Adams in a pulpit is exceedingly droll. He was much too big, too enterprising, too masterful, for such a cage. He would have resembled the wolf of the story, who could never keep himself wholly covered by the old dame's cloak. His irrepressibly secular nature would have been constantly protruding at one point or another from beneath the clerical raiment. It would have been inevitable that sooner or later he should escape altogether from the uncongenial thralldom, at the cost of a more or less serious waste of time and somewhat ridiculous process of change. Fortunately his good sense or sound instinct saved him from a too costly blunder. Yet for many months his diary is sprinkled with remarks concerning the flinty theology and the intense, though very unchristian, Christianity of those days. Nevertheless the truth constantly peeps out; disputatious enough, and severe upon backslidings, he appears not sufficiently narrow in intellect and merciless in disposition; he could not squeeze himself within the rigid confines which hemmed in the local divine. It is to no purpose that he resolves "to rise with the sun and to study the Scriptures on Thursday, Friday, Saturday, and Sunday mornings," and that occasionally he writes "Scripture poetry industriously" of a morning. The effort is too obvious. Yet he was religiously inclined. The great Lisbon earthquake of 1755, which filled Europe with infidels, inspired him with a sense of religious awe. "God Almighty," he says, "has exerted the strength of his tremendous arm, and shook one of the finest, richest, and most populous cities in Europe into ruin and destruction by an earthquake. The greatest part of Europe and the greatest part of America have been in violent convulsions, and admonished the inhabitants of both that neither riches nor honors nor the solid globe itself is a proper

basis on which to build our hopes of security."
The Byronic period of his youth even takes a
religious form.   He gloomily reflects that : —

"One third of our time is consumed in sleep, and
three sevenths of the remainder is spent in procuring
a mere animal sustenance ; and if we live to the age
of threescore and ten, and then sit down to make an
estimate in our minds of the happiness we have enjoyed and the misery we have suffered, we shall find,
I am apt to think, that the overbalance of happiness
is quite inconsiderable. We shall find that we have
been, through the greater part of our lives, pursuing
shadows, and empty but glittering phantoms, rather
than substances. We shall find that we have applied
our whole vigor, all our faculties, in the pursuit of
honor or wealth or learning, or some other such delu-
sive trifle, instead of the real and everlasting excellences of piety and virtue. Habits of contemplating
the Deity and his transcendent excellences, and correspondent habits of complacency in and dependence
upon Him ; habits of reverence and gratitude to God,
and habits of love and compassion to our fellow-men,
and habits of temperance, recollection, and self-govern-
ment, will afford us a real and substantial pleasure.
We may then exult in a consciousness of the favor of
God and the prospect of everlasting felicity."

A young man of twenty who, in our day,
should write in this strain would be thought fit
for nothing better than the church ; but Adams
was really at war with the prevalent church

spirit of New England. Thus one evening in a conversation with Major Greene "about the divinity and satisfaction of Jesus Christ," the major advanced the argument that "a mere creature or finite being could not make satisfaction to infinite justice for any crimes," and suggested that "these things are very mysterious." Adams's crisp commentary was: "Thus mystery is made a convenient cover for absurdity." Again he asks: "Where do we find a precept in the gospel requiring ecclesiastical synods? convocations? councils? decrees? creeds? confessions? oaths? subscriptions? and whole cartloads of other trumpery that we find religion incumbered with in these days?" Independence in thought and expression soon caused him to be charged with the heinous unsoundness of Arminianism, an accusation which he endeavored neither to palliate nor deny, but quite cheerfully admitted. A few such comments, more commerce even with the tiny colonial world around him, a little thinking and discussion upon doctrinal points, sufficed for his shrewd common sense, and satisfied him that he was not fitted to labor in the ministerial vineyard as he saw it platted and walled in. Accordingly, upon August 21, 1756, he definitely renounced the scheme. On the following day he writes gravely in his diary : —

" Yesterday I completed a contract with Mr. Putnam to study law under his inspection for two years. . . . Necessity drove me to this determination, but my inclination, I think, was to preach; however, that would not do. But I set out with firm resolutions, I think, never to commit any meanness or injustice in the practice of law. The study and practice of law, I am sure, does not dissolve the obligations of morality or of religion; and, although the reason of my quitting divinity was my opinion concerning some disputed points, I hope I shall not give reason of offense to any in that profession by imprudent warmth."

Thus fortunately for himself and for the people of the colonies, Adams escaped the first peril which threatened the abridgment of his great usefulness. Yet the choice was not made without opposition from " uncles and other relations, full of the most illiberal prejudices against the law." Adams says that he had " a proper veneration and affection " for these relatives, but that, being " under no obligation of gratitude " to them, he " thought little of their opinions." Young men nowadays are little apt to be controlled by uncles or even aunts in such matters, but John Adams's independence was more characteristic of himself than of those times.

CHAPTER II

On August 23, 1756, Adams says that he
"came to Mr. Putnam's and began law, and
studied not very closely this week." But he
was no sluggard in any respect save that he
was fond of lying abed late of mornings. Jus-
tinian's Institutes with Vinnius's Notes, the
works of Bracton, Britton, Fleta, Glanville,
and all the other ponderous Latin tomes behind which the law of that day lay intrenched,
yielded up their wisdom to his persistency. He
had his hours of relaxation, in which he smoked
his pipe, chatted with Dr. Savil's wife, and read
her Ovid's "Art of Love," a singular volume,
truly, for a young Puritan to read aloud with
a lady! Yet in the main he was a hard student; so that by October, 1758, he was ready to
begin business, and came to Boston to consult
with Jeremiah Gridley, the leader and "father"
of that bar, as to the necessary steps "for an
introduction to the practice of law in this country." Gridley was very kind with the young
man, who seems to have shown upon this occa-

sion a real and becoming bashfulness. Among other pieces of advice, the shrewd old lawyer gave to the youngster these two: first, " to pursue the study of the law rather than the gain of it; pursue the gain of it enough to keep out of the briars, but give your main attention to the study of it;" second, "not to marry early, for an early marriage will obstruct your improvement, and in the next place it will involve you in expense." On Monday, November 6, the same distinguished friend, with a few words of kindly presentation, recommended Adams to the court for the oath. This formality being satisfactorily concluded, says Adams, "I shook hands with the bar, and received their congratulations, and invited them over to Stone's to drink some punch, where the most of us resorted and had a very cheerful chat." Through this alcoholic christening the neophyte was introduced into the full communion of the brethren, and thereafter it only remained for him to secure clients. He had not to wait quite so long for these trailing-footed gentry as is often the wearisome lot of young lawyers; for the colonists were a singularly litigious race, suing out writs upon provocations which in these good-natured days would hardly be thought to justify hard words, unconsciously training that contradictory and law-loving temper which really went far to

bring about the quarrels with Parliament, so
soon to occur. Fees were small, mercifully
adapted not to discourage the poorest client,
so that the man who could not afford "to take
the law" might as well at once seek the tranquil shelter of the "town farm." Accordingly,
though Adams was anxious and occasionally
dispirited, he seems to have done very well.

He had many admirable qualifications for
success, of which by no means the least was his
firm resolution to succeed; for throughout his
life any resolution which he seriously made was
pretty sure to be carried through. He was, of
course, honest, trustworthy, and industrious; he
exacted of himself the highest degree of care
and skill; he cultivated as well as he could
the slender stock of tact with which nature had
scantily endowed him; more useful traits, not
needing cultivation, were a stubbornness and
combativeness which made him a hard man to
beat at the bar as afterwards in political life.
In a word, he was sure to get clients, and soon
did so. He followed the first part of Gridley's
advice to such good purpose that he afterwards
said: "I believe no lawyer in America ever did
so much business as I did afterwards, in the
seventeen years that I passed in the practice
at the bar, for so little profit." Yet this
"little profit" was enough to enable him to

treat more lightly Gridley's second item, for on October 25, 1764, he took to himself a wife. The lady was Abigail Smith, daughter of William Smith, a clergyman in the neighboring town of Weymouth, and of his wife, Elizabeth (Quincy) Smith. But the matrimonial venture was far from proving an "obstruction to improvement;" for "by this marriage John Adams became allied with a numerous connection of families, among the most respectable for their weight and influence in the province, and it was immediately perceptible in the considerable increase of his professional practice." In other respects, also, it was a singularly happy union. Mrs. Adams was a woman of unusually fine mind and noble character, and proved herself a most able helpmate and congenial comrade for her husband throughout the many severe trials as well as in the brilliant triumphs of his long career. Not often does fate allot to a great man a domestic partner so fit to counsel and sustain as was Abigail Adams, whose memory deserves to be, as indeed it still is, held in high esteem and admiration.

History depicts no race less fitted by character, habits, and traditions to endure oppression than the colonists of New England. Numerically the chief proportion of them, and in point of influence nearly all who were worthy of consideration, were allied with the men who had successfully defied and overthrown the British monarchy. The surroundings and mode of life of settlers in a new country had permitted no deterioration in the physical courage and hardihood of that class which, in Cromwell's army, had constituted as fine a body of troops as the world has seen to the present day. It was simply impossible to affect New Englanders through the sense of fear. Far removed from the sight of monarchical power, and from contact with the offensive display of aristocracy, they had ceased to hate this form of government, and even entertained feelings of loyalty and attachment towards it. But these sentiments throve only upon the condition of good treatment; and on the instant when harshness destroyed the sense of reciprocity, the good-will of the dependent body disappeared. Even while the rebellious temper slumbered, the independent spirit had been nourished by all the conditions of social, intellectual, even of civil life. The chief officers of government had been sent over from England, and some legislation had taken place in Parliament; but the smaller laws and regulations, which, with the ministers thereof, touched the daily lives and affairs of the people, had been largely established by the colonists themselves. They were a thinking race, intelligent, disputatious, and combative. The religion which absorbed much of their mental activity had cherished these qualities; and though their creed was narrow, rigid, and severe, yet they did not accept it, like slaves of a hierarchy, without thought and criticism. On the contrary, their theology was notably polemical, and discussion and dispute on matters of doctrine were the very essence of their Christianity. Their faith constituted a sort of gymnasium or arena for the constant matching of strength and skill. They were ready at every sort of intellectual combat. The very sternness of their beliefs was the exponent of their uncompromising spirit, the outgrowth of a certain fierceness of disposition, and by no means a weight or pall which had settled down upon their faculties of free thought. Men with such bodies, minds, and morals, not slow to take offense, quick to find arguments upon their own side, utterly fearless, and of most stubborn mettle, furnished poor material for the construction of a subservient class. Moreover, they were shrewd, practical men of business, with the aptitude of the Anglo-Saxon for affairs, and with his taste for money-getting, his proneness for enterprise, his passion for worldly success; hence they were very sensitive to any obstacle cast in the way of their steady progress towards material prosperity. The king and the ruling classes of Great Britain had no comprehension whatsoever of all these distinguishing traits of the singular race with whom they undertook to deal upon a system fundamentally wrong, and of which every development and detail was a blunder.

In nearly every respect John Adams was a typical New Englander of the times; at least it may be said that in no one individual did the colonial character find a more respectable or a more comprehensible development than in him, so that to understand and appreciate him is to understand and appreciate the New England of his day; and to draw him is to draw the colonists in their best form. It was inevitable from the outset that he should be a patriot; if men of his mind and temper could hesitate, there could be no material out of which to construct a " liberty party " in the province. At first, of course, older and better known men took the lead, and he, still a *parvus Iulus*, was fain to follow with unequal steps the vigorous strides of the fiery Otis, and of that earliest of genuine democrats, Samuel Adams. But the career of Otis was like the electric flash which so appropriately slew him, brief, brilliant, startling, sinking into melancholy darkness; and

John Adams pressed steadily forward, first to the side of his distinguished cousin, and erelong in advance of him.

It was in 1761 that Otis delivered his daring and famous argument against the writs of assistance. This was the first log of the pile which afterward made the great blaze of the Revolution. John Adams had the good fortune to hear that bold and stirring speech, and came away from the impressive scene all aglow with patriotic ardor. The influence of such free and noble eloquence upon the young man was tremendous. As his son classically puts it: "It was to Mr. Adams like the oath of Hamilcar administered to Hannibal." He took some slight notes of the argument at the time, and in his old age he proved the indelible impression which it had made upon him by writing out the vivid story. His memoranda, though involving some natural inaccuracies, constitute the best among the meagre records of this important event. He said afterward that at this scene he had witnessed the birth of American Independence. "American Independence was then and there born. The seeds of patriots and heroes, to defend the *non sine diis animosus infans*, to defend the vigorous youth, were then and there sown. Every man of an immense, crowded audience appeared to me to go away, as I did, ready to take arms against writs of assistance. Then and there was the first scene of the first act of opposition to the arbitrary claims of Great Britain. Then and there the child Independence was born. In fifteen years, *i. e.* in 1776, he grew up to manhood and declared himself free." Such impassioned language, written in the tranquillity of extreme age, nearly three-score years after the occurrence, shows what feelings were aroused at the time. The seed which Otis flung into the mind of this youth fell upon a sufficiently warm and fertile soil.

In this initial struggle of the writs of assistance the royal government obtained a nominal victory in the affirmation of the technical legality of the process; but the colonists enjoyed the substance of success, since the attempt to issue the obnoxious writ was not repeated. The troubled waters, not being soon again disturbed, recovered their usual placidity of surface, but the strong under-current of popular thought and temper had been stimulated not in the direction of loyalty. From the day of Otis's argument Adams, for his part, remained a patriot through his very marrow. Yet he continued to give close attention to his own professional business, which he steadily increased. Gradually he gained that repute and standing among his fellow citizens which careful study, sound sense, and a strong character are sure in time to secure. He held from time to time some of the smaller local offices which indicate that a young man is well thought of by his neighbors. Such was his position when in 1765 the Stamp Act set the province in a flame and launched him, altogether unexpectedly, upon that public career which was to endure to the end of his active years. This momentous piece of legislation was passed in Parliament innocently and thoughtlessly enough by a vote of 294 to 49, in March, 1765. It was to take effect on November 1 of the same year. But the simple-minded indifference of the English legislators was abundantly offset by the rage of the provincials. The tale of the revolt is too familiar to be repeated; every child knows how the effigy of stamp-distributor Oliver was first hanged and then burned; how he himself was compelled by the zealous "Sons of Liberty" to resign his office; how his place of business was demolished; how his house and the houses of Hutchinson and of other officials were sacked by the mob. These extravagant doings disgusted Adams, whose notions of resistance were widely different. In his own town of Braintree he took the lead of the malcontents; he drew up and circulated for signatures a petition to the selectmen asking for a town meeting, at which he presented a draft of instructions to the representative of the town in the colonial General Court. These, being carried unanimously, were "published in Draper's paper, and . . . adopted by forty other towns of the province as instructions to their respective representatives." Adams became a man of prominence.

When the time came for putting the new statute in operation, divers expedients for evading it were resorted to. But Chief Justice Hutchinson in the county of Suffolk prevented the opening of the courts there and the transaction of business without stamps. On December 18 Adams wrote gloomily: —

"The probate office is shut, the custom house is shut, the courts of justice are shut, and all business seems at a stand. . . . I have not drawn a writ since the first of November. . . . This long interval of indolence and idleness will make a large chasm in my affairs, if it should not reduce me to distress and incapacitate me to answer the demands upon me. . . . I was but just getting into my gears, just getting under sail, and an embargo is laid upon the ship. Thirty years of my life are passed in preparation for business. . . . I have groped in dark obscurity till of late, and had but just become known and gained a small degree of reputation when this execrable project was set on foot for my ruin as well as that of America in general, and of Great Britain."

Adams was not alone in feeling the stress of this enforced cessation of all business. On the very day when he was writing these grievous forebodings a town meeting was holding in Boston, at which a memorial was adopted, praying the governor and council to remove the fatal obstruction out of the way of the daily occupations of the people. The next day news came to Mr. Adams at Braintree that he had been associated with the venerable Jeremiah Gridley and James Otis as counsel for the town to support this memorial. This politico-professional honor, which was the greater since he was not a citizen of Boston, surprised him and caused him no little perturbation. He saw in it some personal peril, and, what he dreaded much more, a sure opposition to his professional advancement on the part of the government and the numerous body of loyalists. Moreover, he distrusted his capacity for so momentous and responsible a task. But there is no instance in Adams's life when either fear of consequences or modesty seriously affected his action. Upon this occasion he did not hesitate an instant. "I am now," he at once declared, "under all obligations of interest and ambition, as well as honor, gratitude, and duty, to exert the utmost of my abilities in this important cause." On the evening of the very next day, with no possibility for preparation, with few hours even for thought or consultation, the three lawyers were obliged to make their arguments before the governor and council. Mr. Adams had to speak first. "Then it fell upon me," he said, "without one moment's opportunity to consult any authorities, to open an argument upon a question that was never made before, and I wish I could hope it never would be made again, that is, whether the courts of law should be open or not."

John Quincy Adams alleges, not without justice, that his father placed the demands of the colonists upon a stronger, as well as upon a more daring basis than did either of his colleagues. "Mr. Otis reasoned with great learning and zeal on the judges' oaths, etc., Mr. Gridley on the great inconveniences that would ensue the interruption of justice." Mr. Adams, though advancing also points of expediency, "grounded his argument on the invalidity of the Stamp Act, it not being in any sense our Act, having never consented to it." This was recognized as the one sufficient and unanswerable statement of the colonial position from this time forth to the day of Independence, — the injustice and unlawfulness of legislation, especially for taxation, over persons not represented in the legislature. But in British ears such language was rebellious, even revolutionary.

No historian has conceived or described the condition of affairs, of society, of temper and feeling, at least in the southern part of this country, at the time of the Stamp Act, with anything like the accuracy and vividness which illuminate the closing pages of "The Virginians." With a moderation happily combined with force, and with a frank recognition of the way he would have been struck by his own arguments had he listened to them from the other side, Thackeray puts into the mouth of George Warrington the English justification of English policy. It may be admitted that, if Parliament could not tax the colonists, then there was the case of a government which could exact no revenue from its subjects, and which, therefore, could only take with thanks their voluntary contributions. In any theory of government such a proposition is an absurdity. It may further be admitted that Englishmen "at home" were a much more heavily taxed community than there was any endeavor to make the expatriated colonial Englishmen. It is also true that Great Britain acknowledged and performed reasonably well the duties which are part of the function of government. Against these weighty arguments there was but one which could prevail, and that was the broad and fundamental one advanced by Mr. Adams: it reached deeper than any of the English arguments; it came before them and settled the controversy before one could get to them. Great Britain said: A government without a power of taxation is an impossible absurdity. The colonies replied with a still earlier fact: But taxation cannot be exercised without representation. The truth at the very bottom was fortunately the American truth, and this Mr. Adams saw clearly and said boldly, so that the "liberty party" never forgot the exposition. There was a question which he did not shirk, though he contemplated it with something like a shudder. If there could be no government without taxation, and no taxation without representation, and there was no chance that representation would be conceded, — what then? Only independence. Such a chain of logic was enough to make so thoughtful a man as Adams very serious, and one is not surprised to find these brief, pregnant entries in his diary : —

"Sunday.   At home with my family, thinking."
"Christmas.   At home, thinking, reading, searching, concerning taxation without consent."

But he never had any doubt of the soundness of his position. He reiterated it afterwards in court in behalf of John Hancock, who was sued for duties on a cargo of madeira wine, which had been landed at night, smuggler-fashion. Adams, as counsel for the defendant, impugned the statute because "it was made without our consent. My client, Mr. Hancock, never consented to it; he never voted for it himself, and he never voted for any man to make such a law for him." This cause, by the way, gave Adams plenty of business for one winter, since the government lawyers seemed "determined to examine the whole town as witnesses." It was finally disposed of in a manner less formal, though not less effective, than the usual docket entry, "by the battle of Lexington."

By the share which he took in this business of the Stamp Act, Adams conclusively cast in his lot with the patriot party, and thereafter stood second only to such older leaders as Otis, Samuel Adams, and Hancock. He continued, however, to devote himself sedulously to his law business, accepting only the not very onerous public office of selectman in the spring of 1766. He was advised to apply to the governor for the position of justice of the peace, then a post of substantial honor and value. But he refused to do so, because he feared that a "great fermentation of the country" was at hand, and he had no fancy for hampering himself with any "obligations of gratitude."

Early in 1768, through the persuasion of friends, he removed to Boston, and occupied the " White House," so called, in Brattle Square, taking the step, however, not without misgivings on the score of his health, which at this time was not good and gave him no little concernment. He had not been long in his new quarters when his friend, Jonathan Sewall, attorney-general of the province, called upon him, and, with many flattering words as to his character and standing at the bar, offered him the post of advocate-general in the court of admiralty. It was a lucrative office, " a sure introduction to the most profitable business in the province, ... a first step in the ladder of royal favor and promotion." Unquestionably the proposal was insidious, since the policy of such indirect bribes was systematically pursued at this juncture by Bernard and Hutchinson. But Sewall endeavored, of course, to gloss over the purport of his errand by stating that he was specially instructed by the governor to say that there was no design to interfere with Adams's well-known political sympathies. Words, however, could not conceal the too obvious trap. Adams was prompt and positive in his refusal. Sewall declined to take No for an answer, and returned again to the charge a few weeks later. But he gathered nothing by his persistence. It was time lost to endeavor to mould a man whose distinguishing trait was a supreme stubbornness, which became preëminently invincible upon any question of personal independence.

In October, 1768, the two regiments which Hutchinson had advised the king's ministers to send over debarked and marched through Boston town "with muskets charged, bayonets fixed, drums beating, fifes playing," and all the circumstance of war! Overflowing their barracks, these unwelcome guests took possession of the town-house and other public buildings, and by their cannon commanded the state-house and court-house. The officers certainly endeavored to maintain a conciliatory bearing, and kept the troops creditably quiet and orderly. But it was impossible to give an amiable complexion to a military occupation. The townspeople obstinately regarded the redcoats as triumphant invaders, and hated, and, it must be confessed, taunted them continually as such. The odiousness of the situation was especially forced upon Adams by the daily drill of a regiment in the great square before his house. But in the evening the "Sons of Liberty" pointedly sought to cleanse his ears from the offense of the British military music by serenading beneath his windows. Long afterwards, writing of this time, recalling the confidence placed in him by the patriots and his resolve not to disappoint them, Adams said : " My daily reflections for two years at the sight of those soldiers before my door were serious enough. . . . The danger I was in appeared in full view before me ; and I very deliberately and indeed very solemnly determined at all events to adhere to my principles in favor of my native country, which, indeed, was all the country I knew, or which had been known by my father, grandfather, or great-grandfather." Yet he held himself in prudent restraint, and declined to attend or speak at the town meetings. " That way madness lies," he used to say, with a reference to the sad condition of Otis. Yet he was destined to perform a singularly trying task in connection with these same redcoats, in spite of his desire to stand aloof from any public appearance.

It was a mere question of time when a serious collision with the troops should take place. It came at last, as every one knows, upon the memorable evening of March 5, 1770, in the shape of the famous " Boston Massacre." On that fatal day a crowd of the disorderly loafers and boys of the town, with their natural weapons of sticks and stones, so threatened and abused the solitary sentry pacing upon King Street that he called for aid. To his summons speedily responded Captain Preston, bringing six more soldiers. The force of the civilian tormentors also received large accessions. The mob, pressing angrily upon the officer and his little force, so far alarmed them that they fired a volley. Each musket was loaded with two balls, and each ball found its human mark. Five men were slain outright; others were wounded. Forthwith the whole regiment turned out and formed in defensive array across the street upon the northerly side of the town-house. Before it a great and unterrified crowd swelled and raged. An awful conflict was impending. Fortunately Hutchinson appeared upon the scene, and by wise words checked the tumult at its present stage. He promised that the officer and the men should at once be placed under arrest and tried for murder. The people, with the native respect of their race for law, were satisfied, and further bloodshed was averted. During the night Preston and the soldiers were arrested.

The very next morning, the heat of the turmoil still seething, there came into Mr. Adams's office one Forrest, pleasantly nicknamed the " Irish infant." This emissary was charged to induce Adams to act as counsel for the accused, and he evidently expected to find his task difficult of accomplishment; but Adams acceded to

the request as soon as it was preferred, making
some remarks to the point of professional duty,
trite and commonplace in their ethical aspect,
but honorably distinguished in that they were
backed by instant action at a moment of grave
trial. With him acted Josiah Quincy, junior,
then a young man lately called to the bar. It
was no welcome duty which professional obligation and perhaps still higher sentiments thus
thrust upon these two lawyers. It has been
suggested that the choice of Mr. Adams, especially, was due to the astute cowardice of Hutchinson, who wished first to handicap a strong
patriot by rendering him an object of suspicion
among the less reasonable malcontents, and next,
in case of being ultimately compelled to pardon
the accused men, to interpose between himself
and an angry people the character and influence
of the most highly considered lawyer on the
popular side. It may well be supposed, however, that Captain Preston, on trial for his life
amid strange and hostile surroundings, selected
his counsel with a single eye to his own interest.
Mr. C. F. Adams regards this engagement in
this cause as constituting one of the four great
moral trials and triumphs marking his grandfather's career. Undoubtedly it was so. It
was not only that, so far as his own feelings
were concerned, the position was odious, but he

was called upon to risk losing the well-earned
confidence of those of his fellow townsmen with
whom he was in profound sympathy in matters
of momentous importance; to imperil a reputation and popularity won by twelve long years
of honest labor, and necessary to his success
and even to his livelihood. It is difficult to
admire too highly the spirit which saw no cause
even for an hour's hesitation in the sudden
demand for such sacrifices. That he was unquestionably right is now so evident that it is
hard to appreciate that he could have incurred
great censure and peril at the time. Yet this
was the case. The cooler and more intelligent
patriots could be counted upon to appreciate
the case justly, and in time also a large proportion of the party would follow. But at first
there was a great clamor of rebuke and wrath.
Even Josiah Quincy, senior, a man from whom,
if from any one, better judgment might have
been anticipated, wrote to his son a letter mingled of incredulity, indignation, and remonstrance. It seems ridiculous to find that long
years afterwards, after the Revolution, after
Adams had signed the Declaration of Independence, had been insulted at the English court,
and had served as Vice-President with Washington, this legal service of his was dragged out
by his opponents as evidence of his subjection

to British influence; yet such folly actually occurred.

The trial of Preston began October 24, and closed October 30. It resulted in an acquittal, since it was of course impossible to adduce satisfactory evidence that he had given the command to fire. The trial of the soldiers followed, which a shorthand writer endeavored to report; but he failed lamentably in catching the tenor of the counsel's arguments. Of these defendants all were acquitted save two, who were found guilty of manslaughter. They claimed their privilege of clergy, and so saved their lives, but were branded on the hand with a hot iron, a disgrace which they keenly felt to be undeserved, and which won for them the honest sympathy of Mr. Adams. It may be remarked that Adams was much annoyed at a story, to which a sort of corroboration was afterward given by some unfair language of Hutchinson in his history, that his motive in engaging for the prisoners came in the shape of a large fee. In fact, his entire remuneration for all services rendered to all his eight clients was only nineteen guineas, which were not accompanied or followed by so much as even a courteous word of thanks from Preston. But he had the comfort of appreciating the character of his own conduct at least as well as if he were judging the behavior of another person. He said of it two or three years later: "It was one of the most gallant, manly, and disinterested actions of my whole life, and one of the best pieces of service I ever rendered my country." So fairly could he at times estimate himself and his doings!

One gratification, however, was his besides the *mens conscia recti* and the paltry guineas. After his acceptance of the position of defendant's counsel had become known, and before the trial, a vacancy occurred in the representation of the town of Boston in the General Court. Upon June 3 Adams was elected to fill this place by the handsome vote of 418 out of a total of 536, good evidence that the people had come to their senses concerning the true character of his action. But gratifying as such a testimonial of popularity was at the moment, when he had staked his good repute upon a question of principle, yet in other respects the honor was less welcome. Heretofore he had carefully abstained from entanglement in public affairs, contenting himself with a bold profession of patriotic sentiment, and shunning sedulously that active share which he was often and inevitably urged and tempted to assume. He had devoted himself with steady and almost exclusive persistence to the practice of his pro-

fession, recognizing no object superior to that.
Success in this he was already grasping. Twelve
years he had been in practice, and now "had
more business at the bar than any man in the
province." He felt that an entry upon a public
career would rob him of the ripening harvest of
his years of toil; that it would expose him to
anxiety, complications, and personal danger,
and his family perhaps to poverty. His later
reminiscence of his feelings upon accepting this
office is impressively pathetic : —

"My health was feeble. I was throwing away as
bright prospects as any man ever had before him,
and I had devoted myself to endless labor and anxiety, if not to infamy and to death, and that for nothing, except what indeed was and ought to be in all
a sense of duty. In the evening I expressed to Mrs.
Adams all my apprehensions. That excellent lady,
who has always encouraged me, burst into a flood of
tears, and said she was very sensible of all the danger to her and to our children, as well as to me, but
she thought I had done as I ought; she was very
willing to share in all that was to come, and to place
her trust in Providence."

Thus solemnly, with a sense of costly self-
sacrifice to duty, and with dark presagings,
Adams consented to enter upon that public
career which in the inscrutable future proved to
be laden with such rich rewards for his noble

courage, and such brilliant confutation of his melancholy forebodings.

This first incursion into the domain of public life, undertaken in so grave a temper, was not of long duration. Considering the hale and prolonged old age which Mr. Adams came to enjoy, his health in what should have been vigorous years seems to have given him a surprising amount of solicitude. So now, within a few months after his election, he fell into such a condition with "a pain in his breast, and a complaint in his lungs, which seriously threatened his life," that he felt sure that city life was disagreeing with him. Accordingly in the spring of 1771, just three years after coming to town, he removed his household back to Braintree, and of course at the end of his year of service he could not again be returned as a member from Boston. He was very despondent at this time. He held the inhabitants of Boston in "the most pleasing and grateful remembrance." He said : " I wish to God it was in my power to serve them, as much as it is in my inclination. But it is not; my wishes are impotent, my endeavors fruitless and ineffectual to them, and ruinous to myself." He fell occasionally into moods of melancholy like this, doubtless by reason of ill-health. Probably, also, after having tasted the singular fascination of active concernment in public affairs, he was not able altogether without regret to contemplate his apparent future, with "no journeys to Cambridge, no General Court to attend," nothing but "law and husbandry." He had come to be a man of some note, which is always pleasant, whatever disingenuous professions prominent men may sometimes make. Already, many months before, when stopping at a tavern on his way to Plymouth, he was surprised by having a fellow-traveler, unknown to him, go out to saddle and bridle his horse and hold the stirrup for him, saying, " Mr. Adams, as a man of liberty, I respect you; God bless you! I 'll stand by you while I live, and from hence to Cape Cod you won't find ten men amiss." Now, too, upon coming to Braintree, the representative from that town, who once had been pleased to call Mr. Adams "a petty lawyer," complimented him as the "first lawyer in the province," and offered to stand aside if Mr. Adams would be willing to represent Braintree in the General Court. One could not lightly throw away such prestige.

From the farm at Braintree he rode habitually to his office in Boston, and by this wholesome life regained his good health, and fortunately suffered no material loss in the popular estimation. His interest in colonial affairs continued unabated. He set down, for the instruction of his family, "if this wretched journal should ever be read" by them, that he was the unwavering enemy of Hutchinson and of Hutchinson's system, and he predicted that the governor had inaugurated a contention, which would "never be fully terminated but by wars and confusions and carnage." "With great anxiety and hazard, with continual application to business, with loss of health, reputation, profit, and as fair prospects and opportunities of advancement as others, who have greedily embraced them, I have for ten years together invariably opposed this system and its fautors." So Pym or Hampden might have spoken concerning Strafford. But now there came one of those lulls in the political storm when sanguine people sometimes think that it has spent its force and is to give way to fairer days. Adams beheld this with some bewilderment and regret, but with constancy of spirit. "The melodious harmony, the perfect concords, the entire confidence and affection that seem to be restored, greatly surprise me. Will it be lasting? I believe there is no man in so curious a situation as I am; I am, for what I can see, quite left alone in the world." He had not, however, to wait long before the tranquillity passed, the gales were blowing anew more fiercely than ever, and the old comrades were all in company again.

In truth, it was ridiculous for Mr. Adams to fancy that he could remain permanently a villager of Braintree, a long hour's journey from Boston. That redoubtable young town, though for a while it was making such a commotion in the world, had only about 16,000 inhabitants, and it could not have been sufficiently metropolitan to justify Mr. Adams in fleeing from its crowds into the wholesome solitudes of the country. It was a morbid notion on his part. By the autumn of 1772 he came to this conclusion, and found his health so reëstablished that he not only moved back to town, but actually bought a house in Queen Street, near the court-house. He, however, registered a pledge to himself " to meddle not with public affairs of town or province. I am determined my own life and the welfare of my whole family, which is much dearer to me, are too great sacrifices for me to make. I have served my country and her professed friends, at an immense expense to me of time, peace, health, money, and preferment, both of which last have courted my acceptance and been inexorably refused, lest I should be laid under a temptation to forsake the sentiments of the friends of this country. . . . I will devote myself wholly to

my private business, my office, and my farm,
and I hope to lay a foundation for better fortune to my children and a happier life than
has fallen to my share."   Yet these sentiments,
which he seems not to have kept to himself,
brought upon him some harsh criticism. James
Otis, the fiery zealot, one day sneeringly said
to him, with a bluntness which sounds somewhat startling in our more cautious day, that
he would never learn military exercises because
he had not the heart. "How do you know?"
replied Adams. "You never searched my
heart." "Yes, I have," retorted Otis; "tired
with one year's service, dancing from Boston to
Braintree and from Braintree to Boston; mop-
ing about the streets of this town as hypped as
Father Flynt at ninety, and seemingly regard-
less of everything but to get money enough to
carry you smoothly through this world." This
was the other side of the shield from that upon
which Mr. Adams was wont to look, and which
has been shown in the sundry communings
cited from his diary concerning his sacrifices.
Otis was impetuous and extravagant of tongue,
and probably his picture was the less fair of
the two. Yet truly Mr. Adams appears a little
absurd in putting on the airs and claiming the
privileges of "an infirm man," as he calls himself, at the age of thirty-seven. But at times

he could give way to patriotic outbursts such
as would not have misbecome even the pungent
and reckless Otis himself.   One evening at Mr.
Cranch's " I said there was no more justice
left in Britain than there was in hell; that I
wished for war, and that the whole Bourbon
family was upon the back of Great Britain;
avowed a thorough disaffection to that country;
wished that anything might happen to them,
and, as the clergy prayed of our enemies in
time of war, that they might be brought to
reason or to ruin."   Yet he was afterward penitent for this language, and took himself to
task " with severity, for these rash, inexperienced, boyish, raw, and awkward expressions.
A man who has no better government of his
tongue, no more command of his temper, is unfit
for anything but children's play and the company of boys," etc., etc.

In justice to Mr. Adams it should be said
that, so far as any records show, he had not
often to blame himself in this manner; habitually he was not less moderate than firm and
courageous.   One is greatly struck with the
change of tone which insensibly steals over the
diary as the young man, at first having only
himself to care for, develops into the man of ma-
ture years with the weighty and difficult interests of the province at heart.   The tendency to

James Otis

selfishness and narrow egotism, the heartburn-
ings, jealousies, suspicions, carpings, and harsh
criticisms, which do not give a very amiable impression of the youth, all disappear as the times
change. A loftier elevation and finer atmosphere are insensibly reached. A grave, resolute, anxious air pervades the pages; a trust
and sense of comradeship towards fellow patriots; almost as much of regret as of rancor
towards many of those who should be standing
by the province but are not; hostility, of course,
but a singular absence of personal abuse and
acrimony, even towards such men as Hutchinson. No unmeasured rage, no flames of anger
and ill-considered words, but an immutable
conviction and a stubborn determination are
characteristics which he shares with the great
bulk of the "liberty party." There is no
excitement exhausting itself with the effervescence of its own passion, there are no protestations too extravagant to be fulfilled; the exte-
rior is all coolness and persistence; the heat
glows fiercely far inside. Thus one clearly
reads in Mr. Adams's diary the temper of his
coadjutors and of the times; and if the same
perusal could have been had in England, it is
barely possible that events might have been
different. Cromwell and the Puritans were not
in so remote a past that the royal government

could be justified in an utter failure to appreciate the moral and mental traits of the people of New England, if only those traits could once be got beneath the eyes of the king and cabinet. But Adams's diary was for himself alone.

CHAPTER III

THE FIRST CONGRESS

It has been seen that nearly three years
before the time at which we have now arrived
Mr. Adams had experienced no small solicitude
and misgivings when summoned to take a part
in public life. He had soon escaped from functions which were really distasteful to him, and
had gladly resumed the practice of his profession
and that care for his private interests which
naturally lay close to the heart of a shrewd and
prudent man, bred in the practical and business-
like atmosphere of the New England of those
days, and having a wife and children to support.
Hitherto he has been seen holding aloof so far
as possible from any prominent and active share
in the disturbed and exciting, but certainly also
the perilous politics of the times. Even within
a few weeks of the event which was to make
his career permanently and irrevocably that of
the public man, he writes to a friend that he
can send no interesting news, because " I have
very little connection with public affairs, and I
hope to have less." Nevertheless it is perfectly

obvious that if the services of men having his
qualities of mind and character could not be
commanded by the patriots, then the sooner
submission was made to Great Britain the better.   At the ripe age of thirty-eight, well read
in private and in public law, of a temperament
happily combining prudence and boldness, notably trustworthy, active, and energetic, standing
already in the front rank of his profession if
not actually at its head in the province, it
was inevitable that he should be compelled to
assume important and responsible duties in the
momentous contest so rapidly developing.   His
reluctance was not of the mouth only, not the
pretended holding back of a man who nevertheless desired to be driven forward; he was sincere in his shrinking from a prominent position,
yet he could surely be counted upon ultimately
to take it, because refusal would have been contrary to his nature.

It was apparently in March, 1774, that Mr.
Adams was contemplating a project somewhat
amusing in view of the near future.   "Have I
patience and industry enough," he says, "to
write a history of the contest between Britain
and America?   It would be proper to begin,"
etc.   Comical enough was this proposition for
writing an historical narrative before the material even for the introductory chapter had been
completed.

A few days later he gives to James Warren his opinion: "that there is not spirit enough on either side to bring the question to a complete decision, and that we shall oscillate like a pendulum, and fluctuate like the ocean, for many years to come, and never obtain a complete redress of American grievances, nor submit to an absolute establishment of parliamentary authority, but be trimming between both, as we have been for ten years past, for more years to come than you and I shall live. Our children may see revolutions," etc., etc. Evidently he was not well pleased at these predictions, which his despondent judgment forced from him. But the "revolutions," so much more to his taste than the "trimming," were already at hand. Less than three months later, on June 17, the provincial assembly was sitting with closed doors; the secretary of the governor, with a message for their dissolution in his hand, was knocking in vain for admittance, while the members were hastily choosing five persons to represent Massachusetts at a meeting of committees from the several colonies to be held at Philadelphia on September 1. One hundred and seventeen members voted "aye," twelve voted "no;" the doors were opened, and the "last provincial assembly that ever acted under the royal authority in Massachusetts" was at an end.   The five representatives to the first Congress of North America were: James Bowdoin, Thomas Cushing, Samuel Adams, John Adams, and Robert Treat Paine.   It so happened that at the very hour when this nomination was making, John Adams was presiding at Faneuil Hall over a meeting of citizens engaged in considering what measures should be taken concerning the recent acts of Parliament for the destruction of the commerce of the town.

The first glimpse of Mr. Adams's feeling at this juncture comes in a few hurried, disjointed sentences, written in his diary three days later; he is "in Danvers, bound to Ipswich," still attending closely to his law business, starting on the eastern circuit.   He says : —

"There is a new and grand scene open before me : a Congress.   This will be an assembly of the wisest men upon the continent, who are Americans in principle, that is, against the taxation of Americans by authority of Parliament.   I feel myself unequal to this business.   A more extensive knowledge of the realm, the colonies, and of commerce, as well as of law and policy, is necessary, than I am master of. What can be done?   Will it be expedient to propose an annual Congress of Committees? to petition? Will it do to petition at all? — to the King? to the Lords? to the Commons?   What will such consultations avail?   Deliberations alone will not do.   We must petition, or recommend to the Assemblies to petition, or — "

The alternative to be introduced by this " or " gives him pause; it is too terrible, doubtless also as yet too little considered in all its vague, vast, and multiform possibilities, to be definitely shaped in words, even on these secret pages. He will not be run away with by a hasty pen, though his only reader is himself. Five days later he comes back from " a long walk through . . . corn, rye, grass," and writes : —

" I wander alone and ponder. I muse, I mope, I ruminate. I am often in reveries and brown studies. The objects before me are too grand and multifarious for my comprehension. We have not men fit for the times. We are deficient in genius, in education, in travel, in fortune, in everything. I feel unutterable anxiety. God grant us wisdom and fortitude ! Should the opposition be suppressed, should this country submit, what infamy and ruin ! God forbid ! Death in any form is less terrible."

On June 25 he writes to his friend Warren, who had been instrumental in appointing him to Congress : —

" I suppose you sent me there to school. I thank you for thinking me an apt scholar, or capable of learning. For my own part I am at a loss, totally at a loss, what to do when we get there ; but I hope to be there taught. It is to be a school of political

prophets, I suppose, a nursery of American statesmen."

Mr. Adams estimated with much candor and
fairness the deficiencies which he recognized as
likely to stand in the way of his usefulness and
success in Congress.   But in speaking of his
qualifications he did not mention, and doubtless
did not at all appreciate, one fact which told
largely in his favor.   In our day men habitually
go to Congress with only such crude training in
the oral discussion of public questions as they
have gained in the juvenile debating societies of
school or college, or possibly through an occasional appearance "on the stump."   But Adams
had enjoyed the advantage of a peculiar and
singularly admirable schooling, and it was only
because this had been a matter of course in his
life ever since he had come of age that he failed
now to set it down at its true value.   He had
been accustomed always to take an active part
in the town meetings, that old institution of New
England, than which nothing finer as a preparatory school of debate has ever existed in the
world.   In these assemblages, at which nearly
all the voters of the town were present, every
public question was discussed with that ardor
which the near personal interest of the speakers
can alone supply.   There was no indifference.
Every one made it a point to be present, and the

concourse was a more striking one than many more pretentious and dignified gatherings. The colonists were a disputatious, shrewd, and hard-headed race. When they met to arrange all those matters of domestic polity, which by virtue of their nearness seemed much more important than grander but more distant and abstract questions, there was no lack of earnestness or of keen ability in their debates. Men learned the essential elements of vigorous and able discussion. They did not perhaps learn all the intricacies of parliamentary tactics, but they did acquire a good deal of skill in the way of observation and of management. It was a democratic political body,[1] wherein perfect equality prevailed so far as privilege or the distinction of the individual were concerned, but where the inequality arising from difference in natural ability counted for all that it was worth. In such conflicts every man learned to strike with all the skill and strength that he could master, and learned also to take as good and often better than he could give back. Behind it all lay the

[1] Gordon, in his *History of Independence*, says: "Every town is an incorporated republic;" and Mr. Hosmer, in an admirable pamphlet lately published upon this subject, calls the town meeting the "proper primordial cell of a republican body politic," and says that it existed "in well developed form only in New England."

fundamental Anglo-Saxon feeling of respect for
law and order, for common sense and the sounder
reason.   It was generally the stronger argument
which prevailed.   It was to the judgment, not
to the emotions, that appeal had to be made in
bodies composed of such material.   A throng
of Yankee farmers or merchants listening to a
speaker for the purpose of detecting the weak
points in his speech compelled the ablest and
the coolest man to do his best.   No one could
afford to lose either his temper or his head.
Service in such tournaments, though the con-
tests were not of national moment, very soon
made veterans of the active participants.   Courage, independence, self-control, thoroughness,
readiness, were soon acquired amid the rough
but strong and honest handling of such encoun-
ters.   From these fields Adams came to one
more conspicuous, with his mental sinews more
toughened and more active than could have been
expected by any one who had not witnessed the
scenes of the rude arena.   He had learned how
to prepare himself for an argument and to study
a question which was to be discussed, how to
put his points with clearness, force, and brevity ;
he was at home in addressing a body of hearers ;
he was not discomposed by attacks, however
vigorous ; he could hold his position or assail
the position of an opponent with perfect cool-

ness and dangerous tenacity; he had learned self-confidence and to fear no man, though by the fortunes of war he must sometimes be defeated. Altogether, he was much better fitted for parliamentary labors than he himself suspected.

From this period of his life for nearly thirty years Mr. Adams continued to expand in popular estimation, unfortunately also in his own estimation, through constantly enlarging measures of greatness. But at no time does he appear to the student of his character so noble, so admirable, or so attractive as during two or three years about this time. The entries in the diary are brief, and often made at provokingly long intervals; nor do very many letters remain. Yet there are dashes of strong color sufficient to give a singularly vivid picture of his state of mind and feeling. There is a profound consciousness of being in the presence of great events, of living in momentous and pregnant times. This develops him grandly. Before the immensity of the crisis all thoughts of self, all personal rivalries, even political enmities, disappear. There is perceptible scarcely any trace of that unfortunate vanity and egotism which so marred his aspect when time had taught him that he was really a great man. At present he does not know that he is great; he is simply one meaning to do his best, and harassed with a genuine, modest doubt how good that best will be. Amid the surroundings his new duties impress him with a sense of awe. Who is he to take counsel for his fellow citizens, — he who has only studied the few books which he has been able to afford to import from England; who has never seen a town with more than sixteen thousand inhabitants, nor ever had any experience whatsoever of statecraft; who gathers only by hearsay his ideas concerning the power and resources of England, the temper of her rulers and her people; and who really has scarcely more knowledge of any province south of Massachusetts? How can he weigh, and compare, and judge wisely? Yet he has at least the wisdom to measure his own exceeding ignorance, and obviously he will commit no such rash blunders as those into which he will by and by be led by the overweening self-confidence of later years. Now he will ponder and reflect, and will act prudently and moderately; for he feels most gravely his immense responsibility. But though he feels this, it does not make a coward of him; the courage and the spirit of John Adams were the same from the cradle to the grave. There is not a shadow of timidity; modesty and self-distrust do not take that shape, nor betray him into irresolution. In every line that he writes the firm and manly temper is distinctly seen. If he will be anxious, so also he will be bold and will fear no consequences either for his country or for himself. His nerve is good; he is profoundly thoughtful, but not in the least agitated. His own affairs must give him some thought, but not for himself, only for his family. He does not say this; if he did, the fact might be less sure; but his letters, clear, brief, blunt, straightforward, written often in haste and always with unquestionable simplicity and frankness, leave no doubt concerning his generous courage in all matters of his private interests. The only direct recognition of his personal risk is in a passage of a letter to James Warren:—

"There is one ugly reflection. Brutus and Cassius were conquered and slain, Hampden died in the field, Sidney on the scaffold, Harrington in jail, etc. This is cold comfort. Politics are an ordeal path among red-hot ploughshares. Who, then, would be a politician for the pleasure of running about barefoot among them? Yet somebody must."

After he had been a short while in Congress he writes reassuringly to his wife:—

" Be not under any concern for me. There is little danger from anything we shall do at the Congress. There is such a spirit through the colonies, and the members of Congress are such characters, that no danger can happen to us which will not involve the whole continent in universal desolation ; and in that case, who would wish to live ? "

He was willing to take his turn and to do his share ; but he insisted that after he had contributed his fair proportion of toil and sacrifice, and had assumed his just measure of peril, others should come forward to succeed him and play their parts also. In truth, at this crisis a prominent public position did not hold out those lures to ambition which exist in established governments ; there were no apparent prizes of glory, power, or prosperity ; there were alarming visible chances of utter destruction. The self-seeking and aspiring class saw meagre temptations. So Adams may be rigidly believed when he writes :

" To say the truth, I was much averse to being chosen, and shall continue so ; for I am determined, if things are settled, to avoid public life. . . . At such a time as this there are many dangerous things to be done, which nobody else will do, and therefore I cannot help attempting them ; but in peaceful times there are always hands enough ready."

The letters of Adams to his wife from the time of his appointment to Congress are delightful reading. Not because they communicate interesting historical facts, which indeed it was not safe to set down in correspondence, but rather because in a thousand little ways they cast such a vivid light upon the very striking character of the man himself, and give us his personal surroundings, also that atmosphere of the times which was intense to a degree which we hardly picture to ourselves as we read cold sketches of them. We see his anxiety sometimes transiently darkening into despondency; for his energetic, impatient temperament chafes occasionally at the delays of more timid souls. But anon his high spirit gives him gleams of bright hope; no one who has a cause so near at heart as Adams had the cause of America ever despairs more than temporarily in hours of fatigue. Generally Adams's courage is of the stubborn and determined sort; he feels with something of bitterness the sacrifices which he seems to be making at the cost of his family, and meets them as might be expected of such a typical descendant of the New England Puritans.

"We live, my dear soul, in an age of trial. What will be the consequence, I know not. The town of Boston, for aught I can see, must suffer martyrdom. It must expire."

"I go mourning in my heart all the day long, though I say nothing. I am melancholy for the public and anxious for my family. As for myself, a frock and trousers, a hoe and a spade, would do for my remaining days. For God's sake make your children *hardy*, *active*, and *industrious*; for strength, activity, and industry will be their only resource and dependence."

This he reiterates : —

"The education of our children is never out of my mind. Train them to virtue. Habituate them to industry, activity, and spirit. Make them consider every vice as shameful and unmanly. Fire them with ambition to be useful."

On August 10, 1774, Mr. Adams set forth upon a journey which was to give him his first opportunity to see other places than the small town of Boston and the eastern villages, to meet persons whose habits of thought and ways of life differed from those prevalent among the descendants of the Pilgrims. With three of his fellow delegates [1] he started in a coach, " and rode to Coolidge's," whither a " large number of gentlemen " had gone before and had " pre-pared an entertainment for them." The part-ing after dinner " was truly affecting, beyond all description affecting." The following days proved most interesting and agreeable. At every place of any consequence the travelers were received with flattering attentions. The people turned out in crowds ; bells were rung, even cannon were fired ; the feasting was fre-

[1] Bowdoin declined ; Sam Adams, Cushing, Paine, and John Adams went.

quent and plentiful; every person of any note called on them; and they had ample opportunities to learn the opinions and to judge the feelings of the influential citizens all along the route. Adams was naturally much pleased; he began to have that sense of self-importance which expanded so rapidly during many years to come. "No governor of a province or general of an army," he complacently remarks, "was ever treated with so much ceremony and assiduity." But he modestly translates the "expressions of respect to us" into "demonstrations of the sympathy of this people with the Massachusetts Bay and its capital." He told his wife: —

"I have not time nor language to express the hospitality and the studied and expensive respect with which we have been treated in every stage of our progress. If Camden, Chatham, Richmond, and St. Asaph had traveled through the country, they could not have been entertained with greater demonstrations of respect than Cushing, Paine, and the brace of Adamses have been. . . . I confess the kindness, the affection, the applause which have been given to me, and especially to our province, have many a time filled my bosom and streamed from my eyes."

It was the period when gentlemen, dining and shaking hands, were full of noble patriotism and a generous sense of brotherhood, before the problems and hardships of a tedious and painful conflict had bred weariness and doubt, before the rivalries of office and authority had given rise to jealousy and division.

But amid the courtesies the Massachusetts men had not been without instructive hints as to what difference of opinion they must expect to encounter, and how it would be prudent for them to bear themselves. Forthwith after his appointment Adams had written to the shrewd old lawyer, the Nestor of the Massachusetts patriots, Joseph Hawley, and in reply had received a singularly wise as well as kindly letter of advice. Having disposed of Adams's expressions of diffidence with some friendly words of encouragement, this sagacious counselor said : —

"You cannot, sir, but be fully apprised, that a good issue of the Congress depends a good deal on the harmony, good understanding, and I had almost said brotherly love of its members. . . . Now there is an opinion which does in some degree obtain in the other colonies, that the Massachusetts gentlemen, and especially of the town of Boston, do affect to dictate and take the lead in continental measures ; that we are apt, from an inward vanity and self-conceit, to assume big and haughty airs. Whether this opinion has any foundation in fact I am not certain. . . . Now I pray that everything in the conduct and behavior of our gentlemen, which might tend to beget or strengthen such an opinion, might be most carefully avoided.   It is highly probable, in my opinion, that you will meet gentlemen from several of the other colonies fully equal to yourselves, or any of you, in their knowledge of Great Britain, the colonies, law, history, government, commerce, etc. . . . And by what we from time to time see in the public papers, and what our assembly and committees have received from the assemblies and committees of the more southern colonies, we must be satisfied that they have men of as much sense and literature as any we can or ever could boast of."

Do these cautious words indicate that this keen reader of men had already seen in John Adams the presumptuous and headstrong temperament which was to make life so hard for him in the years to come? But the sound admonition, well meant and well taken, was corroborated by occurrences on the journey.   In New York, McDougall, an eminent patriot, advised the Massachusetts men " to avoid every expression here which looked like an allusion to the last appeal."   A party in that province, he said, were "intimidated, lest the leveling spirit of the New England colonies should propagate itself into New York.   Another party are prompted by Episcopalian prejudices against New England."   At an entertainment in the city Mr. Philip Livingston, "a great, rough, rapid mortal," with whom "there is no holding any conversation," seemed "to dread New England, the leveling spirit," etc., threw out distasteful hints "of the Goths and Vandals," and made unpleasant allusions to "our hanging the Quakers," etc. Perhaps it is to the self-restraint which Mr. Adams had to impose on his resentful tongue at these interviews that we must attribute his harsh criticism of the city and its people : —

"We have been treated," he admitted, "with an assiduous respect; but I have not seen one real gentleman, one well-bred man, since I came to town. At their entertainments there is no conversation that is agreeable; there is no modesty, no attention to one another. They talk very loud, very fast, and all together. If they ask you a question, before you can utter three words of your answer they will break out upon you again, and talk away."

But if Mr. Adams was a little pettish at not being listened to with a gentlemanlike deference by the New Yorkers, he had worse to endure before he set foot in Philadelphia. A party of Philadelphian "Sons of Liberty" came out to meet the Massachusetts travelers, and warned them they had been represented as "four desperate adventurers," John Adams and Paine being young lawyers of "no great talents, reputation, or weight," who were seeking to raise themselves into consequence by "courting popularity." Moreover, they were "suspected of having independence in view;" but if they should utter the word they would be "undone," for independence was as "unpopular in Pennsylvania and in all the middle and southern states as the Stamp Act itself."

All this could hardly have been gratifying, even if it were wholesome. But the quartette took it wonderfully well, and shrewdly acted upon it. They were even so far reticent and moderate in the debates as to be outstripped by many in rebellious expressions; and though really more sternly in earnest and more advanced in their views than any others, they skillfully so managed it that for a long while they were not recognized as constituting a vanguard, or as being either leaders or drivers of the rest. Indeed, their visible moderation provoked some uncomplimentary utterances of surprise. While they measured their words rather within than beyond the limits of what their colony was anxious to make good, the impetuous southerners vented more reckless language, and soon found themselves committed to the forward movement by this hasty and unintentional assumption of a position at the head of the column. "The gentlemen from Virginia" pleased Mr. Adams much. They "appear to be the most spirited and consistent of any," he said. "Young Rutledge," who "was high enough," apparently astonished and perhaps not a little amused Mr. Adams, heretofore without experience of a temperament so unlike the restrained but stubborn spirit of the old-fashioned New Englander. Sometimes tongues moved freely under artificial stimulus; thus one day "we went with Mr. William Barrell to his store, and drank punch, and ate dried smoked sprats with him;" in the evening, at Mr. Mifflin's, there was "an elegant supper, and we drank sentiments till eleven o'clock. Lee and Harrison were very high. Lee had dined with Mr. Dickinson, and drank burgundy the whole afternoon." There were enough treasonable toasts that festal night to have seriously troubled the patriotic revelers, had the royal authorities found it more convenient to punish such vinous disaffection.

Not much real work could be done by this first Congress. In fact it was simply a conclave of selected citizens convened to talk over the imminent crisis. The people had invested them with no authority, and could expect only wise counsel. Thus the sole definite result of their deliberations was a recommendation of a non-exportation and non-importation league of all the provinces. It was a poor medicine, but it was according to the knowledge of the times; heroic but mistaken surgery, reminding one of the blood-letting which used to be practiced in those same days at the very times when all the vigor of the system seemed likely to be taxed to the uttermost. On the verge of a war with Great Britain, the colonists were bidden by their wise men to impoverish themselves as much as possible, and to cut off the supply of all the numerous articles of common necessity and daily use, which they would only be able to replenish after the war should be over. It is true that they hoped to avoid war by this commercial pressure upon England, and there is so much plausibility in the argument that, had not the folly of the policy been demonstrated by its palpable failure before the war of the Revolution, and again, a generation later, before the war of 1812, it might possibly still be believed in to this day. It is now known that commercial pressure has often hastened peace, but never averted war. But when the first Congress met, experiments had not yet manifested this truth. Mr. Adams apparently had some glimmering appreciation of the case, for he only favored half of the measure, approving of non-exportation, but not of non-importation. This was foolish, being a plan for putting out money without taking it back.

Upon another question which arose also, Mr. Adams was very imperfectly satisfied with the result of the deliberations. A great committee was formed, upon which each colony was represented by two of its members, and which was charged with the duty of drafting a declaration of rights. A second committee, of half the size, was also deputed to specify wherein the enumerated rights had been infringed. The report of the second committee, when rendered, was referred to the first committee, which was at the same time increased in numbers. Mr. Adams was an original member of the first committee, which afterward for a time became of such importance as to supersede the regular sittings of the full Congress, and at last suffered very naturally from the jealousy of those who were not included in it. Adams was also one of the sub-committee appointed to draft the report, and he struggled hard to have embodied in the declaration an assertion of "natural rights," as a general basis. "I was," he said, "very strenuous for retaining and insisting on it, as a resource to which we might be driven by Parliament much sooner than we were aware." But after long and earnest discussion he was defeated, as has been supposed, through the "influence of the conservative Virginia members." [1]

---

[1] Mr. C. F. Adams, in his *Life of John Adams.*

The really important function, which this Congress fulfilled efficiently and with the best results, was the establishment of a sense of unity among the colonies. Not only were their representative men enabled to know each other, but, through the reports which they carried home and spread abroad among their neighbors, the people of each province could form some fair estimate of the prevalent temper and the quality of sentiment in every other province. The temperature of each colony could be marked with fair accuracy on the patriotic thermometer. The wishes and the fears of the several communities, based on their distinct interests, were appreciated with a near approach to accuracy. The leaders in the movement could discern the obstacles which they had to encounter. The characters and opinions of influential men were learned; it was known how far each could be relied upon, and at what point of advance one or another might be expected to take fright. On the whole, the outcome of all this comparison and observation was satisfactory. There was a substantial concordance, which left room indeed for much variety in schemes of policy, in anticipations of results, in doctrines concerning rights, and in theories as to the relationship of the colonies to that step-dame called the mother country.

But in the main there was a fundamental consent that England was exercising an intolerable tyranny, and that resistance must be made to whatever point might prove necessary. Also there was a manifest loyalty towards each other, and a determination to stand together and to make the cause of one the cause of all. To the delegation from Massachusetts this feeling was all-important and most reassuring. Adams seized eagerly upon every indication of it. By nature he was a man of action rather than of observation; and upon the present errand he had to do violence to his native qualities in many ways. It is droll to see this impetuous and imperious creature seeking to curb himself, this most self-asserting of men actually keeping himself in the background by an exertion of will nothing less than tremendous. His painful consciousness of the necessities of the situation, impressed upon him by others and confirmed by his own common sense, is constantly apparent. For two months the rash and outspoken man is politic and reticent, the headstrong leader assumes moderation in the middle rank. In September he wrote: " We have had numberless prejudices to remove here. We have been obliged to act with great delicacy and caution. We have been obliged to keep ourselves out of sight, and to feel pulses, and to sound the depths; to insinuate our sentiments, designs, and desires by means of other persons, sometimes of one province, sometimes of another."

No reports of the debates remain which can give us any just knowledge of the part he played or the influence he exercised. It was not prudent for semi-rebels to keep such records. But his diary and his letters, especially those to his wife, from which most of the foregoing quotations have been made, reflect with picturesque and delightful naturalness his struggles with himself, his opinions of others, his anxiety, his irritations, his alternate hopes and fears, and intermittent turns of despondency and reassurance. The reader of these memorials, which Adams has left behind him, will be struck to see how very emotional he was; varying moods succeed each other, as shadow and sunshine chase one another over the face of the fields in springtime. Excitement, hopefulness, kindliness, weariness, dislikings, mistrust, doubt, pleasure, ennui, moralizings, checker in lively succession records only too brief for so varied a display. Beyond this personal element they also give much of the atmosphere of Congress. At first he burst forth in enthusiastic admiration of that body: "There is in the Congress a collection of the greatest men upon this continent in point of abilities, virtues, and fortunes. The magnanimity and public spirit which I see here make me blush for the sordid, venal herd which I have seen in my own province." Again he wrote to Warren: "Here are fortunes, abilities, learning, eloquence, acuteness, equal to any I ever met with in my life. . . . Every question is discussed with a moderation, an acuteness, and a minuteness equal to that of Queen Elizabeth's privy council." But the moderation and minuteness, admirable qualities as they were, involved vexation in the shape of "infinite delays." So occasionally Adams finds his pulse beating somewhat faster than that of others, and says with less satisfaction: "But then, when you ask the question, 'What is to be done?' they answer: 'Stand still. Bear with patience. If you come to a rupture with the troops all is lost!' Resuming the first charter, absolute independency, etc., are ideas which startle people here." "They shudder at the prospect of blood," he says, yet are "unanimously and unalterably against submission" by Massachusetts to any of the acts of Parliament. Adams felt very keenly the inconsistency between these sentiments. He knew that the choice lay between submission and blood, and he was irritated at seeing Congress guilty of what seemed to him the weakness, unquestionably wholly alien from his own character,

of recoiling from the consequences of that
which they acknowledged to be the proper
course. He noted with disgust the " general
opinion here, that it is practicable for us in the
Massachusetts to live wholly without a legislature and courts of justice as long as will be
necessary to obtain relief." "A more adequate
support and relief to the Massachusetts should
be adopted," he said, than "figurative pane-
gyrics upon our wisdom, fortitude, and temperance," coupled with " most fervent exhortations
to perseverance." "Patience, forbearance, long-
suffering are the lessons taught here for our
province," — lessons which oftentimes severely
taxed his " art and address," though he did his
best to receive them with a serene countenance.

But anon these expressions of impatience and
discontent were varied by outbursts of enthusiastic joyousness. A rumor came of a bombard-
ment of Boston, and he writes : " War ! War !
War ! was the cry, and it was pronounced in a
tone which would have done honor to the oratory of a Briton or a Roman. If it had proved
true,[1] you would have heard the thunder of an
American Congress." When the spirited resolutions from Suffolk County, Massachusetts,
were presented to Congress, and received in a
warm, kindred temper, he exclaims in joyous

---

[1] The rumor was quickly contradicted.

triumph : " This day convinced me that America will support the Massachusetts, or perish with her." He was profoundly affected by manifestations of sympathy for his province. The intensity of such times is brought home to us as we read his words : " The esteem, the affection, the admiration for the people of Boston and the Massachusetts, which were expressed yesterday, and the fixed determination that they should be supported, were enough to melt a heart of stone. I saw the tears gush into the eyes of the old, grave, pacific Quakers of Pennsylvania."

All the while, through these trying alternations, he more and more accustomed himself to think, though never openly to speak, of the end towards which events were surely tending, an end which he anticipated more confidently, and contemplated more resolutely, than probably any of his comrades. Let our people, he advised, drill and lay in military stores, but " let them avoid war, *if possible, — if possible*, I say." Many little indications show how slender, in his inmost thought, he conceived this possibility to be. On September 20, 1774, he was in a very ardent frame of mind. " Frugality, my dear," he wrote to a wife who needed no such admonitions, " frugality, economy, parsimony must be our refuge. I hope the ladies are every day diminishing their ornaments, and the gentlemen too.   Let us eat potatoes and drink water.   Let us wear canvas and undressed sheepskins, rather than submit to the unrighteous and ignominious domination that is prepared for us."   These injunctions to abstemiousness were perhaps merely reactionary after some of the "incessant feasting" which was trying the digestion of the writer.   For these patriots at this early stage of the troubles were not without alleviations amid their cares and toils.   From nine in the morning till three in the afternoon they attended to business, "then we adjourn and go to dine with some of the nobles of Pennsylvania at four o'clock, and feast upon ten thousand delicacies, and sit drinking madeira, claret, and burgundy till six or seven, and then go home fatigued to death with business, company, and care."   Similar allusions to " a mighty feast," " an elegant feast," to turtle, rich dishes, and glorious wines abound.   It was probably when the gastric resources had been too sorely taxed by these fiery hospitalities that he became irritated and impatient, so that he said to his wife : " Tedious indeed is our business, — slow as snails."   " I am wearied to death with the life I lead."

As the October days glided by and the end of the session did not seem to be at hand, his natural impatience frequently broke out, expressed with that sarcastic acerbity which he so often displayed.

"The deliberations of Congress are spun out to an immeasurable length. There is so much wit, sense, learning, acuteness, subtlety, eloquence, etc., among fifty gentlemen, . . . that an immensity of time is spent unnecessarily."

"This assembly is like no other that ever existed. Every man in it is a great man, an orator, a critic, a statesman ; and therefore every man upon every question must show his oratory, his criticism, and his political abilities. The consequence of this is, that business is drawn and spun out to an immeasurable length. I believe, if it was moved and seconded that we should come to a resolution that three and two make five, we should be entertained with logic and rhetoric, law, history, politics, and mathematics ; and then — we should pass the resolution, unanimously, in the affirmative."

"These great wits, these subtle critics, these refined geniuses, these learned lawyers, these wise statesmen, are so fond of showing their parts and powers, as to make their consultations very tedious. Young Ned Rutledge is a perfect bob-o-lincoln, — a swallow, a sparrow, a peacock ; excessively vain, excessively weak, and excessively variable and unsteady ; jejune, inane, and puerile."

The Adams censoriousness was bubbling to the surface. Even the "perpetual round of feasting" began to pall upon his simple New England stomach, and he grumbles that "Phil- adelphia, with all its trade and wealth and regularity, is not Boston. The morals of our people are much better; their manners are more polite and agreeable; they are purer English; our language is better; our taste is better; our persons are handsomer; our spirit is greater; our laws are wiser; our religion is superior; our education is better." But by November 28, when he was able at last to start for home, he recovered his good-nature, and though he had to depart in "a very great rain," yet he could speak of "the happy, the peaceful, the elegant, the hospitable and polite city of Philadelphia," and declared his expectation "ever to retain a most grateful, pleasing sense of the many civilities" he had received there.

In truth there were sound reasons to account for Mr. Adams's irritability and critical outbursts. Though he had sense enough not to say so, yet evidently he was dissatisfied with the practical achievements of the Congress. In a momentous crisis, with events pressing and anxious throngs hanging expectant upon the counsels of the sages in debate, those sages had broken up their deliberations, and were carrying home to their constituents only a recommendation of commercial non-intercourse. One half of this scheme Adams plainly saw to be foolish; the mischief of the other half he did not comprehend; yet he was shrewd enough to

give it small credit for efficiency. Of an active,
impatient temperament, he was sorely discouraged at this outcome of a gathering to which
he had gone with high hopes. He could hardly
be expected to appreciate that a greater rate
of speed would probably have resulted in a
check and reaction. By doing too much Congress would have stimulated a revulsion of popular feeling ; by doing too little it tempted
the people to demand more. The really serious
misfortune was, that the little which was done
was unpopular. On his way home Mr. Adams
learned that non-intercourse was so ill-received
in New York that the Tories were jubilant, and
expected to obtain conclusive possession of the
province.

CHAPTER IV

MR. ADAMS came home only to change the scene of his public labor. The provincial assembly at once summoned him for consultation, and directly afterward he was chosen a member of that body as a delegate from Braintree. No sooner had it adjourned, in December, than he found himself involved in a new undertaking. The lively newspaper discussions, conducted after the fashion of the times by essays and arguments in the form of letters, constituted an important means of influencing popular sentiment. The Tory "Massachusettensis"[1] was doing very effective work on the king's side, and was accomplishing a perceptible defection from the patriot ranks. Adams took up his pen, as "Novanglus," in the Boston Gazette, and maintained the controversy with absorbing ardor and gratifying success until the bloodshed at Lexington put an end to merely inky warfare. The last of his papers, actually in type at the time of the fray, was never published.

[1] Judge Leonard.

Shortly after that conflict Mr. Adams rode over the scene of action and pursuit, carefully gathering information. On his return he was taken seriously ill with a fever, and before he was fairly recovered he was obliged to set forth on his way to Philadelphia, where Congress was to meet again on May 5, 1775. He traveled in a "sulky," with a servant on horseback, and arrived on May 10. It was no light matter in those troubled times, within a few days after bloody collisions between British troops and Yankee farmers, to leave his wife and small children alone in a farmhouse not many miles from the waters on which rode his majesty's ships of war. He wrote to Mrs. Adams: "Many fears and jealousies and imaginary dangers will be suggested to you, but I hope you will not be impressed by them. In case of real danger, of which you cannot fail to have previous intimations, fly to the woods with our children." But he was happy in being well mated for the exigencies of such days. His admirable wife would perhaps have not been less distinguished than himself had she not been handicapped by the misfortune of sex. She was a woman of rare mind, high courage, and of a patriotism not less intense and devoted than that of any hero of the Revolution. Mr. Adams found infinite support and comfort in her and gratefully acknowledged it. His account of Dickinson, by way of comparison with his own case, is at once comical and pathetic. That gentleman's mother and wife, he says "were continually distressing him with their remonstrances. His mother said to him: 'Johnny, you will be hanged; your estate will be forfeited and confiscated; you will leave your excellent wife a widow, and your charming children orphans, beggars and infamous.' From my soul I pitied Mr. Dickinson. . . . If my mother and my wife had expressed such sentiments to me, I was certain that, if they did not wholly unman me and make me an apostate, they would make me the most miserable man alive." But he was "very happy" in that his mother and wife, and indeed all his own and his wife's families, had been uniformly of the same mind as himself, "so that I always enjoyed perfect peace at home." Thus free from any dread of a fusillade in the rear, he could push forward faster than many others.

Everywhere along his route towards Philadelphia he beheld cheering signs of the spirit which he longed to see universal among the people. In New York the Tories "durst not show their heads;" the patriots had "shut up the port, seized the custom-house, arms, ammunition, etc., called a provincial Congress," and agreed "to stand by whatever shall be ordered by the continental and their provincial Congress." The great Tory, Dr. Cooper, had fled on board a man-of-war. "The Jerseys are aroused and greatly assist the friends of liberty in New York. North Carolina has done bravely." In Connecticut "everything is doing . . . that can be done by men, both for New York and Boston." In Philadelphia he saw a "wonderful phenomenon, . . . a field-day, on which three battalions of soldiers were reviewed, making full two thousand men" of all arms. Colonel Washington was showing his opinion of the situation by appearing in Congress in his uniform. On all sides were the tokens of warlike preparation. Adams was overjoyed. "We shall see better times yet!" he cheerily exclaimed. "The military spirit which runs through the continent is truly amazing." He himself caught some whiff of the enthusiasm for actual gunpowder. "I have bought," he said, "some military books, and intend to buy more." "Oh that I were a soldier! I will be. I am reading military books. Every one must, and will, and shall be a soldier." But in cooler moments he concluded that his age and health rendered it foolish for him to think of undertaking camp life. He was right, of course; his proper place was among the civilians. Yet he accepted it not without some grumbling. A

little later, when he rode out with a great caval-
cade to honor Washington and others on their
departure for the leaguer around Boston, he
wrote home, describing the "pride and pomp"
of the occasion: "I, poor creature, worn out
with scribbling for my bread and my liberty,
low in spirits and weak in health, must leave
others to wear the laurels which I have sown."
He seemed at times to have an unpleasant jealousy that the military heroes appeared to be
encountering greater dangers than the civilians,
and he argued to show that, in one way and
another, his risk was not less than that of an
officer in the army. He says that sometimes
he feels "an ambition to be engaged in the more
active, gay, and dangerous scenes; dangerous, I
say, but I recall the word, for there is no course
more dangerous than that which I am in." But
he had no need to defend either his courage or
his capacity for self-devotion; neither could be
arraigned, even by malicious opponents.

Naturally the display of activity and zeal on
the part of the disaffected disturbed those who,
without being Tories, were yet of a less determined temper, less hopeless of reconciliation,
more reluctant to go fast, and dreading nothing so much as an inevitable step towards
separation. Independence was still spoken of
deprecatingly, with awe and bated breath, and

its friends were compelled to recognize the
continuing necessity of suppressing their views
and maintaining for the present only a sort
of secret brotherhood. Yet it was inevitable
that their sentiments should be divined by the
keen observers who thought differently. The
moderatist or reconciliationist party not only
understood the temper prevalent, though not
universal, in the New England section, but they
read Mr. Adams with perfect accuracy, — a
perusal never, it must be confessed, very difficult to be made by any clever man. It was
not without disappointment after his encouraging journey that he "found this Congress like
the last; . . . a strong jealousy of us from
New England, and the Massachusetts in particular; suspicions entertained of designs of independency, an American republic, presbyte-
rian principles, and twenty other things." He
had to admit that his "sentiments were heard
in Congress with great caution, and seemed to
make but little impression." The reticence
and self-restraint practiced by him in the early
weeks of the preceding summer session had not
long retarded a just estimate both of his opinions and his abilities. This is proved by the
fact that the moderates now singled him out as
their chief and most dangerous antagonist. It
was this respect and hostility manifested pre-

eminently towards him by the opponents of separation which, combined with his own strenuous force, placed him during this winter at the head of the party of independence.

In strong contrast with him, upon the other side, was Dickinson, leader of the conciliationists, rich, courteous, popular, cultivated, plausible, amiable, moderate by nature, and handicapped by the ladies at home. This tardy, though really sincere patriot, now insisted that a second petition, another "olive-branch," should be sent to the king. Adams wrought earnestly against "this measure of imbecility," the success of which he afterward said "embarrassed every exertion of Congress." Dickinson prevailed, though only narrowly and imperfectly; and Adams was extremely disgusted. His views were well established; he had a permanent faith that "powder and artillery are the most efficacious, sure, and infallible conciliatory measures we can adopt." During the debate he left the hall, and was followed by Mr. Dickinson, who overtook him in the yard, and berated him with severe language in an outburst of temper quite unusual with the civil Pennsylvanian. Mr. Adams retorted, according to his own account, "very coolly." But from this time forth there was a breach between these two, and though in debate they were able to preserve the amenities, they spoke no more with each other in private.

But there were more horses harnessed to the congressional coach than Mr. Dickinson could drive. Many necessities were pressing upon that body, and many problems were imminent, which could not readily be solved in consistence with loyalist or even with moderatist principles. Adams, hampered by no such principles, would have had little difficulty in establishing a policy of great energy — possibly of too great energy — had he been allowed to dictate to the assembly. Many years afterwards, in writing his autobiography, he gave a very graphic and comprehensive sketch of his views at this time. It is true that he was looking back through a long vista of years, and his memory was not always accurate, so that we may doubt whether at the actual moment his scheme was quite so bold and broad, so rounded and complete, as he recalled it. But unquestionably his feelings are substantially well shown.

"I thought," he says, "the first step ought to be to recommend to the people of every state in the Union to seize on all the crown officers and hold them, with civility, humanity, and generosity, as hostages for the security of the people of Boston, and to be exchanged for them as soon as the British army would release them ; that we ought to recommend to the people of all the states to institute governments for themselves, under their own authority, and that without loss of time ; that we ought to declare the colonies free, sovereign, and independent states, and then to inform Great Britain that we were willing to enter into negotiations with them for the redress of all grievances and a restoration of harmony between the two countries upon permanent principles. All this I thought might be done before we entered into any connection, alliances, or negotiations with foreign powers. I was also for informing Great Britain, very frankly, that hitherto we were free ; but, if the war should be continued, we were determined to seek alliances with France, Spain, and any other power of Europe that would contract with us. That we ought immediately to adopt the army in Cambridge as a continental army, to appoint a general and all other officers, take upon ourselves the pay, subsistence, clothing, arming, and munitions of the troops. This is a concise sketch of the plan which I thought the only reasonable one ; and from conversation with the members of Congress I was then convinced, and have been ever since convinced, that it was the general sense of a considerable majority of that body. This system of measures I publicly and privately avowed without reserve."

It is evident from some contemporary statements that, at least in the early days of the session, these avowals were not quite so open and unreserved as Mr. Adams afterward remembered them to have been. Though it is true that the chief parts of this plan were soon adopted, and though it is altogether credible that the feeling which led to that adoption was already very perceptible to Mr. Adams in his private interviews with individual delegates, yet it is tolerably certain that, had he exploded such a box of startling fireworks in the face of Congress during the first days of its sitting, the outcry and scattering would have stricken him with sore dismay. Fortunately, though burning with impatience, he was more politic than he afterwards described himself, and he had sufficient good sense to wait a little until events brought the delegates face to face with issues which the moderatists could rationally and consistently decide only in one way. He did not like the waiting, he chafed and growled, but he wisely endured, nevertheless, until his hour came. When and how that hour advanced is now to be seen.

Mr. Dickinson had not carried his motion for a second memorial to King George without paying a price for it; Congress simultaneously declared that, by reason of grave doubt as to the success of that measure, it was expedient to put the colonies chiefly threatened, especially New York, into a condition for defense. This was a practical measure, bringing some comfort to the party of action. Soon also there came from the

Massachusetts Assembly a letter, setting forth the condition of that province now so long without any real government, and asking "explicit advice respecting the taking up and exercising the powers of civil government." This missive presented a problem which many gentlemen would gladly have shunned, or at least postponed, but which could be shunned and postponed no longer; a large and busy population could not exist for an indefinite period without civil authorities of some sort; the people of Massachusetts Bay had already been in this anomalous condition for a long while, and though they had done wonderfully well, yet the strain was not much longer to be endured. If Congress, thus supplicated, refused to take some action in the premises, it would be open to the charge of abdicating its function of adviser to the colonies, and so would lose a large part of its *raison d'être*. The letter was referred to a committee, and upon their report a long debate ensued. The Massachusetts delegates were much consulted, and at last, on June 9, Congress replied that, "no obedience being due to the act of Parliament for altering their charter, nor to any officers who endeavor to subvert that charter, letters should be written to the people in the several towns requesting them to elect representatives to an assembly, who should in their turn elect a council, and these two bodies should exercise the powers of government for the time."

This was very good, but a much more important matter was still to be disposed of. From the beginning of the session it had been a main object with Mr. Adams to induce the Congress to adopt, so to speak, the army which was engaged in besieging the British forces in Boston. At present this extraordinary martial assemblage was in the most singular condition ever presented by such a body. It could not be said that the officers commanded by any lawful title or authority, or that the rank and file obeyed otherwise than by virtue of their own willingness to do so. The whole existing condition of military as well as of civil affairs was based upon little more than general understanding and mutual acquiescence. Mr. Adams was profoundly resolved that the army should become the army of Congress, for nondescript as that body still was, yet at least the army, when adopted by it, would become more the army of all the provinces and less that of Massachusetts alone than it might now be described. He was overwhelmed with letters, both from influential civilians of Massachusetts and from the principal military officers, imploring him in urgent terms to carry through this measure. It was no easy matter ; for, besides the inevitable opposition of the moderates and conciliationists, he had to encounter many personal jealousies and ambitions. The adoption of the army involved the nomination of a commander-in-chief, and of subordinate generals, and there were many who either wished these positions, or had friends and favorite aspirants whose possible pretensions they espoused. Mr. Adams found that he could make little progress towards unanimity by private interviews, arguments, and appeals. Accordingly, at last, he came to a very characteristic decision. More than once in his life he showed his taste and capacity for a *coup d'état* in politics. When he dealt such a blow, he did it in the most effectual way, vigorously, and without warning ; thus he confounded his opponents and carried his point. We shall see more than one other striking instance of this sudden strategy and impetuous courage, in his future career. Now, finding not only that he could not control the delegation from his own State, but that even the gentlemen from Virginia would not agree to unite upon their own fellow citizen, " full of anxieties concerning these confusions, and apprehending daily " the receipt of distressing news from Boston, despairing of effecting an agreement by personal persuasion, but recognizing that here again was a case where the

issue, if forced, could have but one conclusion,
he one morning, just before going into the hall,
announced to Samuel Adams that he had resolved to take a step which would *compel* his
colleagues from Massachusetts and all the other
delegates " to declare themselves for or against
something. I am determined this morning to
make a direct motion that Congress should adopt
the army before Boston, and appoint Colonel
Washington commander of it. Mr. Adams
seemed to think very seriously of it, but said
nothing."

The move was made with the same decisive
promptitude which marked this divulging of the
intention. Upon the opening of that day's
session Mr. Adams obtained the floor, and made
the motion for the adoption. He then pro-
ceeded briefly to sketch the imperative necessities of the time, and closed with a eulogy upon
a certain gentleman from Virginia, " who could
unite the cordial exertions of all the colonies
better than any other person." There was no
doubt who was signified ; even the modest gentleman himself could not pretend to be ignorant, and hastily sought refuge in the library.
Washington was not the only person who was
startled out of his composure by this sudden
thrusting forward of a proposal which heretofore had only been a subject of private and by

no means harmonious discussion. Mr. Hancock, in the president's chair, could not conceal his mortification, for he had his own aspirations in this same direction. Many gentlemen expressed doubts as to the propriety of placing this southerner at the head of an army in New England, chiefly composed of New England troops, and now commanded by New England officers apparently equal to their functions. Mr. Pendleton, though himself from Virginia, was especially prominent in this presentation of the case ; so was Mr. Sherman of Connecticut ; and even Mr. Adams's own colleague, Mr. Cushing, allowed it to be understood that he was of the same opinion. But Mr. Adams had dealt a master-stroke. There must be some wriggling of individuals, who might thereafter remain his enemies ; but of enemies he was never afraid. It was inevitable that he should carry his point, that Congress should accept his measure ; so he had the satisfaction of seeing the delegates, one by one, many pleased, some doubtful, a few sorely grumbling, fall into line behind the standard which he had so audaciously planted. A little work was shrewdly done outside the hall, a few days were prudently suffered to elapse for effervescence ; the reluctant ones were given sufficient opportunity to see that they were helpless, and then, upon the formal motion of Thomas Johnson of Maryland, George Washington was unanimously chosen commander-in-chief of the united forces of the colonies. On June 17, the day of the gallant battle of Bunker's Hill, Adams wrote in joyous triumph to his wife: "I can now inform you that the Congress have made choice of the modest and virtuous, the amiable, generous, and brave George Washington, esquire, to be general of the American army. This appointment will have a great effect in cementing and securing the union of these colonies." With some natural anxiety to have his action justified by the good acceptance of his fellow citizens of Massachusetts, he adds: "I hope the people of our province will treat the general with all that confidence and affection, that politeness and respect, which is due to one of the most important characters in the world. The liberties of America depend upon him in a great degree." The next day he wrote, still in the highest spirits: "This Congress are all as deep as the delegates from the Massachusetts, and the whole continent as forward as Boston. We shall have a redress of grievances, or an assumption of all the powers of government, legislative, executive, and judicial, throughout the whole continent, very soon." He had been conducting an arduous struggle, he had gained

two points, deserving to be regarded not only as
essential but as finally decisive of the success of
his policy.   He chiefly had induced Congress to
recommend Massachusetts to establish a rebellious government; he had compelled Congress to
adopt an army conducting open war against
King George.   Thus, as he said, he had got all
the other provinces as deep in rebellion as his
own Massachusetts, and the two acts logically
involved independence.

Concerning this nomination of Washington,
Mr. C. F. Adams says: " In the life of Mr.
Adams, more than in that of most men, occur
instances of this calm but decided assumption
of a fearful responsibility in critical moments.
But what is still more remarkable is that they
were attended with a uniformly favorable result." Without now discussing the other instances, it may be admitted that the present
one deserves even this somewhat magniloquent
laudation. The measure brought the possibility
of a hearty union of the colonies in real war
to a sharp, immediate, practical test. It was
the extreme of audacity for this one man to
stand forth alone, having secured no support-
ers, apparently not having even felt the pulse
of New England, to propose that there should
be set over an army of New England troops,
led by New England officers, encamped on

New England soil, supported by New England resources, fighting in what was thus far chiefly if not solely a New England quarrel, and which had met with no reverses, a commander from a distant and, in a proper sense, even a foreign state. Had the New Englanders received this slightly known southerner with dissatisfaction, a more unfortunate and fatal move could not have been made. In truth the responsibility assumed was sufficiently great! But the stake to be won was the union of the thirteen provinces, and the irrevocable assurance that the quarrel to its end was to be not that of one but that of all. Unless this stake could be won, all must be lost. But to determine when and how to play the test card in so momentous a game called for the highest nerve. Adams acted upon an implicit faith in the liberal intelligence of the people of his region. The result proved his thorough comprehension of them, and set the seal of wisdom upon his fearless assumption of one of the greatest political risks recorded in the world's history. It was to this sufficiency on his part for an emergency, instinctively felt rather than plainly formulated, that Adams owed in his lifetime, and has owed since his death a great respect and admiration among the people, as being a strong, virile man, who could be trusted at the crucial moment in spite of all sorts of somewhat ignoble foibles and very inexcusable blunders.

As if to encourage men of moderate capacity by showing that no one is always and evenly wise, we have now to see in a small matter the reverse of that sagacious judgment just displayed in a great matter. Throughout life Mr. Adams startled his friends by his petty mistakes not less constantly than he astounded his enemies by his grand actions. Repeatedly he got into trouble through an uncontrollable propensity to act without forethought, upon sudden impulse. This was a poor development of the same trait which, in happier moments, led to such prompt, daring, and fortunate movements as the nomination of Washington. A few weeks after that event it happened that a young man, whose patriotism had been under a cloud, was about to leave Philadelphia for the neighborhood of Boston. Opportunities for sending letters by safe hands being then gladly availed of, this person begged to be allowed to carry home some letters for Mr. Adams. But Adams had none written and declined the offer. Then the youth became importunate, urging that to carry only a few lines from Mr. Adams would set right his injured reputation. Foolishly Mr. Adams yielded, or rather the folly lay in what he wrote. By persons in whom he could place

perfect confidence he had for months been sending the most guarded communications; now he
seized this dubious chance to put in writing
remarks which a prudent statesman would not
have uttered in conversation without sealing
every keyhole. To General Warren he began:
" I am determined to write freely to you this
time," and thoroughly did he fulfill this determination. The other letter to his wife was a little
less distinctly outspoken; but between the two
the doings and the plans of Adams and his advanced friends in Congress were boldly sketched,
and some very harsh remarks were indulged in
concerning delegates who were not fully in harmony with him. In Rhode Island the British
intercepted the bearer and captured the letters,
which were at once published and widely distributed on both sides of the water. They
were construed as plainly showing that some
at least among the Americans were aiming at
independence; and they made a great turmoil,
stimulating resentment in the mother country,
alarming the moderates in the provinces, and
corroborating the extreme charges of the Tories.
It was afterward insisted that they did more
good than harm, because they caused lines to
be drawn sharply and hastened the final issue.
Adams himself sought consolation in this view
of the matter in his autobiography. But if

this effect was really produced, yet it could not have been foreseen, and it therefore constituted no excuse for Mr. Adams's recklessness, which had been almost incredible.

Neither did this dimly visible result act as an immediate shelter against the flight of evils from this Pandora's box. To Warren, Adams had said: "A certain great fortune and piddling genius, whose fame has been trumpeted so loudly, has given a silly cast to our whole doings." He closed the letter to his wife with this unfinished sentence: "The fidgets, the whims, the caprice, the vanity, the superstition, the irritability of some of us are enough to —;" words failed him for the expression of his disgust. "No mortal tale can equal it," as he had already said. The "piddling genius" was easily recognized as Mr. Dickinson, and the unfortunate victims of the fidgets, etc., were of course the conciliationists. Widespread wrath naturally ensued; and Mr. Adams was made for a while extremely uncomfortable. Dickinson cut him; many more treated him little better; he walked the streets a marked and unpopular man, shunned, distrusted, and disliked by many. He put the best face he could upon it, and said that the letters did not amount to so very much, after all the talk about them; but it is plain enough that he would have been glad to recall them. If they were nothing worse, at least they were crying evidence of his incorrigible and besetting weakness. He lived to be an old man and had his full share of severe lessons, but neither years nor mortifications could ever teach him to curb his hasty, ungovernable tongue. The little member was too much for him to the end, great, wise, and strong-willed as he was.

CHAPTER V

CONGRESS adjourned for the summer vacation of 1775, which enabled Mr. Adams to spend August at home. But during nearly all this brief recess he was busy with the provincial executive council, and got little rest. On the last day of the month he set out again for Philadelphia, where he arrived in the middle of September. In addition to public cares, he was for many weeks harassed with ill news from home. Dysentery became epidemic in the neighborhood of Boston during this summer and autumn. His brother had died of it before he left home; his wife's mother died in September; his wife herself and three of his four children were in turn stricken with the disease. Besides these troubles, the complexion of Congress gave him much disquietude. During the recess a reaction had set in, or at best the momentum acquired prior to the adjournment had been wholly lost. From the first secret committee Massachusetts was conspicuously omitted. Dickinson, Deane, and Jay, conciliationists all, seemed to lead a majority, and to give color to the actions of the whole body. Those unfortunate letters of Mr. Adams had been efficiently used by the moderates to alarm the many who dreaded political convulsion, prolonged war, and schemes for independence. Even old friends and coadjutors of the detected correspondent now looked coldly on him, since intimacy with him had become more than ever compromising. Yet he stood stoutly to his purposes.

"I assure you," he wrote to his wife, "the letters had no such bad effects as the Tories intended and as some of our short-sighted Whigs apprehended; so far otherwise that I see and hear every day fresh proofs that everybody is coming fast into every political sentiment contained in them. I assure you I could mention compliments passed upon them, and if a serious decision could be had upon them, the public voice would be found in their favor."

More and more zealously he was giving his whole heart and soul, his life and prospects, to the great cause. Almost every day he was engaged in debate; almost every day he had something to say about instituting state governments, about the folly of petitions to the king and of conciliatory measures. A paragraph from one of his letters to his wife, October 7, 1775, though long, is worth quoting, to show the intense and lofty spirit which animated him in these critical days : —

" The situation of things is so alarming that it is our duty to prepare our minds and hearts for every event, even the worst. From my earliest entrance into life I have been engaged in the public cause of America; and from first to last I have had upon my mind a strong impression that things would be wrought up to their present crisis. I saw from the beginning that the controversy was of such a nature that it never would be settled, and every day convinces me more and more. This has been the source of all the disquietude of my life. It has lain down and risen up with me these twelve years. The thought that we might be driven to the sad necessity of breaking our connection with Great Britain, exclusive of the carnage and destruction which it was easy to see must attend the separation, always gave me a great deal of grief. And even now I would gladly retire from public life forever, renounce all chance for profits or honors from the public, nay, I would cheerfully contribute my little property, to obtain peace and liberty. But all these must go and my life too before I can surrender the right of my country to a free Constitution. I dare not consent to it. I should be the most miserable of mortals ever after, whatever honors or emoluments might surround me."

Solemn words of faith and self-devotion! Yet the man who spoke them was still a subject of Great Britain, a rebel. No wonder that he chafed at the names, and longed rather to be called a free citizen and a patriot.

In spite of the hostility which he had excited, he was acquiring great influence. His energy and capacity for business compelled recognition at a time when there was more work to be done than hands to do it. The days of feasting and of comfortable discussion at the tables of Philadelphia magnates belonged to the past. Hard labor had succeeded to those banquetings. Adams thus sketches his daily round in the autumn of 1775: "I am really engaged in constant business from seven to ten in the morning in committee, from ten to four in Congress, and from six to ten again in committee." The incessant toiling injured by degrees his constitution, and within a few months he began to fear that he should break down before his two great objects, independence and a confederation, could be attained, at the present creeping pace, as it seemed to him.

This lukewarmness, so prevalent this autumn, struck him the more painfully because he had just come from a neighborhood where the aroused people were waging real war, and had set their hot hands to the plow with a dogged determination to drive it to the end of the furrow. The change to the tepid patriotism of the

Quaker City embittered him. To his diary he confided some very abusive fleers at the manners and appearance of many of his co-delegates. "There appears to me," he says, "a remarkable want of judgment in some of our members." Chase he describes as violent, boisterous, tedious upon frivolous points. So, too, is E. Rutledge, who is likewise an uncouth, ungraceful speaker, with offensive habits of shrugging his shoulders, distorting his body, wriggling his head, rolling his eyes, and speaking through his nose. John Rutledge also "dodges his head" disagreeably; and both "spout out their language in a rough and rapid torrent, but without much force or effect." Dyer, though with some good qualities, is long-winded, roundabout, obscure, cloudy, very talkative, and very tedious. Sherman's air is the "reverse of grace" when he keeps his hands still, but when he gesticulates "it is stiffness and awkwardness itself, rigid as starched linen or buckram, awkward as a junior bachelor or sophomore," so that Hogarth's genius could have invented nothing worse. Bad as Sherman is, Dickinson's "air, gait, and action are not much more elegant." Thus wrote the father of that bitter-tongued son, who, it is clear, took his ruthless sarcasm and censoriousness as an honest inheritance. But the words were only an impetuous outburst of irritation due to a pass-

ing discontent, which disappeared altogether
soon afterward, when the business of Congress
began to run more to the writer's taste. There
had to be some private safety-vent, when he
must so repress himself in public. "Zeal and
fire and activity and enterprise," he acknowledged, "strike my imagination too much. I
am obliged to be constantly on my guard, yet
the heat within will burst forth at times." Very
soon, however, the stern logic of facts, the irresistible pressure of events, controlled the action
of this session of Congress not less conclusively
than the preceding. Men might prattle of olive-
branches and the restoration of harmony, but
scarcely concealed behind the thin fog raised by
such language stood the solid substance of a
veritable rebellion. An American army was
besieging a British army; governments, not
rooted in royal or parliamentary authority, were
established in several provinces. The Congress
which had adopted that army, given it a commander, and provided for its maintenance, which
also had promoted the organization of those
governments, was a congregation of rebels, if
ever there were rebels in the world. Dickinson
and Deane were as liable to be hanged as were
the Adamses and the Lees; and Washington
himself was in scarcely more danger than any
of these civilians. In this condition of affairs

advance was inevitable. All history shows that the unresting pressure of a body of able men, resolutely striving for a definite end, furnishes a motive power which no inertia of a reluctant mass can permanently resist. Progression gains point after point till the conclusion is so assured that resistance ceases. A fresh indication of this truth was now seen in the movement to establish a fleet at the continental charge. "This naked proposition," Mr. C. F. Adams tells us, "was at once met with a storm of ridicule," in which some delegates joined who might have been looked for on the other side. But the tempest spent itself in a few days, and then a committee was appointed, charged to procure vessels, to be placed under the control of Washington. Within less than two months a real navy was in course of active preparation. Mr. Adams was a member of the committee and set zealously about the work; he sought information on all sides and exhaustively; and besides the practical equipment and manning of the vessels, he was soon ready with a maritime code.

About the same time an application from New Hampshire for advice concerning its internal policy was answered by a recommendation for calling a "full and free representation of the people;" and with advice that "the representatives, if they think it necessary, establish

such a form of government as in their judgment
will best produce the happiness of the people
during the continuance of the present dispute."
The ease with which this resolution passed, almost unchallenged by the Dickinson party, was
very encouraging. During this autumn also was
made the first effort to organize foreign embassies. Mr. Adams described this endeavor as
follows : —

"In consequence of many conversations between
Mr. Chase and me he made a motion . . . for sending ambassadors to France. I seconded the motion.
You know the state of the nerves of Congress at that
time. . . . Whether the effect of the motion resembled the shock of electricity, of mesmerism, or of gal-
vanism the most exactly, I leave you philosophers to
determine, but the grimaces, the agitations and convulsions were very great."

Vehement debates ensued, of his own share
in which Mr. Adams says : " I was remarkably
cool and, for me, unusually eloquent. On no
occasion, before or after, did I ever make a
greater impression on Congress." " Attention
and approbation were marked on every countenance." Many gentlemen came to pay him their
compliments, and even Dickinson praised him.
Nevertheless his oratory failed to secure the
practical reward of success ; the step was too far
in advance of the present position of a majority

of members.   There were "many motions" and much "tedious discussion," but "after all our argumentation the whole terminated in a committee of secret correspondence."   So Mr. Adams was again relegated to the odious duty of waiting patiently.   But he and his abettors had insured ultimate success; indeed, it was only a question how far the colonies would soon go in this direction.   It even appeared that there were some persons who desired to push foreign connections to a point much beyond that at which Mr. Adams would have rested.   Thus, Patrick Henry was in favor of alliances, even if they must be bought by concessions of territory; whereas Adams desired only treaties of commerce, advising that "we should separate ourselves as far as possible and as long as possible from all European politics and wars."   He anticipated the "Monroe Doctrine."

On December 9, 1775, Mr. Adams set out on a short visit to Massachusetts.   He was anxious to learn accurately the present temper of the people.   While there, besides advising Washington upon an important question concerning the extent of his military jurisdiction, he also arranged a personal matter.   He had lately been appointed chief justice of the province, apparently not with the expectation of securing his actual presence on the bench, but for the sake of the strength and prestige which his name would give to the newly-constituted tribunal of justice. He now accepted the office upon the clear understanding that he should not take his seat unless upon some pressing occasion.

On January 24, 1776, having found both the leaders and the people in full accord with his own sentiments, he set out in company with Elbridge Gerry on his return to Philadelphia. The two carried with them some important instructions to the Massachusetts delegates, possibly the fruit of Mr. Adams's visit, or at least matured and ripened beneath the heat of his presence. These gentlemen were bidden to urge Congress " to concert, direct, and order such further measures as shall to them appear best calculated for the establishment of right and liberty to the American colonies, upon a basis permanent and secure against the power and art of the British administration, and guarded against any future encroachments of their enemies."

But again the change from the patriotic atmosphere of Massachusetts to the tamer climate of Philadelphia dispirited Adams seriously. He wrote home, February 11, to his wife : " There is a deep anxiety, a kind of thoughtful melancholy, and in some a lowness of spirits approaching to despondency, prevailing through the

southern colonies at present." But he had at last
learned to value these intermissions correctly;
he had seen them before, even in Massachusetts,
and he recognized them as transitory. " In
this or a similar condition we shall remain, I
think, until late in the spring, when some critical
event will take place; perhaps sooner. But the
arbiter of events . . . only knows which way
the torrent will be turned. Judging by experience, by probabilities and by all appearances, I
conclude it will roll on to dominion and glory,
though the circumstances and consequences may
be bloody." This was correct forecasting; late
in the spring of 1776 a very " critical event " did
happen, entailing " bloody consequences," " dominion," and " glory." " In such great changes
and commotions," he says, " individuals are but
atoms. It is scarcely worth while to consider
what the consequences will be to us." The
" effects upon the present and future millions,
and millions of millions," engage his thoughts.
The frequent recurrence of such expressions indicates a peculiar sense of awe on his part. He
felt, to a degree that few others did at this time,
that he was in the presence of momentous events.
The prescience of a shadowy but grand future
was always with him, and impressed him like
a great religious mystery. This feeling lent a
solemn earnestness to his conduct, the wonderful

force of which is plainly perceptible, even to this day, in the meagre fragmentary records which have come down to us.

As the winter of 1776 advanced it could no longer be doubted that the American provinces were rapidly nearing an avowed independence. The middle states might be reluctant, and their representatives in Congress might set their backs towards the point which they were approaching; but they approached it nevertheless. They were like men on a raft, carried by an irresistible current in one direction, while obstinately steering in the other. Adams listened to their talk with contempt; he had no sympathy with their unwillingness to assert an undeniable fact. " I cannot but despise," he said, " the understanding which sincerely expects an honorable peace, for its credulity, and detest the hypocritical heart, which pretends to expect it when in truth it does not." He spoke with bitter irony of the timid ones who could not bring themselves to use a dreaded phrase, who were appalled by a word. " If a post or two more should bring you unlimited latitude of trade to all nations, and a polite invitation to all nations to trade with you, take care that you do not call it or think it independency; no such matter; independency is a hobgoblin of such frightful mien that it would throw a delicate person into fits to look it in the face." But by degrees he was able plainly to see the features of this alarming monster drawing nearer and nearer. He beheld an unquestionable and great advance by the other provinces towards the faith long since familiar to New England minds. " The newspapers here are full of free speculations, the tendency of which you will easily discover. The writers reason from topics which have been long in contemplation and fully understood by the people at large in New England, but have been attended to in the southern colonies only by gentlemen of free spirits and liberal minds, who are very few."

The "barons of the south" and the proprietary interests of the middle states had long been his *bêtes noires*. " All our misfortunes," he said, " arise from a single source, the reluctance of the southern colonies to a republican government." But these obstacles were beginning to yield. With the influence of Virginia in favor of independence, it was a question of no very long time for the rest of the southern provinces to fall into line, even at the sacrifice of strong prejudices. Still the conciliationists, not giving up the struggle, spread reports that commissioners were coming from the king on an errand of peace and harmony. Their talk bred vexatious delay and aroused Mr. Adams's ire. "A more egregious bubble," he said, "was never blown up, yet it has gained credit like a charm, not only with, but against, the clearest evidence." "This story of commissioners is as arrant an illusion as ever was hatched in the brain of an enthusiast, a politician, or a maniac. I have laughed at it, scolded at it, grieved at it, and I don't know but I may at an unguarded moment have rip'd at it. But it is vain to reason against such delusions."

Still, among these obstructions the great motive power worked ceaselessly and carried steadily forward the ship of state, or rather the fleet of thirteen ships which had lashed themselves together just sufficiently securely to render uniform movement a necessity. Fastened between New England and Virginia, the middle states had to drift forward with these flanking vessels. Chief engineer Adams fed the fires and let not the machinery rest. A personal attack upon him made at this time was really a hopeful symptom of the desperation to which his opponents were fast being reduced. Maryland instructed her delegates to move a self-denying ordinance, of which the implication was that Mr. Adams was urging forward independence because he was chief justice of Massachusetts, and so had a personal gain to achieve by making the office permanent. But not much could be gained by this sort of strategy. By the spring he was very sanguine. "As to declarations of independency," he said to his wife, "be patient. Read our privateering laws and our commercial laws. What signifies a word?" Yet the word did signify a great deal, and he was resolved that it should be spoken bluntly and with authority.

He saw that it would be so spoken very soon. On May 29, 1776, he wrote cheerfully: "Maryland has passed a few eccentric resolves, but these are only flashes which will soon expire. The proprietary governments are not only incumbered with a large body of Quakers, but are embarrassed by a proprietary interest; both together clog their operations a little, but these clogs are falling off, as you will soon see." The middle colonies had " never tasted the bitter cup," " never smarted," and were " therefore a little cooler; but you will see that the colonies are united indissolubly." Of this union he was assured: " Those few persons," he said, " who have attended closely to the proceedings of the several colonies for a number of years past, and reflected deeply upon the causes of this mighty contest, have foreseen that such an unanimity would take place as soon as a separation should become necessary." One immense relief he was now enjoying, which probably contributed

not a little to raise his spirits. The odious
season of reticence was over; he was at last
able to work in the cause openly and incessantly, in Congress and out of it, in debate, on
committees, and in conversation. His influence was becoming very great; his hand was
felt everywhere; during the autumn of 1775,
the winter and spring of 1776, he says that
he unquestionably did more business than any
other member of the body. He had broad ideas;
he practiced a deep and far-reaching strategy.
Long since he had conceived and formulated a
complete scheme of independence, and he laid
his plans to carry this through piece by piece,
with the idea that when every item which went
to the construction of the composite fact should
be accomplished, so that the fact undeniably
existed, then at last its declaration, even if
postponed so late, could no longer be withstood.
The three chief articles in his scheme, still
remaining to be accomplished, were, "a government in every colony, a confederation among
them all, and treaties with foreign nations to
acknowledge us a sovereign state." In fact, "a
government in every colony" really covered
the whole ground, and *was independence*. A
league between these free governments, and
connections with foreign states, were logically
only natural and desirable corollaries, not inte-

gral parts of the proposition; but practically they were very useful links to maintain it.

By the month of May the stage had been reached at which the general organization of free governments among the states, many of which had not yet gone through the form, seemed possible. On May 6 Mr. Adams brought forward a resolution, which, after being debated three days, was passed upon May 9. It recommended to those several colonies, wherein no government "sufficient to the exigencies of their affairs" had yet been established, to adopt such a government as should "best conduce to the happiness and safety" of themselves and of America. Good so far as it went, this resolve was yet felt to be somewhat vague and easy of evasion. To cure these defects Mr. Adams, Mr. Rutledge, and Mr. Lee were directed to prepare a preamble. They reported, on May 15, a paragraph which covered the whole ground of separation from Great Britain and independence of the colonies. This skillful composition recited that his Britannic Majesty, in conjunction with the Lords and Commons, had "excluded the inhabitants of these United Colonies from the protection of his crown; that the whole force of his kingdom, aided by foreign mercenaries, was being exerted for the destruction of the good people of these colonies; that it was

irreconcilable to reason and good conscience for
the colonists now to take oaths and affirmations
for the support of any government under the
crown of Great Britain ; that it was necessary
that every kind of authority under that crown
should be totally suppressed, and that all the
powers of government should be exerted under
the authority of the people of the colonies," etc.

This was plain speaking, which no one could
pretend to misunderstand. It involved independence, though it was not a formal and
explicit declaration ; but it was the substance,
the thing itself ; only verbal recognition of the
fact remained to be made, and was of course
inevitable. This was sufficiently well appreciated; Mr. Duane said that this was a "piece
of mechanism to work out independence." The
moderatists fought hard and not without bitterness, though they recognized that they were
foredoomed to defeat. Finally the preamble was
adopted. Mr. Adams was profoundly happy in
his triumph, but he was too deeply impressed
with the grandeur of the occasion, too much
overawed by a consciousness of his own leading
part and chief responsibility, to be jubilant or
elated as over a less momentous victory. He
writes almost solemnly to his wife : —

"Is it not a saying of Moses : 'Who am I, that
I should go in and out before this great people?'

When I consider the great events which are passed and those greater which are rapidly advancing, and that I may have been instrumental in touching some springs and turning some small wheels, which have had and will have such effects, I feel an awe upon my mind which is not easily described. Great Britain has at last driven America to the last step, a complete separation from her, a total, absolute independence, not only of her parliament but of her crown. For such is the amount of the resolve of the 15th. Confederation among ourselves or alliances with foreign nations are not necessary to a perfect separation from Great Britain. . . . Confederation will be necessary for our internal concord, and alliances may be so for our external defense."

Mr. Adams was of opinion that this step could have been wisely taken at a much earlier date, had it not been for the foolish delays interposed by delegates who " must petition and negotiate," notably the Pennsylvanians, aided by a few New Yorkers and some others from the lukewarm middle states. He believed that twelve months before " the people were as ripe as they are now." But this must be doubted. Looking back upon the progress, it seems to have been sufficiently rapid for safety and permanence.

The thorough approbation entertained for this action of Congress was at once made manifest in the alacrity with which the several colonies prepared to assume the functions of independence. Even Pennsylvania recognized that the gift of freedom was proffered to her accompanied by such a pressure of circumstances that she could not reject it. Her effete assembly of conciliationists was dying of inanition. A body of representatives was chosen by the people, and voted "that the government of this province is not competent for the exigencies of our affairs."

But it was desirable that a fact of such supreme importance as the birth of thirteen new nations should not remain merely a matter of logical inference. It must be embodied in a declaration incapable of misinterpretation, not open to be explained away by ingenious constructions or canceled by technical arguments. Independence could not be left to be gathered among the recitals of a preamble. Readers will probably forgive me for narrating in the briefest manner the familiar story of the passage of the great Declaration. On June 7 Richard Henry Lee of Virginia moved "certain resolutions respecting independency." John Adams seconded the motion. Its consideration was referred to the next morning at ten o'clock, when members were "enjoined to attend punctually." A debate of three days ensued. It appeared that four New England colonies and three southern colonies were prepared to vote at once in the affirmative; but unanimity was desirable and could probably be obtained by a little delay. So a postponement was voted until July 1. There was abundance of work to be done in the mean time, not only in the provinces, but in Congress also, where the machinery for the new order of things was all to be constructed and set in order, ready for immediate use so soon as the creative vote could be taken. Three committees were appointed; one was charged with drafting the document itself, so that it should be ready for adoption on July 1. The members of this committee, in order of precedence, were Jefferson, John Adams, Franklin, Sherman, and R. R. Livingston. A second committee was deputed to devise a scheme for a confederation between the colonies; a third had the duty of arranging a plan for treaties with foreign powers. Upon this last committee also Adams was placed, though in company with colleagues by no means of his way of thinking. On the following day he was further put at the head of a "board of war and ordnance," consisting of five members of Congress and charged with a multiplicity of laborious duties. Evidently these were busy days for him. But they were days of triumph in which work was a pleasure. All those matters which had been promoted by him more zealously than by any other delegate seemed now on the eve of accomplishment; and then, he said, "I shall think that I have answered the end of my creation, and sing my *nunc dimittis*, return to my farm, ride circuits, plead law, or judge causes." So confident was he of the sure and speedy achievement of his purpose that he actually began now to preach patience to others.

When it came to the matter of writing the Declaration, some civilities were exchanged between Mr. Adams and Mr. Jefferson, each politely requesting the other to undertake it. But as it had been probably generally expected, if not tacitly understood, that Jefferson should do the composition, he readily engaged to try his hand. In old age Jefferson and Adams made statements slightly differing from each other concerning this transaction. Jefferson said that he submitted his paper to Franklin and Adams separately, that each interlined in his own handwriting such corrections as occurred to him, but that these were "two or three only and merely verbal;" that the instrument was then reported by the committee. Adams said that after the paper was written he and Jefferson conned it over together, that he was delighted with its "high tone and flights of oratory," and that, according to his recollection, he neither made nor suggested any alteration, though he felt sure that the passage concerning slavery would be rejected by the southern delegates, and though there were some expressions which he did not wholly approve, especially that which stigmatized George III. as a tyrant. The paper, he says, was then read before the whole committee of five, and he could not recall that it was criticised at all. The variance between these two accounts is insignificant, and, in view of the fact that they were made nearly half a century after the events took place, it is only surprising that they were not more discordant. The controversy excited some interest at the time and afterwards ; though, as Mr. C. F. Adams truly says, the question " does not rise beyond the character of a curiosity of literature." Yet he himself cares enough about it to endeavor to show that his grandfather's statement has not been discredited by the evidence. But the contrary seems to be the more correct conclusion. The only evidence of any real value which exists in the case is the original draft of the Declaration in Jefferson's handwriting, bearing two or three trifling alterations interlined in the handwritings of Adams and Franklin. It should be noted, too, that Jefferson assumes to speak positively, while Adams carefully limits his statement by saying that it is according to his present memory. His memory was not a perfectly trustworthy one.

On July 1 debate was resumed in committee
of the whole on the original resolution of Mr.
Lee, which was reported to Congress and carried
by that body on the next day. The Declaration
was then at once reported and discussed until
late on July 4. There was no doubt that it
would be carried, but Dickinson and others who
remained strongly opposed to it were determined,
as a sort of solemn though hopeless duty, to
speak out their minds against it. Jefferson,
utterly helpless in debate, sat silent and very
uncomfortable while the hot battle raged. John
Adams, in this supreme hour, bore the whole
burden of supporting a measure which he regarded as the consummation of all the labor
expended by him since he came into public life,
— substantially as " the end of his creation," as
he had said. His intense earnestness, his famil-
iarity with every possible argument, compelled
him to be magnificently eloquent. He himself
did not know what a grand effort he was making, but his hearers have borne their testimony
to his power and impressiveness in many tributes
of ardent praise. Jefferson uttered words of
warmest admiration and gratitude. Adams, he
said, was the " Colossus of that debate." Stock-
ton called him the " Atlas of independence."
His praise was in every mouth.

On July 3 Adams wrote two letters to his

But the Day is past — The Second Day of July 1776, will be the most memorable Epocha, in the History of America. — I am apt to believe that it will be celebrated, by succeeding Generations, as the great anniversary Festival. It ought to be commemorated, as the Day of Deliverance by solemn Acts of Devotion to God Almighty. It ought to be solemnized with Pomp and Parade with shews, Games, Sports, Guns, Bells, Bonfires and Illuminations from one End of this Continent to the other from this Time forward forever more.

wife. In one he said : "Yesterday the greatest question was decided which ever was debated in America, and a greater perhaps never was nor will be decided among men." In the other: " The second day of July, 1776, will be the most memorable epoch in the history of America. I am apt to believe that it will be celebrated by succeeding generations as the great Anniversary Festival. It ought to be commemorated as the day of deliverance, by solemn acts of devotion to God Almighty. It ought to be solemnized with pomp, and parade, with shows, games, sports, bells, bonfires, and illuminations, from one end of this continent to the other, from this time forward for evermore. You will think me transported with enthusiasm, but I am not. I am well aware of the toil and blood and treasure that it will cost us to maintain this Declaration, and support and defend these states. Yet through all the gloom I can see the rays of ravishing light and glory. I can see that the end is more than worth all the means ; and that posterity will triumph in that day's transaction, even though we should rue it, which I trust in God we shall not." Posterity has selected for its anniversary July 4, instead of July 2, though the question was really settled on the earlier day.

CHAPTER VI

AMID the exultation and excitement attendant upon these closing hours of American colonialism, Adams gave striking evidence of the cool judgment and statesmanlike comprehension which constituted a solid stratum beneath his impetuous temper. He wrote to Samuel Chase : —

" If you imagine that I expect this Declaration will ward off calamities from this country, you are much mistaken. A bloody conflict we are destined to endure. This has been my opinion from the beginning. . . . Every political event since the nineteenth of April, 1775, has confirmed me in this opinion. If you imagine that I flatter myself with happiness and halcyon days after a separation from Great Britain, you are mistaken again. I do not expect that our new government will be so quiet as I could wish, nor that happy harmony, confidence, and affection between the colonies, that every good American ought to study and pray for, for a long time. But freedom is a counterbalance for poverty, discord, and war, and more. It is your hard lot and mine to be called into life at such a time. Yet even these times have their pleasures."

In such words there spoke a cool statesman as well as a warm patriot, accurately measuring a great victory even in the flush of it, appreciating justly the struggles yet to come.

The enthusiastic gentleman, who called Mr. Adams the Atlas of American independence, confused the fact of independence with the declaration of it. The only Atlas of American independence was the great leader who won the war of the Revolution. He established the fact; Mr. Adams induced Congress to declare it. To Mr. Adams belongs, accurately speaking, the chief credit for having not only defended the Declaration triumphantly in debate, but for having brought his fellow delegates to the point of passing votes which, prior to the formal declaration, involved it as a logical conclusion. His earnestness in this cause appears to have been greater than that of any other member; he pressed upon his object as a beleaguering army presses upon a city; he captured one outwork after another; week by week he made the ultimate result more and more inevitable by inducing Congress to take one step after another in the desired direction; his intensity of purpose affected others, as it always will; his tenacity was untiring; his eloquence was never silent; so thoroughly did he study the subject that no individual could cope with the force, variety,

readiness, and breadth of his arguments; so
keen did his perceptions become beneath the
influence of his deep resolve that he was able so
far to subdue his own nature as to become diplomatic, ingenious, and patient in his methods.
The same result would without doubt have been
reached had John Adams never existed, so that,
in a certain sense of the words, the declaration
was not due to him; but as that phrase is ordi-
narily used, to signify that his efforts were the
most conspicuous visible impulse, it is proper to
say that the achievement was his work.

Foolish as it generally is to speculate upon
what would have been if historical events had
not occurred as they did, yet occasionally a sup-
position seems sure enough to be of interest and
value in enabling us to appreciate the importance of an individual, and the relationship of
some prominent man to the public affairs in
which he is concerned. No one doubts that the
American colonies would at some time or other
have become independent states, though George
Washington had never lived. But no one who
has carefully studied that period can doubt that
independence would not have been achieved in
the especial struggle of 1776 without George
Washington. His existence was essential to
American success in that war. With him the
colonies were on the verge of failure; without

him they would inevitably have passed over that verge, and would have had to wait during an uncertain period for a better opportunity. The combination of his moral and mental qualities was so singular that he is an absolutely unique character in history. Other men belong to types and classes, and individual members of any type or class may be compared with each other. Washington is the only man of his type or class. Thus it happens that no one has yet succeeded in describing his character. Every effort that has been made is avowedly a total failure. There have been men as honest, as just, as patriotic, as devoted, as persistent, as noble-minded, as dignified, as much above suspicion, men as capable of inspiring that confidence which leads to willing obedience, men infinitely more magnetic, and able to excite much warmer personal allegiance, men of larger brains, of greater strategic abilities natural and acquired, of wider aptitude for statesmanship. Yet still Washington stands by himself, a man not susceptible of comparison with any other, whether for praise or disparagement; a man who never did a single act indicative of genius, yet who, amid problems as novel and perplexing as ever tortured the toiler in public affairs, never made a serious mistake. One writer will tell us that it was the grand morality of his nature which brought him success; another prefers to say that it was his judgment; but neither of these mere suggestions of leading traits accomplishes the explanation, or guides us to the heart of the undiscoverable secret. This lurks as hidden from the historian as does the principle of life from the anatomist.

John Adams's character, on the other hand, can puzzle no one; his broad, earnest, powerful, impetuous, yet simple humanity is perfectly intelligible, equally in its moral and in its mental developments. In his department he promoted independence more efficiently than any one else, he would have been a greater loss than any other one man in Congress to that cause; but independence would not have been lost in his loss, — would probably not even have been seriously postponed. Popular sentiment would have demanded it, and Congress would have reflected that sentiment almost as soon, though the tongue of Mr. Adams had never moved. Adams, however, could never fully realize this essential difference between the value of his own personality and the value of that of Washington. Throughout life he felt that, in the preëminence universally given to Washington, he was robbed of insignia properly appurtenant to his glory. In 1822, in a letter to Mr. Pickering, he recalled the jealousy and distrust towards New England

in the earlier stages of the struggle, and the resulting necessity upon him of keeping somewhat in the rear in order to give an apparent leadership to Virginia. The whole policy of the United States, he said, had been subsequently colored and affected by this same state of feeling, and this consequent according of precedence to southerners. " Without it Mr. Washington would never have commanded our armies; nor Mr. Jefferson have been the author of the Declaration of Independence; nor Mr. Richard Henry Lee the mover of it; nor Mr. Chase the mover of foreign connections ; . . . nor had Mr. Johnson ever been the nominator of Washington for general." There was some justice in Mr. Adams's feeling; the suspicion entertained towards Massachusetts had compelled him to yield to others a conspicuousness really belonging to himself. Jefferson, Lee, Chase, and Johnson together were far from constituting an equivalent for him. But his unconquerable blunder, originating in 1776–77, before he left Congress, and acquiring much greater proportions afterwards, lay in his utter incapacity to see that there could be no comparison between Washington and himself, that not even any common measure could exist for them, since it is impossible to establish a proportion between the absolutely essential and the highly important.

Before Mr. Adams left Congress in the spring of 1777 he was obliged to witness such a train of disasters as made every one despondent, — the defeat on Long Island, the evacuation of New York, the retreat through the Jerseys, the abandonment of Philadelphia. Deep discouragement prevailed, certainly not without reason. The times were critical, and the colonies were terribly near ruin. General Greene reiterated to Mr. Adams that the business was hopeless. Such a series of events naturally produced some feeling of doubt concerning the capacity of Washington; personal and less honorable motives also exercised a like influence in some quarters. There was an effort to set up Gates as a rival, after the surrender of Burgoyne. Adams was fortunately no longer a member of Congress when these designs had come near maturity. It is probable that he thus fortunately escaped any share in them; but his affiliations had been so largely with those who became anti-Washingtonians, and his predilections were already so far known, that he was regarded as of that connection and sympathy. Mr. C. F. Adams endeavors to clear his grandfather from the obloquy attendant upon such sentiments, but he is obviously uncomfortable beneath the necessity and performs his task unsatisfactorily. Really his best sentences are those in which he

shapes not so much a denial as a palliation, —
"Neither is it any cause of wonder or censure
that the patriots in Congress, who had not yet
any decisive experience of his [Washington's]
true qualities, should have viewed with much
uneasiness the power which circumstances were
accumulating in his hands. History had no
lesson to prompt confidence in him, and on the
other hand it was full of warnings. In this
light the attempt, whilst organizing another
army in the north, to raise up a second chief
as a resource in case of failure with the first,
must be viewed as a measure not without much
precautionary wisdom." This "attempt," he
acknowledges, was "actively promoted" by John
Adams. In spite of the plausible skill with
which this argument is put, it remains an excuse
rather than a vindication. It was John Adams's
business to form a correct judgment of men and
measures; so far as he failed to do so he failed
to show the ability demanded by his position:
if his error was wholly of the head, it affects
only our opinion of the soundness of his judgment in military matters and in reading men;
if any personal motive, though unrecognized by
himself, likewise interfered, this fact may lower
a little our opinion of his character.

Mr. Adams had spoken of the Declaration
of Independence as the "end of his creation."

The arduous and exhausting efforts which he
made to achieve it told so severely upon his
health that his words threatened to be fulfilled
in a sense quite different from that in which
he had uttered them. But, worn out as he was,
the consummation brought him no rest. The
Declaration at once proved to be a beginning of
more than it had brought to an end. The thirteen embryotic nations, created by it, were to
be united into a single nationality, or federation,
of a character so peculiar that no historical precedent afforded any real aid in the task. In
this direction Mr. Adams was able to render
very important services. From the beginning
he had given much thought to the subject of
government. " Would that we were good archi-
tects ! " had been his anxious cry long before the
conciliationists had been worsted, or permanent
separation had appeared other than a remote
possibility. His services in promoting independence have naturally monopolized attention
almost to the entire exclusion of his other labors.
But in fact, though more showy, they were not
so greatly more valuable than other matters
which he was caring for at this time, and which
have been very little heard of. They were in
their nature destructive ; it was at the anni-
hilation of royal domination that they were
aimed, from which independence was the inevi-

table result. But destruction seldom demands
the highest order of intellectual effort; a de-
stroyer is not a statesman; and if John Adams
had only been the chief mover in substituting
independence for dependence, it would be more
complimentary than accurate to say that he was
the statesman of the Revolution. There were
enough other destroyers in those days, and that
work was sure to be thoroughly done. But
Adams had the higher, constructive faculty.
Many remarks and sentences, scattered through
his contemporaneous writings during the revolutionary period, show his quick natural eye for
governmental matters; he seems to be in a cease-
less condition of observation and thought concerning them. The influence which he exerted
was so indefinite that it can be estimated hardly
with a valuable approximation to accuracy; but
it must have been very great.

He was constantly engaged in studying the
forms of government in the middle and in the
southern sections, each differing widely from
those of New England as well as from each
other. He used to speculate upon the varying
influences of these forms, and to consider what
changes must be effected in order to accomplish
unanimity of feeling and of action. From an
early day his eye had ranged forward to the
time when the existing systems must be suc-

ceeded by different ones, and he busied himself much with thinking what new principles should be incorporated in the new machinery. He watched with anxiety all indications of opinion in this direction, and lost no opportunity to inculcate his own ideas, which were clear and decided. Many months prior to the time at which we are now arrived, Tom Paine published "Common Sense." Adams, to whom this anonymous but famous publication was by many attributed, was in fact greatly disgusted at the lack of the architectural element in it, and was soon stirred to write and publish another pamphlet, also anonymous, which was designed to supply the serious deficiency of Paine's. This paper profoundly discussed plans and forms of government in a practical way, for the purpose of meeting the near wants of the colonies. Its authorship being shrewdly surmised, it was widely circulated and read with great interest, especially by those men in the several provinces who were soon to be chiefly concerned in framing the new constitutions. Adams modestly said of it, that it had at least "contributed to set people thinking on the subject," so that the "manufacture of governments" became for the time "as much talked of as that of saltpetre was before." Of course it is impossible to say what effect this pamphlet had; yet that it had very much is more than probable.

With his habit of noticing such matters, Adams had early remarked upon the difference between the theories of state polity at the North and at the South, a difference much wider apparently in the spirit of administration than in the description of the apparatus. He himself was saturated, so to speak, with the doctrines and practice of New England, and whether in writing or in talk he was never backward to enforce his faith with the extreme earnestness of deep conviction. By correspondence and conversation with leading men in every quarter, he efficiently backed his pamphlet. When, therefore, the innovation of a more popular and democratic spirit is observable in one and another of the new constitutions, it is fair to presume that Adams had done much to bring about the change. In a letter to Patrick Henry, accompanying his pamphlet, Adams said: " The dons, the bashaws, the grandees, the patricians, the sachems, the nabobs, call them by what name you please,[1] sigh, groan, and fret, and sometimes stamp and foam and curse; but all in vain. The decree is gone forth and it cannot be recalled, that a more equal liberty than has prevailed in other parts of the earth must be established in

[1] Elsewhere he called them, by a better nomenclature, " the barons of the south."

America. That exuberance of pride, which has produced an insolent domination in a few, a very few, opulent, monopolizing families, will be brought down nearer to the confines of reason and moderation than they have been used to." To Mr. Hughes of New York he writes, deprecating any scheme "for making your governor and counselors for life or during good behavior. I should dread such a constitution in these perilous times. . . . The people ought to have frequently the opportunity, especially in these dangerous times, of considering the conduct of their leaders, and of approving or disapproving. You will have no safety without it." He says that Pennsylvania is "in a good way. . . . The large body of the people will be possessed of more power and importance, and a proud junto of less." In a letter to Richard Henry Lee he rejoices because there will be "much more uniformity in the governments than could have been expected a few months ago," a result presumably due in large part to his own unremitting exertions. His "Thoughts on Government" had done good work in Virginia, far beyond his expectations, and generally he was "amazed to find an inclination so prevalent throughout all the southern colonies to adopt plans so nearly resembling that" which he had enforced in his political sermons.

Immediately following independence came also a necessity for the formation of a federation. Some sort of a bond, a league, must be devised for tying the thirteen nations together for a few purposes. Nevertheless, the alliance was not to have the effect of creating a single nationality, was not to deprive each ally of its character of absolute sovereignty as an individual state. Mr. Adams recognized that this could not be done at once in any perfect or permanent form. Whatever should be arranged now would necessarily be an experiment, a temporary expedient, out of which, by a study of its defects as they should develop, there might in time be evolved a satisfactory system. But none the less zealously did he enter upon the task of making the federation as efficient as possible under the circumstances, and he did much hard and important work in this department. No sketch of it can well be given in this limited space, nor perhaps would such a sketch be very valuable except to a student of constitutional history. Therefore, after July 4, 1776, the remainder of Adams's congressional career, though laborious to the point of exhaustion, gives no salient points for description. It was in the routine of business that his time was now consumed, and very largely in work upon the committees. It would seem that there could not have been many of these upon which he had not a place; for he was a member of upwards of ninety which were recorded, and of a great many others which were unrecorded. He says that he was kept incessantly at work from four o'clock in the morning until ten o'clock at night. Besides the arduous business of forming the federation, he was also obliged to devote himself to that subject, with which his previous efforts had already allied him in the minds of members, the establishment of connections with European powers. Independence would not permit this important matter to be longer postponed; and a committee, of which Adams was an important working member, was charged to consider and report a system of foreign policy for the thirteen colonies, and to suggest forms of commercial treaties.

But labors more difficult, more vexatious, more omnivorous of time, were entailed upon Mr. Adams by his position at the head of the War Department. The task of organization was enormous; the knowledge and arrangement of details were appalling. Nor was this all. The power of Congress, if any real power it had, over the army, was so undefined even in theory, so vague in its practical bearing upon the officers, so difficult of enforcement, that the relationship of the congressional committee, which really constituted the War Department, with that body was excessively delicate. Adams's jealous and hasty temperament was subjected to some severe trials. Aggrieved officers would sometimes become not only disrespectful but insubordinate. But in such crises he acquitted himself well. A sense of weakness in the last resort perhaps prevented his giving loose to any outburst of anger, while his high spirit and profound earnestness lent to his language an impressive force and an appearance of firmness almost imperious. His deep sincerity inspired all his communications, and gave them a tone which procured respect and turned aside resentment. He breathed into others an honesty of purpose, a vigor, a devotedness akin to his own. Being also a man of much business ability and untiring industry, he made substantially a war minister admirably adapted to the peculiar and exacting requirements of that anomalous period.

But it was impossible that a man not enjoying a rugged physique could endure for an indefinite time labors so engrossing and anxieties so great, away from the comforts of home, and in a climate which, during many months of the year, appeared to him extremely hot. His desire for relief, more and more earnestly expressed, at last took a definite and resolute shape. He wanted to have the Massachusetts delegation so increased in numbers that the members could take turns in attending Congress and in staying at home. If this could not be done, he tendered his resignation. The reply came in the shape of a permission to take a long vacation, which he did in the winter of 1776–77. Then he returned to spend the spring, summer, and autumn of 1777 in a continuance of the same labors which have just been described. At last the limit of specific duties which he had long ago set for himself having been achieved and even overpast, he definitively carried out his design of retirement.

CHAPTER VII

IT was on November 11, 1777, that John Adams, accompanied by his kinsman, Samuel Adams, set forth from Philadelphia on his homeward journey. He was at last a private citizen, rejoiced to be able again to attend to his own affairs, and to resume the important task of money-gathering at his old calling. Yet he was hardly allowed even to get on his professional harness. He was arguing an admiralty cause in Portsmouth when a letter reached him, dated December 3, 1777, from Richard Henry Lee and James Lovell, announcing his appointment as commissioner at the court of France, wishing him a quick and pleasant voyage, and cheerfully suggesting that he should have his dispatch-bags sufficiently weighted to be able to sink them instantly in case of capture. The day after he received this letter he accepted the trust, though the duty imposed by it was far from attractive. Besides the ordinary discomforts and perils of a winter passage in a sailing vessel, he had to consider the chances of seizure by British ships, which covered the ocean and were taking multitudes of prizes. If captured, he would be but a traitor, having in prospect certainly the Tower of London and possibly all the penalties of the English statutes against high treason. If he should arrive safely, he would be only one of three commissioners at the French court; and France, though kindly rendering courteous services, had not yet become the ally of the states, and was still in nominal friendship with Great Britain. Moreover, he was to step into an uninviting scene of dissension and suspicion. The states were represented by Franklin, Arthur Lee, and Silas Deane; Adams was to supersede Deane, who had been embarrassing Congress by reckless engagements with French military officers, and who in many other ways had shown himself, to say the best of it, eminently unfit for diplomatic functions. There was much ill-feeling, of which the new ambassador could not expect to escape a share. Altogether, it was greatly to his credit that he promptly agreed to fill the post.

On February 13, 1778, he set sail in the frigate Boston, accompanied by his young son, John Quincy Adams. On the 20th an English ship of war gave them chase. Adams urged the officers and crew to fight desperately, deeming it "more eligible" for himself "to be killed on board the Boston or sunk to the bottom in her, than to be taken prisoner." But a favoring breeze saved him from the choice between such melancholy alternatives, and on March 31 he found himself riding safely at anchor in the river at Bordeaux.

At the French court he was pleasantly received. People, he says, at first supposed that he was "the famous Adams;" but when somebody asked him if this were so, he modestly explained that he was only a cousin of that distinguished person. Thereafter he received less attention. It was unfortunate, too, that he knew nothing of the language; but he got along, sometimes by the aid of an interpreter, sometimes by "gibbering something like French." This deficiency, however, rather diminished his pleasure than his usefulness; for he soon found that his chief labors were to be with his own countrymen and colleagues. The affairs of the mission he found much worse than he had anticipated. The jealousies and hostilities among the American representatives there were very great. He wrote in his diary: "It is with much grief and concern that I have learned, from my first landing in France, the disputes between the Americans in this kingdom; the animosities between Mr. Deane and Mr. Lee; between Dr. Franklin and Mr. Lee; between Mr. Izard and Dr. Franklin; between Dr. Bancroft and Mr. Lee; between

Mr. Carmichael and all. It is a rope of sand. I am at present wholly untainted with these prejudices, and will endeavor to keep myself so." He heard that Deane and Bancroft had made fortunes by "dabbling in the English funds, and in trade, and in fitting out privateers;" also that "the Lees were selfish." "I am sorry for these things; but it is no part of my business to quarrel with anybody without cause." All the business and affairs of the commission had been conducted in the most lax manner; no minute-book, letter-book, or account-book had been kept, expenditure had been lavish, "prodigious," as he said, but there was no way to learn how the money had gone, or how much was still owing. Utterly inexperienced as he was in such affairs, he yet showed good sense and energy. He endeavored to avoid allying himself with any faction, siding now with Franklin and again with Lee, according to his views of the merits of each specific discussion, and seeking at the same time not to lose the confidence of the Count de Vergennes, the French minister of foreign affairs, who was very partial to Franklin and inimical to Lee. Further, he set himself zealously to bring the business department of the mission into a proper condition. The commissioners had complete control over the fiscal affairs of the states abroad, and had heretofore

managed them in a manner inconceivably loose
and careless.   As Mr. Adams wrote home to the
commercial committee of Congress: "Agents of
various sorts are drawing bills upon us, and the
commanders of vessels of war are drawing on
us for expenses and supplies which we never
ordered. . . . We find it so difficult to obtain
accounts from agents of the expenditure of
moneys and of the goods and merchandises
shipped by them that we can never know the
true state of our finances."   All this shocked
Mr. Adams, who had the notions and habits of
a man of business, and he at once endeavored
to arrange a system of rigorous accuracy and
accountability in spite of the indifference, and
occasionally the reluctance, of his colleagues.
Henceforth records were kept, letters were
copied, accounts were accurately set down.

But the reforms in matters of detail which he
could accomplish were by no means sufficient
to counteract the clumsy and inefficient way in
which the business of the states was conducted,
and to which he had no mind to be even a silent
party.   An entire reorganization was evidently
needed, and on May 21, 1778, he wrote a plain
and bold letter, which he addressed to Samuel
Adams, since, apart from his colleagues, he
could not properly communicate with Congress.
He urged the gross impropriety of leaving the

salaries of the ministers entirely uncertain, so
that they spent what they chose and then sent
their accounts (such as they were) to be allowed
by Congress; the error of blending the business
of a public minister with that of a commercial
agent; and, most important of all, the folly of
maintaining three commissioners where a single
envoy would be vastly more serviceable. By
such advice he knowingly advised himself out of
office; for Dr. Franklin was sure to be retained
at the French court, Lee already had a letter of
credence to Madrid, and no niche was left for
him. But he was too honest a public servant
to consider this, and he repined not at all when
precisely this result came about. Congress lost
no time in following his suggestions, leaving
Franklin in Paris, and ordering Lee to Madrid,
at the same time in a strange perplexity over-
looking Mr. Adams so entirely as not even to
order him to return home. He was greatly
vexed and puzzled at this anomalous condition.
Dr. Franklin, who was finding life near the
French court very pleasant, advised him tranquilly to await instructions. But this counsel
did not accord with his active temperament or
his New England sense of duty. He wrote to
his wife: " I cannot eat pensions and sinecures;
they would stick in my throat." Rather than
do so, he said that he would again run the

gauntlet of the British cruisers and the storms
of the Atlantic. It was no easy matter, however, to get a passage in those days, and his best
endeavors did not bring him back to Boston
until August 2, 1779, after an absence of nearly
a year and a half. In a certain sense his mission had been needless and useless. He had
been away a long while, had undergone great
dangers, and had cost the country money which
could ill be spared; and for all that he had
accomplished strictly in the way of diplomacy
he might as well have spent the eighteen months
at Braintree. But he had aided to break up an
execrable condition of affairs at Paris, and he
had proved his entire and unselfish devotion to
the public interest. These were two important
facts, worth in their fruits all they had cost to
the nation and to himself.

He had, moreover, gathered some ideas concerning Great Britain, France, and Holland.
These ideas were not wholly correct, being colored by the atmosphere of the passing day and
stimulated too much by his own wishes; but
they promoted the temporary advantages of the
states very well. For example, he came back
with a theory of the decadence of Great Britain.
"This power," he said, "loses every day her
consideration, and runs towards her ruin. Her
riches, in which her power consisted, she has

lost with us and never can regain. . . . She
resembles the melancholy spectacle of a great,
wide-spreading tree that has been girdled at the
root."   There was no grain of truth in this sort
of talk, but it was nourishment to the American
Congress.   Towards France his feelings were
of course most friendly.   "The longer I live
in Europe, and the more I consider our affairs,
the more important our alliance with France
appears to me.   It is a rock upon which we may
safely build.   Narrow and illiberal prejudices,
peculiar to John Bull, with which I might perhaps have been in some degree infected when I
was John Bull, have now no influence over me.
I never was, however, much of John Bull, I was
John Yankee, and such I shall live and die."
A very single-minded John Yankee he certainly
was, for amid all his yearning for a French
alliance, which he valued for its practical usefulness, he was jealous of too great a subservience
to that power.

"It is a delicate and dangerous connection. . . .
There may be danger that too much will be demanded
of us.   There is danger that the people and their
representatives may have too much timidity in their
conduct towards this power, and that your ministers
here may have too much diffidence of themselves
and too much complaisance for the court.   There
is danger that French councils and emissaries and

correspondents may have too much influence in our deliberations. I hope that this court may not interfere by attaching themselves to persons, parties, or measures in America."

Again he wrote that it would be desirable to link the two countries very closely together, "*provided* always, that we preserve prudence and resolution enough to receive implicitly no advice whatever, but to judge always for ourselves," etc., etc. Within a few months the need of this watchful independence was abundantly proved; and the early years of the history of the United States fully justified Adams's cautious dread of an undue warmth of sentiment towards France.

CHAPTER VIII

SECOND FOREIGN MISSION: IN FRANCE AND
HOLLAND

SCARCELY was Mr. Adams given time to make his greetings to his friends, after his return through the gauntlet of storms and British cruisers, ere he was again set at work. A convention was summoned to prepare a constitution for Massachusetts, and he was chosen a delegate. It was a congenial task, and he was early assuming an active and influential part in the proceedings when, more to his surprise than to his gratification, he was interrupted by receiving a second time the honor of a foreign mission. The history of the establishment of diplomatic relations between the new states of North America and the old countries of Europe, the narrative of the reluctant and clumsy approaches by England towards a negotiation for peace, and especially the intricate tale of the subtle manœuvres of the French foreign office in connection with its trans-Atlantic allies and supposed dear friends, together form a remarkably interesting chapter in American history. All the complex-

ities of this web, involved beyond the average of
diplomatic labyrinths, have been unraveled with
admirable clearness by Mr. C. F. Adams in his
life of John Adams. A writer more competent
to the difficult task could not have been desired,
and he has so performed it that no successor can
do more than follow his lucid and generally fair
and dispassionate recital. His account of his
grandfather is naturally tinged with the sentiment of the *pius Æneas ;* neither, on the other
hand, can he condone the French minister's selfishness and duplicity, though really not excessive according to the technical code of morals
in European foreign offices of that day. But
otherwise his account of these events is keen,
just, vivid, and exhaustive.

During the period with which we have now
to deal, the Count de Vergennes managed the
foreign affairs of France. He was a diplomate
of that school with which picturesque writers of
historical romance have made us so familiar, a
character as classic as the crusty father of the
British stage ; of great ability, wily, far-sighted,
inscrutable, with no liking for any country save
France, and no hatred for any country except
England, firm in the old-fashioned faith that
honesty had no place in politics, especially in
diplomacy ; apt and graceful in the distinguished
art of professional lying, overbearing and impe-

rious as became the vindicator and the representative of the power of the French monarchy. Such was this famous minister, a dangerous and difficult man with whom to have dealings. From the beginning to the end of his close connection with American affairs he played the game wholly for his own hand, with some animosity towards his opponent, but with not the slightest idea of committing the folly of the pettiest self-sacrifice for the assistance of his nominal partners. They were really to help him; he was apparently to help them. It is now substantially proved that the unmixed motive of the French cabinet in secretly encouraging and aiding the revolted colonies, before open war had broken out between France and England, had been only to weaken the power and to sap the permanent resources of the natural and apparently the eternal enemy of France. After that war had been declared, the same purpose constituted the sole inducement to the alliance with the American rebels. To the government of France, therefore, thus actuated, no gratitude was due from the colonists at any time, and in de Vergennes, as the embodiment of the foreign policy of that government, no confidence could be safely reposed. Yet the kindly feeling of gratitude and the sense of obligation cherished for a generation in America towards France were not wholly erroneous or misplaced; for a considerable proportion of the French people were warmly and generously interested in the success of the Revolution, and many individuals gave it not only sincere good-will but substantial aid. Yet, though it is fair to mention and to remember this latter fact, we shall have nothing more to do with it in this narrative.

Mr. Adams had to deal with the governors, not with the governed. But when he first came to the country he no more understood than did the rest of his countrymen the real difference involved in this distinction. France was but an integral idea for him, and he approached her people and her government alike with an undiscriminating though somewhat cautious feeling of trust. It is important to note this fact, evidence of which may be found in some of his language quoted at the close of the last chapter, because it indicates that his subsequent suspicions of de Vergennes were the outgrowth of observation and not of any original disliking. Neither were these suspicions, which, it must be acknowledged, were soon awakened, stimulated by Mr. Adams's natural temperament; for though he had a strong element of suspicion in him, it was seldom set in action by any other spur than jealousy. The feeling towards the Frenchman was the keen instinct of a man at once shrewd and honest, which had satisfied him of the true condition of affairs even during his first visit to France. Almost alone among his countrymen, he even then saw that it was unwise for the colonies to give themselves blindfold to the guidance of the great French minister. For a long while he was, if not entirely solitary, yet at least with few co-believers in this faith, and at times he occupied an invidious and dangerous position by reason of it. But by good fortune he persisted in it, and in all his action was controlled by it; and if he can hardly be said thereby to have been led to save his country in spite of herself, yet at least it is undeniable that through this he accomplished for her very much which would never have been accomplished by any person holding a different opinion in so vital a matter.

Through the medium of M. Gérard, the French minister, or emissary to Congress, advices came in the autumn of 1779 that England might not improbably soon be ready to negotiate for peace. In order to lose no time when this happy moment should be at hand, it was thought best to have an American envoy, prepared to treat, stationed in Europe to avail of the first opportunity which should occur. For this purpose, as has been said, Mr. Adams was selected; on November 3, 1779, he received notice of his appointment, and on the next day he accepted it, with some expressions of reluctance and diffidence, which were probably sincere, since the mission was attended with both physical danger and the gravest possible responsibility. On November 13 he put to sea in the frigate Le Sensible. She proved to be so unseaworthy that she could barely be brought into the port of Ferrol in safety; and the passengers were compelled to make a long, tedious journey by land to Paris, amid hardships so severe that they seem incredible as occurring in a civilized country of Europe less than a century ago.

Before Mr. Adams's instructions had been drafted, the noxious and perfidious influence of de Vergennes — noxious and perfidious, that is to say, from an American point of view — had had its first effects. For a while that minister's desire had been that the war should draw along a weary and endless length, in order the more thoroughly to drain the vitality of England. How severely the vitality of the colonies might also be drained was matter of indifference, so long as they retained strength enough to continue fighting. To keep them up to their work his plan had been to give them tonics, in the shape of money, arms, and encouragement, secretly administered in such quantities as should be necessary in order to prevent their succumbing; but he had not cared to give them enough assistance, though it might be possible to do so, to enable them quite to conclude the struggle. Even the open outbreak of hostility between France and England had modified his designs only a little, and had affected the details rather than changed the fundamental theory of his action. Now, however, affairs having drifted to that point that the war seemed to be almost fought out, and peace looming apparently not very far away, he recognized only a sole object as necessary so far as the revolted states were concerned. He must see them independent; so mighty a limb must be lopped forever from the parent trunk. Beyond this he cared for nothing else; as for all the points which were of highest moment and dearest interest to those states, his dear and confiding allies, points of boundaries, fisheries, navigation of the Mississippi, and such like, he cared not in the least for any of these. The earliest indication of the feeling in Congress had been that stipulations concerning these three matters should be inserted in the instructions to the American negotiator as *ultimata*. But this by no means consorted with the views of de Vergennes, who saw that such *ultimata* might operate to obstruct a pacification desirable for France, if England should resolutely refuse them; whereas, if they were urgent demands only and not *ultimata*, the sacrifice of them might indirectly effect some gain for France. They might be used as a price to Great Britain, and the thing bought with them might inure to France. Accordingly the strenuous efforts of M. Gérard were put forth, and finally with success, to pare down the congressional instructions to the modest form desired by de Vergennes. It was voted that the envoy in treating for peace should have as his only *ultimatum* the recognition by Great Britain of the independence of the ex-colonies. But, in order not to abandon altogether these other important matters, he received also another and distinct commission for entering into a commercial treaty, and in this he was directed to secure the "right" to the fisheries.

Massachusetts watched all this with extreme anxiety. The fisheries were to her matter of profound concern, far surpassing any question of boundary, and of vastly deeper interest than the navigation of the Mississippi. She was inexorably resolved that this great industry of her people should never be annihilated. To this resolution of so influential a state the appointment of Mr. Adams was largely due. The matter of the foreign representation of the colonies at this time was complicated by many intrigues and quarrels, local jealousies, and personal animosities.   Thus it happened that New York and other states were willing to send Mr. Adams to Spain, but wished Mr. Jay to be the negotiator for peace.   This arrangement would have sufficiently pleased de Vergennes also, whose keen perception and accurate advices had already marked Mr. Adams as a man likely to be obstructive to purely French interests.   But the New Englanders clung with unflinching stubbornness to their countryman.   They are said to have felt that, *ultimatum* or no *ultimatum*, he would save their fisheries if it were a human possibility to do so.   They prevailed. Jay was appointed to Madrid, and Adams got the contingent commissions to England, for both peace and commerce.   In the end Adams was chiefly instrumental in saving the fisheries, and if the choice of him was stimulated by this hope, the instinct or judgment appeared to have been correct.   Yet it is perhaps worth noticing that his sentiments on this subject at this time were hardly identical with his subsequent expressions at Paris.   "Necessity," he said, "has taught us to dig in the ground instead of fishing in the sea for our bread, and we have found that the resource did not fail us.   The fishing was a source of luxury and vanity that did us much injury."   Part of the fish had been exchanged in the West Indies "for rum, and molasses to be distilled into rum, which injured our health and our morals;" the rest came back from Europe in the shape of lace and ribbons. To be compelled to substitute the culture of flax and wool for fishing would conduce to an "acquisition of morals and of wisdom which would perhaps make us gainers in the end." Yet when it came actually to negotiating, Mr. Adams forgot all this horror of rum and frippery, all this desire for flax, wool, and morals, and made a fight for salt fish which won for him even more closely than before the heart of New England.

Mr. Adams was a singular man to be selected for a difficult errand in diplomacy, especially under circumstances demanding wariness and adroitness, if not even craft and dissimulation. He might have been expected to prove but an indifferent player in the most intricate and artificial of invented games. He seemed to possess nearly every quality which a diplomatist ought not to have, and almost no quality which a diplomatist needed. That he was utterly devoid of experience was the least objection, for so were all his countrymen, and it was hoped that the friendly aid of de Vergennes might make up for this defect. But, further than this, he was of a restless, eager temperament, hot to urge forward whatever business he had in hand, chafing under any necessity for patience, disliking to bide his time, frank and outspoken in spite of his best efforts at self-control, and hopelessly incapable of prolonged concealment of his opinions, motives, and purposes in action, his likings and dislikings towards persons. It has been seen, for example, how cautiously he tried to conceal his wish for the declaration of independence, yet every one in Congress soon knew him as the chief promoter of that doctrine; and already, in his brief and unimportant sojourn in France, de Vergennes had got far in reading his mind. Yet it so happened that, with every such prognostic against him, he was precisely the man for the place and the duty. With the shrewdness of his race he had considerable insight into character; a strong element of suspicion led him not quite to assume, as he might have done, that all diplomatists were dishonest, but induced him to watch them with a wise doubt and keenness; he had devoted all the powers of a strong mind to the study of the situation, so that he was thoroughly master of all the various interests and probabilities which it was necessary for him to take into account; he was a patriot to the very centre of his marrow, and so fearless and stubborn that he both made and persisted in the boldest demands on behalf of his country; he was high-spirited, too, and presented such a front that he seemed to represent one of the greatest powers in the civilized world, so that, in spite of the well-known fact that he had only some revolted and more than half exhausted colonies at his back, yet his manly bearing had great moral effect; if it was true that quick-sighted statesmen easily saw what he wanted, it was also true that he impressed them with a sense that he would make a hard fight to get it; they could never expect to bully him, and not easily to circumvent him; if he made enemies, as he did, powerful, dangerous, and insidious ones, he at least showed admirable sturdiness and courage in facing them; he was eloquent and forcible in discussion, making a deep impression by an air of earnest straightforwardness; all these proved valuable qualifications upon the peculiar mission on which he was now dispatched. Had the business of the colonies been conducted by a diplomatist of the European school, burrowing subterraneously in secret mines and countermines, endeavoring to meet art with wiles, and diplomatic lies with professional falsehood, valuable time would surely have been lost, and smaller advantages would probably have been gained; but Adams strode along stoutly, in broad daylight, breaking the snares which were set for his feet, shouldering aside those who sought to crowd him from his path, unceremonious, making direct for his goal, with his eyes wide open and his tongue not silent to speak the plain truth. Certainly this trans-Atlantic negotiator excited surprise by his anomalous and untraditional conduct among the ministers and envoys of the European cabinets; but in the end he proved too much for them all; their peculiar skill was of no avail against his novel and original tactics; their covert indirection could not stand before his blunt directness. So he carried his points with brilliant success.

Yet it is not to be inferred from this record of achievements that Mr. Adams was a good diplomatist, or that in a career devoted to diplomacy he could have won reputation or repeated such triumphs as are about to be narrated. The contrary is probable. His heat, quickness, pugnacity, want of tact, and naïve egotism could not have been compatible with permanent success in this calling. It only so happened that at this special juncture, peculiar and exceptional needs existed which his qualifications fortunately met. Dr. Franklin, who was our minister at Versailles at this time, and with whom, by the way, Mr. Adams did not get along very well, had much more general fitness for diplomacy according to the usual requirements of the profession; cool and dispassionate, keen, astute, and far-sighted, by no means incapable of discovering craft and of meeting it by still craftier craft, no nation in

most emergencies could have wished its affairs
in better hands than those of the distinguished
philosopher, as he was commonly called, though
in fact he was the only living American of note
in 1780 who was a real man of the world. Yet
just now Franklin was almost useless. Leading
the most charming life, caressed by the French
women, flattered by the French men, the com-
panion of the noblest, the wittiest, and the most
dissipated in the realm, visiting, dining, feasting,
he comfortably agreed with de Vergennes, and
quite contentedly fell in with that minister's
policy. It was fortunate for the colonies that
for a time, just at this crisis, the easy-going sage
was forced into unwelcome coupling with the
energetic man of business.

Directly after his arrival in Paris Mr. Adams
wrote to de Vergennes. " I am persuaded," he
says, " it is the intention of my constituents and
of all America, and I am sure it is my own determination, to take no steps of consequence in
pursuance of my commissions without consulting
his majesty's ministers." Accordingly he asks
the count's advice as to whether he shall make
his twofold errand known either to the public or
to the court of London. This was abundantly
civil, and, under all the circumstances, not quite
servile. The response of the Frenchman was
extraordinary. He stated that he preferred to

give no definite reply until after the return from
the states of his emissary, Monsieur Gérard,
"because he is probably the bearer of your instructions, and will certainly be able to make
me better acquainted with the nature and extent
of your commission. But in the mean time I
am of opinion that it will be prudent to conceal
your eventual character, and, above all, to take
the necessary precautions that the object of your
commission may remain unknown at the court
of London." Mr. Adams heard with an indignation which he could not venture to express
this audacious intimation of a design, assumed
to have been successfully carried out, to "pene-
trate into the secrets of Congress," and obtain
"copies of the most confidential communications" between that body and its ministers.
Neither did the advice at all accord with his
own notions. He saw no sound reason for keeping the object of his mission a secret; on the
contrary, he would decidedly have preferred at
once to divulge it, and even formally to communicate it to the British cabinet. Probably he
did not yet suspect what his grandson tells us
was the true state of the case, viz., that de
Vergennes dreaded the possible result of the
commercial portion of his commission, and immediately upon learning it set agents at work in
Philadelphia to procure its cancellation. Never-

theless he answered courteously and submissively, engaging to maintain the desired concealment so far as depended upon himself. He could not do otherwise; it was intended that he should subordinate his own judgment to that of his French friend. But he wrote to the president of Congress to say that the story of his mission and its purpose had not been, as of course it could not have been, kept a close secret, but on the contrary, having been " heard of in all companies," had been used by the English ministerial writers " as evidence of a drooping spirit in America." This, however, concerned only his authority to treat for peace. A few days later, Monsieur Gérard having arrived, de Vergennes did Mr. Adams the honor to say that he found that Mr. Adams had given him a truthful statement of his instructions. He was willing now to have Mr. Adams's " eventual character," but meaning thereby only as an emissary for peace, made public very soon. He still persisted in demanding secrecy as to " the full powers which authorize you to negotiate a treaty of commerce with the court of London. I think it will be prudent not to communicate them to anybody whatever, and to take every necessary precaution that the British ministry may not have a premature knowledge of them. You will no doubt easily feel the motives which induce

me to advise you to take this precaution, and it
would be needless to explain." Mr. Adams did
indeed soon begin to comprehend these "motives" with sufficient accuracy to make explana-
tions almost "needless;" yet for the present he
held his tongue with such patience as he could
command.

This correspondence took place in February,
1780; but it was not till the end of March, and
after further stimulation of de Vergennes' careless memory, that Mr. Adams carried his point
of procuring publication even of the "principal
object" of his mission. "I ought to confess to
Congress," he said, with a slight irony in the
choice of phrases not unworthy of the count
himself, "that the *delicacy* of the Count de
Vergennes about communicating my powers is
not perfectly consonant to my manner of thinking; and if I had followed my own judgment,
I should have pursued a bolder plan, by communicating, immediately after my arrival, to
Lord George Germain my full powers to treat
both of peace and commerce." Yet he modestly
hopes that Congress will approve his deference
to the French minister. There was little danger
that they would not; it was only Mr. Adams's
boldness and independence, never his submis-
siveness, which imperiled his good standing
with that now spiritless body.

Mr. Adams said of himself with perfect truth
that he could not eat the bread of idleness. His
restless energy always demanded some outlet,
whereas now he found himself likely to remain
for an indefinite time without a duty or a task.
He was free to enjoy with a clear conscience all
the novel fascinations of the gayest city in the
world, having the public purse open to his hand
and perfect idleness as his only official function for the passing time.   Such an opportunity
would not have been thrown away by most men ;
but for him the pursuit of ease and pleasure,
even as a temporary recess and with ample excuse, meant wretchedness. Without delay he
set himself to discover some occupation, to find
some toil, to devise some opening for activity.
This he soon saw in the utter ignorance of the
people about him concerning American affairs,
and he entered upon the work of enlightening
them by a series of articles, which he prepared
and caused to be translated and published in
a prominent newspaper, edited by M. Genet, a
chief secretary in the foreign office, father of
Edmond Genet, the famous French minister to
the United States in Washington's time. This
well-meant and doubtless useful enterprise, however, ultimately brought him into trouble, as
his zeal was constantly doing throughout his
life in ways that always seemed to him grossly

undeserved and the hardest of luck. For at the request of de Vergennes, whose attention was attracted by these publications, he now began to furnish often to that gentleman a variety of interesting items of information from the states, of which more will soon be heard. He further kept up an active volunteer correspondence with Congress, sending them all sorts of news, facts which he observed and heard, conjectures and suggestions from his own brain, which he conceived might be of use or interest to them. In a word, he did vigorously many things which might naturally have been expected from Franklin, but which that tranquil philosopher had not permitted to disturb his daily ease.

For a time all went well; Franklin, secure in his great prestige, contemplated with indifference the busy intrusion of Adams; de Vergennes was glad to get all he could from so effusive a source, and Congress seemed sufficiently pleased with the one-sided correspondence. Yet a cautious man, worldly-wise and selfish, would never have done as Adams was doing, and in due time, without any consciousness at all that he deserved such retribution, he found himself in trouble. Early in 1780, Congress issued a recommendation to the several states to arrange for the redemption in silver of the continental paper money at the rate of forty dollars for one.

The adoption of this advice by Massachusetts, and the laying of a tax by that State to provide the money for her share, were announced to Mr. Adams in a letter of June 16, 1780, from his brother-in-law, Richard Cranch. A copy of this letter he promptly sent to de Vergennes. Immediately afterwards he received further news of a resolution of Congress to pay the continental loan certificates according to their value in real money at the time of their issue. A copy of this letter, also, he forwarded to M. de Vergennes, with a letter of his own, explaining, says Mr. C. F. Adams, the "distinction between the action of Congress on the paper money and on the loan certificates, which that body had neglected to make clear." [1]   The letter is brief, and seems fully as much deprecatory as explanatory. But whatever was its character, it was a mistake. Mr. Adams would have done better to allow such disagreeable intelligence to reach the count through the regular channels of communication. He was under no sort of obligation to send the news, nor to explain it, nor to enter on any defense; indeed, had he held his tongue, it was not supposable that the count would ever have known when or how fully he had got his information. Moreover, it was in his discretion to make such communications to the count as he

[1] V. *Dipl. Corr. of the Amer. Rev.* 207.

saw fit; if it was not meddlesome in him to make any, at least it was indiscreet in him to make these especial ones. His punishment was swift. De Vergennes at once took fire on behalf of his countrymen, who were numerously and largely creditors of the colonies. He wrote to Mr. Adams a letter far from pleasant in tone. "Such financial measures," he said, "might be necessary, but their burden should fall on the Americans alone, and an exception ought to be made in favor of strangers."

"In order to make you sensible of the truth of this observation, I will only remark, sir, that the Americans alone ought to support the expense which is occasioned by the defense of their liberty, and that they ought to consider the depreciation of their paper money only as an impost which ought to fall upon themselves, as the paper money was at first established only to relieve them from the necessity of paying taxes. I will only add that the French, if they are obliged to submit to the reduction proposed by Congress, will find themselves victims of their zeal, and I may say of the rashness with which they exposed themselves in furnishing the Americans with arms, ammunition, and clothing, and in a word with all things of the first necessity, of which the Americans at the time stood in need."

Having delivered this severe and offensive criticism, the writer expressed his confidence that Mr. Adams would use all his endeavors to engage Congress to do justice to the subjects of the king, and further stated that the Chevalier de la Luzerne, French minister at Philadelphia, had " orders to make the strongest representations on this subject."

Mr. Adams, thus rudely smitten, began imperfectly to appreciate the position into which his naïve and unreflecting simplicity had brought him. He instantly replied, hoping that the orders to de la Luzerne might be held back until Dr. Franklin could communicate with the French government. It was rather late to remember that the whole business lay properly in Franklin's .department, and unfortunately the tardy gleam of prudence was only a passing illumination. Actually under date of the same day on which this reply was sent, the Diplomatic Correspondence contains a very long and elaborate argument, addressed by Mr. Adams to de Vergennes, wherein the ever-ready diplomate gratuitously endeavored to vindicate the action of Congress. It was a difficult task which he so readily assumed; for though, if it is ever honest for a government to force creditors to take less than it has promised to them, it was justifiable for the colonial Congress and the several states to do so at this time, yet it is by no means clear that such a transaction is ever excusable.

Moreover, apart from this doubt, Mr. Adams
was addressing an argument to a man sure
to be incensed by it, not open to conviction,
and in the first flush of anger. Adams afterwards said that he might easily have shunned
this argument, as Franklin did, by sending the
French minister's letter to Congress, and expressing no opinion of his own to de Vergennes.
But this course he condemned as "duplicity,"
and declared: "I thought it my indispensable
duty to my country and to Congress, to France
and the count himself, to be explicit." Mr.
C. F. Adams also tries to show that his ancestor
could not have shunned this effort without compromising himself or his countrymen. But it is
not possible to take these views. At the outset
Mr. Adams was at perfect liberty to keep silence,
and would have been wise to do so. The trouble
was that keeping silence was something he could
never do. On the same day he wrote to Dr.
Franklin a sort of admonitory letter, phrased in
courteous language certainly, but conveying to
him information which the doctor might well
feel piqued at receiving from such a source, and
intimating that he would do well to bestir himself and to mend matters without more delay.
Shortly after he had thus prodded the minister
of the states, he wrote two letters to Congress,
containing a sufficiently fair narrative of the

facts, but between the lines of which one sees, or easily fancies that he sees, a nascent uneasiness, a dawning sense of having been imprudent. The same is visible in another letter to Franklin dated seven days later, in which the now anxious and for a moment self-distrustful writer begs the doctor, if he is materially wrong in any part of his argument to de Vergennes, to point out the error, since he is " open to conviction," and the subject is one "much out of the way of [his] particular pursuits," so that he naturally may be " inaccurate in some things." The next day brought a curt letter from de Vergennes, embodying a sharp snub. Still a few days more brought a letter from Franklin to de Vergennes, in which the American said that, though he did not yet fully understand the whole business, he could at least see that foreigners and especially Frenchmen should not be permitted to suffer. He added that the sentiments of the colonists in general, so far as he had been able to learn them from private and public sources, " differ widely from those that seem to be expressed by Mr. Adams in his letter to your excellency." Franklin was wrong in these assertions, but he was at least politic; he was turning aside wrath, gaining time, making the blow fall by slow degrees.

So the result of Mr. Adams's well-meant blunders was that he had not affected the opinions

of the French minister in the least, but that he
had secured for himself the ill-will both of that
powerful diplomatist and of Dr. Franklin. They
both snubbed him, and of course quickly allowed
it to be understood by members of Congress
that Mr. Adams was an unwelcome busybody.
This was in a large degree unjust and undeserved, but it was unfortunately plausible. Mr.
Adams could explain in self-defense that he had
been requested by de Vergennes himself to con-
vey information to that gentleman directly from
time to time on American affairs; and the explanation might serve as an excuse for, if not
a full justification of, his encroachment on the
proper functions of Dr. Franklin. But a public man is unfortunately situated when he is so
placed that he is obliged to explain. It seemed
in derogation of Mr. Adams's usefulness abroad
that, whether with or without fault on his own
part, he had incurred the displeasure of de Vergennes and the jealousy of Franklin. Congress
indeed stood manfully by him; yet it was impossible that his prestige should not be rather
weakened than strengthened by what had occurred. Altogether, his ill-considered readiness
had done him a serious temporary hurt on this
occasion, as on so many others, in his outspoken,
not to say loquacious career.

The ill feeling between Adams and Frank-

lin reached a point which it is painful now to
contemplate, as existing between two men who
should have been such hearty co-laborers in the
common cause.   That they did not openly quarrel was probably due only to their sense of propriety and dignity, and to the age and position
of Dr. Franklin.   In fact they were utterly incompatible, both mentally and morally.   From
finding that they could not work in unison, the
step to extreme personal dislike was not a long
one.   In 1811 Mr. Adams put his sentiments
not only in writing but in print with his usual
straightforward and unsparing directness.   He
charged that Franklin had " concerted " with de
Vergennes " to crush Mr. Adams and get possession of his commission for peace ; " and he
stigmatized the conspiracy, not unjustly if his
suspicions were correct, as a " vulgar and low
intrigue," a " base trick."   He said that when
de Vergennes wished to send complaints of him
to Congress, Franklin, who was not officially
bound to interfere in the business, became a
" willing auxiliary . . . at the expense of his
duty and his character."   He said that he had
never believed Dr. Franklin's expressions of
" reluctance," and that the majority of Congress
had " always seen that it was Dr. F.'s heart's
desire to avail himself of these means and this
opportunity to strike Mr. Adams out of exist-

ence as a public minister, and get himself into his place." He denied that he ever intermeddled in Franklin's province, and explained his neglect to consult with the doctor on the ground that he knew the "extreme indolence and dissipation" of that great man. He did not confine himself to accusing Franklin of an ungenerous enmity to himself, but directly assailed his morals and the purity of his patriotism. These bitter pages are not pleasant reading, however much truth there may be in them. In such a misunderstanding, as in a family quarrel, it would have been better had each party rigorously held his peace. Yet since this was not done, and the feud has been published to the world, it may be fairly said that, except in points of discretion at the time, and good taste afterward, it is difficult not to sympathize with Mr. Adams. He had nine tenths of the substance of right on his side.

For a while just now Mr. Adams resembles a ship blundering through a fog bank. Apparently he had taken leave of all discretion. Incredible as it seems, he actually seized this moment of Count de Vergennes's extreme irritation, an irritation of which he himself had been made the unfortunate scape-goat, to write to that minister a letter urging a vigorous and expensive naval enterprise by the French in

American waters, and suggesting that besides its
strictly strategic advantages it would have the
very great moral use of proving the sincerity of
the French in the alliance! Not that he himself, as he graciously said, doubted that sincerity, but others were questioning it. Nothing
could have been more inopportune or more un-
conciliatory than this proposal, made at the precise moment when conciliation would have been
the chief point of a sound policy. The French
treasury was beginning to feel severely the cost
of the war, and however imperfect may have
been the sincerity of the government at other
times and in other respects, they were now at
least doing all they could afford to do in the
way of substantial military assistance. De Vergennes replied with chilling civility. A few
days afterward Mr. Adams touched another
sensitive spot, renewing his old suggestion that
it would be well for him to communicate to the
British court the full character of his commissions. In this he was probably quite right;
but in urging it upon the minister just at this
moment he was again imprudent, if not actually
wrong. He knew perfectly well that de Vergennes did not wish this communication to be
made; it is true also that he more than half
suspected the concealed motives of the minister's reluctance, though he did not fully know

precisely in what shape the ministerial policy was being developed. Still, being aware of the unwelcome character of his proposal, he ought to have refrained from urging it for a little while, until the offense which he had so lately given could drop a little farther into the past. In those days of tardy communication diplomatic matters moved so slowly that a month more or less would not have counted for very much, and certainly he would have been likely to lose less by pausing than he could hope to gain by pushing forward just at this moment. Upon the receipt of the reiterated and unwelcome request, the patience and politeness of de Vergennes at last fairly broke down. His response was curt, and in substance, though not in language, almost insolent. He sent Mr. Adams a paper setting forth categorically his reasons for thinking that the time had not come for informing the English government concerning the congressional commissions. He hoped that Mr. Adams would see the force of these arguments, but otherwise, he said, "I pray you, and in the name of the king request you, to communicate your letter and my answer to the United States, and to suspend, until you shall receive orders from them, all measures with regard to the English ministry." For his own part, he acknowledged that he intended with all expedition to appeal to

Congress to check the intended communication. This was not pleasant; but the reading of the inclosed statement of reasons must have been still less so. They were, said the writer, "so plain that they must appear at first view." After this doubtful compliment to the sagacity of Mr. Adams, who had failed to discern considerations so remarkably obvious, a number of snubs followed. Mr. Adams was told that "it required no effort of genius" to comprehend that he could not fulfill all his commissions at once; that the English ministry would regard his communication, so far as related to the treaty of commerce, as " ridiculous," and would return either "no answer" or "an insolent one;" that Mr. Adams's purpose could never be achieved by the means he suggested, with the too plain innuendo that his suggestion was a foolish one. Finally, but not until the eighth paragraph had been reached in the discussion and disposition of Mr. Adams's several points, the Frenchman said, as if relieved at last to find a break in the chain of ignorance and folly, " This is a sensible reflection." There was a sharper satire in this praise than in the blame which had preceded it; and the subtle minister then continued to show that the " reflection " was " sensible " only because it showed that even Mr. Adams himself could appreciate and admit that under some circumstances he would do well to withhold the communication of his powers.

As a real confutation of Mr. Adams's arguments, this document was very imperfectly satisfactory. As a manifestation of ill-temper it was more efficient; for it was cutting and sarcastic enough to have irritated a man of a milder disposition than Mr. Adams enjoyed. On July 26, however, he replied to it in tolerably submissive form, though not concealing that he was rather silenced by the authority than convinced by the arguments of his opponent, since an opponent de Vergennes had by this time substantially become. But on July 27, Mr. Adams was moved to write a second and a less wise letter. He had overlooked, he said, the count's statement that in the beginning the French " king, without having been solicited by the Congress, had taken measures the most efficacious to sustain the American cause." He sought now to prove, and did prove, that this was an erroneous assertion, inasmuch as the colonists had solicited aid before it had been tendered to them. He would have done better had he continued to overlook the error, rather than be so zealous to prove his countrymen beggars of aid, instead of recipients of it unsought. But if this was a trifling matter, on a following page he committed a gross and unpardonable folly. "I am so convinced," he said, "by experience of the absolute necessity of more consultations and communications between his majesty's ministers and the ministers of Congress, that I am determined to omit no opportunity of communicating my sentiments to your excellency, upon everything that appears to me of importance to the common cause, in which I can do it with propriety." In other words, Dr. Franklin was so outrageously neglecting his duties that Mr. Adams must volunteer to perform them; and though he was even now in trouble by reason of news given to de Vergennes at that gentleman's own request, he actually declares his resolution, untaught by experience, to thrust further unasked communications before that minister. Some very unfriendly demon must have prompted this extraordinary epistolary effort! Two days afterward he received from de Vergennes a sharp and well-merited rebuke. To avoid the receipt of more letters like Mr. Adams's last, the minister now wrote: "I think it my duty to inform you that, Mr. Franklin being the sole person who has letters of credence to the king from the United States, it is with him only that I ought and can treat of matters which concern them, and particularly of that which is the subject of your observations." Then the minister mischievously sent the whole correspondence to Dr. Franklin, expressing the malicious hope that he would forward it all to Congress, so "that they may know the line of conduct which Mr. Adams pursues with regard to us, and that they may judge whether he is endowed, as Congress no doubt desires, with that conciliatory spirit which is necessary for the important and delicate business with which he is intrusted." In a word, de Vergennes had come to hate Adams, and wished to destroy him. Franklin did in fact write to Congress a letter in a tone which could not have been unsatisfactory to Vergennes, and the result came back in the shape of some mild fault-finding for Mr. Adams in an official letter from the President of Congress, a censure much more gentle than he might well have anticipated in view of the powerful influences which he had managed to set in motion against himself. Fortunately, too, such sting as there was in this was amply cured by a vote of December 12, 1780, passed concerning the correspondence relating to the redemption of debts, by which Congress instructed the Committee on Foreign Affairs "to inform Mr. Adams of the satisfaction which they receive from his industrious attention to the interests and honor of these United States abroad, especially in the transactions communicated to them by his letter."

During these two months of June and July,
1780, Mr. Adams had certainly succeeded in
stirring up a very considerable embroilment,
and in making Paris a rather uncomfortable
place of residence for himself for the time being.
It was well for him to seek some new and more
tranquil pastures, at least temporarily. Fortunately he was able to do so with a good grace.
So early as in February preceding he had seen
that a minister in Holland might do good service, especially in opening the way for loans of
money. He had lately been contemplating a
volunteer and tentative trip thither, and had
asked for passports from the Count de Vergennes; these he now received, with an intimation, not precisely that his absence was better
than his company, but at least that for a few
weeks he might rest assured that no negotiations
would arise to demand his attention. So on
July 27 he set out for Amsterdam. This visit,
intended to be brief and of exploration only,
finally ran on through a full year, and covered
the initiation of some important transactions.
Mr. Adams's chief motive was to try the financial prospects, to see what chance there was for
the colonies to delve into the treasure-chests and
deep pockets of the rich bankers and money-
lenders of the Low Countries. He found only
a black ignorance prevalent concerning the con-

dition and resources of his country, and that it
was of no use to talk of loans until he could
substitute for this lack of knowledge abundant
and favorable information. To this end he at
once bent himself by industriously employing
the press, and by seeking to extend his personal
acquaintance and influence as far as possible in
useful directions. At first this was another of
his purely voluntary undertakings, from which
he had not yet been turned aside; but while he
was prosecuting it, direct authority for engaging
a loan reached him from Congress. As ill luck
would have it, however, just at this same crisis
the English captured some papers disagreeably
compromising the relations of the Dutch with
Great Britain. At once the English ministry
became very menacing; the Dutch cowered in
alarm; and for the time all chance of borrowing money disappeared. "Not a merchant or
banker in the place, of any influence," says Mr.
C. F. Adams, "would venture at such a moment
even to appear to know that a person suspected
of being an American agent was at hand." But
after a while the cloud showed symptoms of
passing over; even a reaction against the spirit
of timid submission to England began to set in.
Mr. Adams patiently stayed by, watching the
turn of affairs, and while thus engaged received
from Congress two new commissions. The one

authorized him to give in the adhesion of the
United States to the armed neutrality; the other
appointed him minister plenipotentiary to the
United Provinces, and instructed him to negotiate a treaty of alliance as soon as possible.
Thus he obtained not only new incentives but
fresh points of departure, of which it may be
conceived that he was not slow to avail himself.
He at once announced to the ministers of various European nations at the Hague his power
in relation to the armed neutrality; and soon
afterward presented to the States General a
memorial requesting to be recognized as minister from the United States. But this recognition, involving of course the recognition of
the nation also, was not easily to be obtained.
Against it worked the fear of Great Britain and
all the influence of that court, which, though at
last on the wane, had long been overshadowing
in Holland, and was now strenuously pushed to
the utmost point in this matter. Further, the
influence of France was unquestionably, though
covertly and indirectly, arrayed upon the same
side. No more conclusive evidence could have
been desired as to the precise limits of the good-
will of de Vergennes to the American states.
Had he had their interests nearly at heart, he
would have had every reason to advance this
alliance; but having no other interests save

those of France at heart, he pursued the contrary course; for it best suited a purely French policy to have the colonies feel exclusively dependent upon France, and remain otherwise solitary, unfriended, unsupported. It is not fair to blame de Vergennes for this; his primary, perhaps his sole, duties were to his own country. But the fact undeniably indicates that he was not the disinterested friend of the colonies which he professed to be, and that he could not wisely be trusted in that implicit manner in which he demanded to be trusted by them. He was dishonest, but not to a degree or in a way which the diplomatic morality of that day severely condemned. He only pretended to be influenced by sentiments which he did not really feel, and called for a confidence which he had no right to. Mr. Adams, however, could not fail to suspect him, almost to understand him, and to become more than ever persuaded of the true relationship of the French government to the United States. He wrote to Jonathan Jackson, that the French minister, the Duke de la Vauguyon, doubtless acting upon instructions from de Vergennes, "did everything in his power" to obstruct the negotiation; and that it was only upon the blunt statement made to him by Mr. Adams, that "no advice of his or of the Comte de Vergennes, nor even a requisition from the king, should restrain me," that he desisted from his perfidious opposition and " fell in with me, in order to give the air of French influence " to the measures.

Amid these labors in Holland Mr. Adams was interrupted by a summons to Paris. There were some prospects of a negotiation, which, however, speedily vanished and permitted him to return. Besides his own endeavors, events were working for him very effectually. For the time England was like a man with a fighting mania; wildly excited, she turned a belligerent front to any nation upon the slightest, even imaginary, provocation. Utterly reckless as to the number of her foes, she now added Holland to the array, making a short and hasty stride from threats to a declaration of war. Mr. Adams could have suggested nothing better for his own purposes, had he been allowed to dictate British policy. Still the game was not won; things moved slowly in Holland, where the governmental machine was of very cumbrous construction, and any party possessed immense facilities in the way of obstruction. The stadtholder and his allies, conservatively minded, and heretofore well-disposed towards England, still remained hostile to Mr. Adams's projects; but a feeling friendly to him and to the colonies had rapidly made way among the merchants and popular party in politics. This was attributable in part

to indignation against Great Britain, in part to
the news of the American success in the capture
of Cornwallis's army, and in part to Adams's
personal exertions, especially in disseminating a
knowledge concerning his country, and sketch-
ing probable openings for trade and financial
dealings. At last he became convinced that
these sentiments of good-will had acquired such
strength and extension that a bold measure
upon his part would be crowned with immediate
success.

With characteristic audacity, therefore, he
now preferred a formal demand for a categor-
ical answer to his petition, presented several
months before, asking that he should be recognized by the States General as the minister of
an independent nation. In furtherance of this
move he made a series of personal visits to the
representatives of the several cities. It was a
step, if not altogether unconventional, yet at
least requiring no small amount of nerve and of
willingness for personal self-sacrifice; since, had
it failed, Adams would inevitably and perhaps
properly have been condemned for ill-judgment
and recklessness. This, coming in immediate
corroboration of the unfriendly criticisms of de
Vergennes and Franklin, would probably have
been a greater burden than his reputation could
have sustained. But as usual his courage was

ample. The deputies, one and all, replied to
him that they had as yet no authority to act
in the premises; but they would apply to their
constituents for instructions. They promptly
did so, and the condition of feeling which Mr.
Adams had anticipated, and which he had been
largely instrumental in producing, was manifested in the responses. The constituencies, in
rapid succession, declared for the recognition,
and on April 19, 1782, a year after the presentation of the first memorial, it took place. Mr.
Adams was then formally installed at the Hague
as the minister of the new people. The French
minister, the Duke de la Vauguyon, having covertly retarded the result so far as he well could,
but now becoming all courtesy and congratula-
tion, gave a grand entertainment in honor of
the achievement, and presented Mr. Adams to
the ministers of the European powers as the
latest member of their distinguished body. It
was a great triumph won over grave difficulties.
Mr. C. F. Adams says concerning it: " This
may be justly regarded, not simply as the third
moral trial, but what Mr. Adams himself always
regarded it, as the greatest success of his life;"
and this is hardly exaggeration. Practical advantages immediately followed. The Dutch
bankers came forward with offers to lend money,
and some sorely needed and very helpful loans

were consummated.   Further, on October 7,
Mr. Adams had the pleasure of setting his hand
to a treaty of amity and commerce, the second
which was ratified with his country as a free
nation.   Concerning this Dutch achievement he
wrote: "Nobody knows that I do anything; or
have anything to do.   One thing, thank God! is
certain.   I have planted the American standard
at the Hague.   There let it wave and fly in triumph over Sir Joseph Yorke and British pride.
I shall look down upon the flagstaff with pleasure from the other world."   The Declaration of
Independence, the Massachusetts Constitution,
the French alliance had not given him "more
satisfaction or more pleasing prospects for our
country" than this "pledge against friends and
enemies," this "barrier against all dangers from
the house of Bourbon," and "present security
against England."

CHAPTER IX

THE TREATY OF PEACE: THE ENGLISH MISSION

THE Revolutionary war was protracted by the
English in a manner altogether needless and
wicked. Long after its result was known by
every one to be inevitable, that result was still
postponed at the expense of blood, suffering,
and money, for no better motives than the selfish pride of the British ministry and the dull
obstinacy of the English king. Even the rules
of war condemn a general who sacrifices life
to prolong a battle when the prolongation can
bring no possible advantage; but no court-
martial had jurisdiction over Lord North, and
impeachment has never been used to punish
mere barbarity on the part of a cabinet minister. Mr. Adams appreciated these facts at the
time as accurately as if he had been removed
from the picture by the distance of two or three
generations. It caused him extreme and perfectly just wrath and indignation. Bitter expla-
nations of the truth are sprinkled through his
letters, official and personal, from the time of

his second arrival in Europe. The hope of
coming peace had a dangerous influence in re-
laxing the efforts and lowering the *morale* of
the people in the states. He steadily endeavored to counteract this mischief, and repeated
to them with emphasis, often passing into anger,
his conviction that the end was not near at hand.
He encouraged them, indeed, with occasional
descriptions of the condition of affairs in England, which are a little amusing to read now.
His animosity to the government party was intense, and many of his anticipations were the
offspring of his wishes rather than of his judgment. The nation seemed to him on the brink
of civil war, and to be saved for the time from
that disaster solely because of the utter dearth
of leaders sufficiently trustworthy to gain the
confidence of the discontented people. Thus he
declared, "it may truly be said, that the British
empire is crumbling to pieces like a rope of
sand," so that, if the war should continue, "it
would not be surprising to see Scotland become
discontented with the Union, Asia cast off the
yoke of dependence, and even the West India
islands divorce themselves and seek the protection of France, of Spain, or even of the United
States." In a word, throughout England, "the
stubble is so dry, that the smallest spark thrown
into it may set the whole field in a blaze." "His

lordship talks about the misery of the people in America. Let him look at home, and then say where is misery! where the hideous prospect of an internal civil war is added to a war with all the world!"

But all this did not blind him in the least to the dogged resolve of king and cabinet to fight for a long while yet. The English, he says, "have ever made it a part of their political system to hold out to America some false hopes of reconciliation and peace, in order to slacken our nerves and retard our preparations. . . . But serious thoughts of peace upon any terms that we can agree to, I am persuaded they never had." He said that he would think himself to be wanting in his duty to his countrymen, if he "did not warn them against any relaxation of their exertions by sea or land, from a fond expectation of peace. They will deceive themselves if they depend upon it. Never, never will the English make peace while they have an army in North America." "There is nothing farther from the thoughts of the king of England, his ministers, parliament, or nation (for they are now all *his*), than peace upon any terms that America can agree to. . . . I think I see very clearly that America must grow up in war. It is a painful prospect, to be sure." But he goes on at some length to show that it must and can be encountered successfully. "I am so fully convinced that peace is a great way off," he again reiterates, "and that we have more cruelty to encounter than ever, that I ought to be explicit to Congress." Thus earnestly and unceasingly did he endeavor to make the Americans look the worst possibilities of the future fairly in the face, appreciate all they had to expect, and escape the snare of too sanguine anticipation, with its fatal consequence of languor in the prosecution of the war. France and Spain, he said, cannot desert the states; self-interest binds the trio together in an indissoluble alliance for the purposes of this struggle. But even should these nations abandon America, should his country "be deserted by all the world, she ought seriously to maintain her resolution to be free. She has the means within herself. Her greatest misfortune has been that she has never yet felt her full strength, nor considered the extent of her resources." It was the resolute temper of such patriots as Mr. Adams that was bringing forward the end more rapidly than the prudent ones among them ventured to believe.

If the postponement of that end was wicked on the part of the English government, their ungracious and shambling approaches to it were contemptible and almost ridiculous, their manœuvres were very clumsy, their efforts to save appearances in abandoning substantials were extremely comical and pitiful. There were secret embassies, private and informal overtures made through unknown men, proposals so impossible as to be altogether absurd, ludicrous efforts to throw dust in the eyes of French, Spanish, and American negotiators, endeavors to wean the allies from each other, to induce France to desert the states, even to bribe the states to turn about and join England in a war against France. There was nothing so preposterous or so hopeless that the poor old king in his desperation, and the king's friends in their servility, would not try for it, nothing so base and contemptible that they would not stoop to it, and seek to make others also stoop. There was endless shilly-shallying; there was much traveling of emissaries under assumed names; infinite skirmishing about the central fact of American independence. It was no fact, the English cabinet said, and it could not be a fact until they should admit it; for the present they stoutly alleged that it was only a foolish mirage; yet all the while they knew perfectly well that it was as irrevocably established as if an American minister had been already received by George III. Though they might criminally waste a little time in such nonsense, all the world saw that they could not hold out much longer.

Amid his transactions in Holland Mr. Adams had been interrupted by a summons from de Vergennes to come at once to Paris, and advise concerning some pending suggestions. It was about the time of Mr. Cumberland's futile expedition to Madrid. Immediately after the failure of this originally hopeless attempt, Russia and Austria endeavored to intervene, with so far a temporary appearance of success that some articles were actually proposed. De Vergennes had intended from the outset to be master in the negotiations whenever they should take place, and to this end he had conceived it wise to prevent either Spain or the United States from making demands inconvenient to him, or incompatible with his purely French purposes. Spain he must manage and cajole as best he could; but the states he expected to handle more cavalierly and imperiously. He had no notion of letting this crude people, this embryotic nationality, impede the motions or interfere with the interests of the great kingdom of France. So hitherto he had quietly attended to all the preliminary and tentative business which had been going forward, without communicating anything of it to Mr. Adams. Accordingly now, when affairs had come to a point at which that gentleman could no longer be utterly ignored, he suddenly found himself called upon to speak and act in the middle of transactions of which he did not know the earlier stages. It was much as if a player should be ordered to go upon the stage and take a chief part in the second act of a play, of which he had not been allowed to see or read the first act.

On July 6, 1781, Mr. Adams appeared in Paris and was allowed to know that the basis of negotiation covered three points of interest to him: 1. A negotiation for peace between the states and Great Britain without any intervention of France, or of those mediators who were to act in arranging the demands of the European belligerents. 2. No treaty, however, was to be signed, until the quarrels of these European belligerents should also have been successfully composed. 3. A truce was to be arranged for one or two years, during which period everything should remain *in statu quo*, for the purpose of giving ample time for negotiation. This was divulged to him, but he was not told of a fourth article, though not less interesting to him than these. This was, that when this basis should have been acceded to by all the parties, the mediation should go forward. The difficulty in this apparently simple proposition, a difficulty sufficiently great to induce de Vergennes to indulge in the gross ill faith of concealing it, lay in the stipulation concerning " all the parties." Were the states a party or were they not? Were they a nation, independent like the rest, or were they colonies in a condition of revolt? If they constituted a "party" they were entitled to be treated like the other parties, and to accede to and share in the mediation, appearing before the world in all respects precisely like their comrade nations. To this it was foreseen that England would object, and that she would not consent thus at once to set herself upon terms of equality with those whom she still regarded as rebellious subjects. Also the states, being present at the mediation, might urge in their own behalf matters which would cause new snarls in a business already unduly complicated, whence might arise some interference with the clever ways and strictly national purpose of the count. These were the reasons why de Vergennes refrained from mentioning this fourth point to Mr. Adams.

But if that astute diplomatist fancied that the concealment of this article would carry with it the concealment of the vital point which it involved, he was in error. Though unversed in intrigue, Mr. Adams had not the less a shrewd and comprehensive head, and from the first article he gathered the necessary suggestion. Why should his country be separated from the rest and bidden to treat with Great Britain in a side closet, as it were, apart from the public room in which the European dignitaries were conducting their part of the same business? Proud, independent, and long ago suspicious of the French minister, Mr. Adams not only at once saw this question, but surmised the answer to it. Yet since his belief could after all be nothing more than a surmise, which he had to grope for in the dark, unaided by knowledge which he ought to have received, he framed a cautious reply. With professions of modesty, he said that it seemed to him that an obvious inference from the isolation of the states was, that their independence was a matter to be settled between themselves and Great Britain; and he could not but fear that before the mediation some other power, seeking its own ends, might come to such an understanding with Great Britain as would jeopardize American nationality. Therefore he said fairly that he did not like the plan. The point was put by him clearly and strenuously; subsequently, as will be seen, it proved to be pregnant with grave difficulties. But for the moment he was saved the necessity of pushing it to a conclusion by reason of the failure of the whole scheme of pacification. Indeed, he was detained in Paris but a very short time on this occasion, and quickly returned to his Dutch negotiations. He had, however, corroborated the notion of Count de Vergennes, that he would be an uncomfortable person for that selfish diplomatist to get along with in the coming discussions.

Perfectly convinced of this incompatibility, de Vergennes was using all his arts and his influence with Congress to relieve himself of the anticipated embarrassment. His envoy to the states now prosecuted a serious crusade against the contumacious New Englander, and met with a success which cannot be narrated without shame. To-day it is so easy to see how pertinaciously the French cabinet sought to lower the tone of the American Congress, that it seems surprising that so many members could at the time have remained blind to endeavors apparently perfectly obvious. Even so far back as in 1779, the *ultimata* being then under discussion in Congress, and among them being a distinct recognition by Great Britain of the independence of the states, M. Gérard, the French minister at Philadelphia, had actually suggested, in view of a probable refusal by England of this demand, that Geneva and the Swiss Cantons had never yet obtained any such formal acknowledgment, and still enjoyed "their sovereignty and independence only under the guarantee of France!" The suspicion which such language ought to have awakened might have found corroboration in the hostility to Mr. Adams, the true cause of which was often hinted at. Yet so far were the Americans from being put upon their guard by the conduct of de Vergennes's emissaries, and so far were they from appreciating the true meaning of this dislike to Mr. Adams, that they made one concession after another before the steady and subtle pressure applied by their dangerous ally. In March, 1781, de la Luzerne, M. Gérard's successor, began a series of efforts to bring about the recall of Mr. Adams. In this he was fortunately unsuccessful; he was going too far. Yet his arts and persistence were not without other fruits. In July, 1781, he succeeded in obtaining a revocation of the powers which had been given to Mr. Adams to negotiate a treaty of commerce with England so soon as peace should be established, powers which, as we have seen, were so obnoxious to de Vergennes that he had obstinately insisted that they should be kept a close secret. Further, though Congress persisted in retaining Mr. Adams, they were induced to join with him four coadjutors, the five to act as a joint commission in treating for peace. These four were Dr. Franklin, minister to France, John Jay, minister at Madrid, Laurens, then a prisoner in the Tower of London, and who was released in exchange for Lord Cornwallis just

in time to be present at the closing of the negotiation, and Jefferson, who did not succeed in
getting away from the United States.

There was no objection to this arrangement,
considered in itself, and without regard to the
influence by which it had been brought about.
Indeed, in view of Adams's relations with the
French court, it was perhaps an act of prudence.
It might possibly be construed as a slur on him;
but it had not necessarily that aspect, and he
himself received it in a very manly and generous
spirit, refusing to see in it "any trial at all of
spirit and fortitude," but preferring to regard
it as "a comfort." "The measure is right," he
wrote; "it is more respectful to the powers of
Europe concerned, and more likely to give satisfaction in America." Unfortunately, however,
worse remained behind. Not content with re-
moving all *ultimata* except the fundamental
one of the recognition of American independence, — a recession, of which the foolish and
gratuitous pusillanimity was made painfully apparent by the subsequent progress and result of
the negotiations, — Congress now actually trans-
muted its five independent representatives, the
commissioners, into mere puppets of M. de Vergennes. That effete body, at the express request
and almost accepting the very verbal dictation
of de la Luzerne, now instructed their peace

commissioners "to make the most candid and confidential communications upon all subjects to the ministers of our generous ally, the King of France; to undertake nothing in the negotiations for peace or truce without their knowledge or concurrence," and "ultimately to govern themselves by their advice and opinion." At last bottom was indeed reached; no lower depth of humiliation existed below this, where the shrewd and resolute diplomacy of de Vergennes had succeeded in placing the dear allies of his country, the *protégés*, now properly so called, of the kind French monarch.

The American commissioners abroad took these instructions in different and characteristic ways. Dr. Franklin received them in his usual bland and easy fashion; he was on the best of terms with de Vergennes; he certainly had not pride among his failings, and he gave no sign of displeasure. Mr. Adams's hot and proud temper blazed up amid his absorbing occupations in Holland, and he was for a moment impelled to throw up his position at once; but he soon fell back beneath the control of his better reason, his patriotism, and that admirable independent self-confidence, his peculiar trait, which led him so often to undertake and accomplish very difficult tasks on his own responsibility. He wisely and honorably concluded to stand by his post and do his best for his country, without too much respect for her demands. Mr. Jay was hurt, and felt himself subjected to an unworthy indignity, altogether against his nice sense of right. He had already seen that France was covertly leagued with Spain to prevent the granting of the American request for the privilege of navigating the Mississippi through Spanish territory. He understood the dangerous character of the new American position, and saw that he was so hampered that he could not do his countrymen justice. He would play no part in such a game; and wrote home, not resigning, but requesting that a successor might be appointed. Events, however, marched at last with such speed that this request never was or well could be granted.

At last peace was really at hand. The unmistakable harbingers were to be seen in every quarter. The French cabinet, having gained a controlling influence over the American negotiation, now thought it time to undertake the further task of bringing these confiding friends into a yielding and convenient mood, forewarning them that they must not expect much. They were told that the French king took their submission graciously, and would do his best for them, of course; but if he should " not obtain for every state all they wished, they must attribute the sacrifice he might be compelled to make of his inclinations to the tyrannic rule of necessity." Then came references to " the other powers at war," reminding one of the way in which Mr. Spenlow kept Mr. Jorkins darkly suspended over David Copperfield's head; nor, indeed, could one deny, as an abstract proposition, that, " if France should continue hostilities merely on account of America, after reasonable terms were offered, it was impossible to say what the event might be." The true meaning of such paragraphs had to be sought between the lines. The American negotiators had peculiar perils before them, and more to dread from their allies than from their foes.

England meanwhile was also in her bungling fashion really getting ready for peace. With grimaces and writhings, indicating her reluctance, her suffering, and her humiliation, and so not altogether ungrateful in the eyes of the Americans, who were in some measure compensated for her backwardness by beholding its cause, the mother country at last prepared to let the colonies go. The year 1782 opened with the ministry of Lord North tottering to its fall. General Conway moved an address to the king, praying for peace. The majority against this motion was of one vote only. Lord North resigned; the Whigs, under the Marquis of Rockingham, came in. Even while the cabinet was in a transition state, the first serious move was made. Mr. Digges, an emissary without official character, was dispatched to ask whether the American commissioner had power to conclude as well as to negotiate. His errand was to Mr. Adams, and Mr. C. F. Adams conceives that his real object was to discover whether the Americans would not make a separate peace or truce without regard to France. Nothing came of this. But when the new ministry was fairly installed, with Fox at the head of the department of foreign affairs and Lord Shelburne in charge of the colonies, Dr. Franklin wrote privately to Shelburne, expressing a hope that a peace might now be arranged. In reply Shelburne sent Mr. Richard Oswald, "a pacifical man," to Paris to sound the doctor. But Oswald, though coming from the colonial department, was so thoughtless as to talk with de Vergennes concerning a general negotiation. Fox, finding his province thus invaded, sent over his own agent, Thomas Grenville, to de Vergennes. A graver question than one of etiquette, or even of official jealousy, underlay this misunderstanding, — the question whether the states were to be treated with as colonies or as an independent power, the same about which Adams had already expressed his views to de

Vergennes. Fox and Shelburne quarreled over it in the first instance in the cabinet. Fox was outvoted, and announced that he would retire with his followers At the same critical moment Lord Rockingham died; and then Fox and Shelburne further disputed as to who should fill his place. Shelburne carried the day, unfortunately, as it seemed, for the peace party. For Shelburne was resolved to regard the states as still colonies, who might indeed acquire independence by and through the treaty, but who did not yet possess that distinction. He at once recalled Grenville, and gave Mr. Oswald a commission to treat. But this commission was carefully so worded as not to recognize, even by implication, the independence or the nationality of the states. It authorized Oswald only to treat with " any commissioner or commissioners, named or to be named by the thirteen colonies or plantations in North America, and any body or bodies, corporate or politic, or any assembly or assemblies, or description of men, or any person or persons whatsoever, a peace or truce with the said colonies or plantations, or any part thereof." In such a petty temper did the noble lord approach this negotiation, and by this silly and unusual farrago of words endeavor to save a dignity which, wounded by facts, could hardly be plastered over by phrases.

But if for the English this was mere matter of pride in a point of detail, it wore a different aspect to an American. Mr. Jay had no notion of accepting for his country the character of revolted colonies, whose independence was to be granted by an article in a treaty with Great Britain, and was therefore contingent for the present, and non-existent until the grant should take place. Suppose, indeed, that after such an admission the treaty should never be consummated; in what a position would the states be left? They were, and long had been and had asserted themselves to be, a free nation, having a government which had sent and received foreign ministers. This character was to be acknowledged on all sides at the outset, and they would transact business on no other basis. Independence and nationality could not come to them as a concession or gift from Great Britain, having been long since taken and held by their own strength in her despite. Assurances were offered that the independence should of course be recognized by an article of the treaty; but neither would this do. In this position Jay found no support where he had a right to expect it. Dr. Franklin, with more of worldly wisdom than of sensitive spirit, took little interest in this point; declaring that, provided independence became an admitted fact, he cared

not for the manner of its becoming so. De
Vergennes said that the commission was amply sufficient, and even covertly intimated this
opinion to the British ministry. But from Mr.
Adams, in Holland, Mr. Jay received encouraging letters, thoroughly corroborating his opinions, and sustaining him fully and cheerfully.
Only Mr. Adams suggested that a commission
to treat with the United States of America, in
the same form in which such documents ran as
towards any other country, would seem to him
satisfactory. A formal statement from the British could be waived. The admission might come
more easily than an explicit declaration. This
suggestion gave Lord Shelburne a chance to
recede, of which he availed himself. Mr. Oswald
was authorized to treat with the commissioners
of the United States of America; and the point
was at last reached at which the task of negotiation could be fairly entered upon.

The Americans at once put forward their
claims in brief and simple fashion; these involved questions of boundary, the navigation of
the Mississippi, so far as England could deal
with it, and the enjoyment of the northeastern
fisheries. The English court began, of course,
by refusal and objection, and de Vergennes was
really upon their side in the controversy. The
territory demanded by the United States seemed

to him unreasonably extensive; the navigation
of the Mississippi nearly concerned Spain, who
did not wish the states to establish any claim to
it; and he was anxious for his own purposes to
do Spain a good turn in this particular; while
as for the fisheries, he intended that they should
be shared between England and France. Further than this, the English demanded that the
states should reimburse all Tories and loyalists
in America for their losses in the war; and de
Vergennes said that this requirement, which the
American commissioners scouted, was no more
than a proper concession to England. Matters
standing thus, Franklin and Jay had to fight
their diplomatic battle as best they could, certainly without that valuable aid and potent, generous assistance from the French court of which
Congress had been so sanguine. Fortunately
Mr. Oswald, the "pacifical man," was heartily
anxious to bring about a successful conclusion.
But he had not full powers to grant all that the
Americans desired, and in his frequent communications to the cabinet his good-nature became
so apparent that it was deemed best to dispatch
a coadjutor of a different temper. Accordingly
Mr. Strachey appeared in Paris as the exponent
of English arrogance, insolence, and general
offensiveness.

This new move boded ill; but as good luck

would have it, just at this juncture Mr. Jay also received a no less effective reinforcement. Mr. Adams, having got through with his business in Holland, arrived in Paris on October 26. He at once had a long interview with Mr. Jay, received full information of all that had passed, and declared himself in perfect accord with all the positions assumed by that gentleman. The two fell immediately into entire harmony, and with the happiest results. For a vital question was impending. Matters had just reached the stage at which the final terms of the treaty were to be discussed with a view to an actual conclusion. The instructions of the commissioners, it will be remembered, compelled them to keep in close and candid communication with de Vergennes, and to be guided and governed by his good counsel. Yet two of the three commissioners present thoroughly distrusted him,[1] and

---

[1] About this time Mr. Adams gave to Jonathan Jackson this true and pungent summary of the French policy: "In substance it has been this: in assistance afforded us in naval force and in money to keep us from succumbing, and nothing more; to prevent us from ridding ourselves wholly of our enemies; to prevent us from growing powerful or rich; to prevent us from obtaining acknowledgments of our independence by other foreign powers, and to prevent us from obtaining consideration in Europe, or any advantage in the peace but what is expressly stipulated in the treaty; to deprive us of the grand fishery, the Mississippi River, the western lands, and to saddle us with the Tories."

were assured that obedience to these instructions
would cost their country a very high price.
Should they, then, disobey? Franklin had said
no. Jay had said yes. Adams, now coming
into the business, promptly gave the casting vote
on Jay's side. Thereupon Franklin yielded. It
was a bold step. An immense responsibility was
assumed; a great risk, at once national and personal, was ventured. Men have been impeached
and condemned upon less weighty matters and
more venial charges. But the commissioners
had the moral courage which is so often born
out of the grandeur of momentous events.
Henceforth they went on in the negotiation
without once asking advice or countenance from
de Vergennes; without even officially informing
him of their progress, though Mr. Adams gave
him private news very regularly. If he offered
them no aid under the circumstances, he can
hardly be blamed; but such few criticisms or
hints as he did throw out were by no means upon
their side in the discussions.

Considering that the recognition of independence was the only *ultimatum* which the Americans were ordered to insist upon, they certainly
made a wonderfully good bargain. They did
very well in the way of boundaries; they got all
that the English could grant concerning navigation of the Mississippi; the English claim to

compensation for loyalists they cut down to a
stipulation, which they frankly said would be of
no value, that Congress should use its influence
with the states to prevent any legal impediment
being placed in the way of the collection of
debts.   This was the suggestion of Mr. Adams.
But the question of the fisheries caused their
chief difficulty; it seemed as though the Americans must make a concession here, or else break
off the negotiation altogether.   Mr. Strachey
went to London to see precisely what the cabinet would do, but at the same time left behind
him the distinct intimation that he had no idea
that the ministry would meet the American
demands.   Mr. Vaughan, distrusting the influence which Strachey might exert, set off immediately after him in order to counteract his
contumacy.   The ministry had, however, already
decided, and directed its envoys to insist to the
last point, but ultimately to yield rather than
jeopardize the pacification.   Thus instructed,
they came to a final session.   The question of
the fisheries came up at once; the Americans
appeared resolute, and for a while matters did
not promise well; but soon the Englishmen
began to weaken; they said that at least they
would like to substitute the word " liberty " in
place of the less agreeable word " right."   But
Mr. Adams thereupon arose and with much

warmth and ardor delivered himself of an eloquent exposition of his views. A "right" it
was, he said, and a "right" it should be called.
He even went so far as to say that the conciliation hung upon the point which he urged. The
fervor of his manner, which in moments of excitement was always impressive, lending an air
of earnest and intense conviction to his words,
satisfied the Englishmen that they must avail
themselves of all the latitude of concession
which had been allowed to them. They yielded;
and a "right" in the fisheries became and has
ever since remained a part of the national property. They had to yield once more, as has
been stated, on the question of compensation to
Tories, and then the bargain was finally struck,
substantially upon the American basis.

The agreement was signed, and the conclusion
was reported to de Vergennes. At first he took
the announcement tranquilly enough; he had
been pushing forward his own negotiations with
England for some time very smoothly, and had
been satisfied to have the Americans take care
of themselves and keep out of his way. But in
the course of a fortnight after the American
conclusion the aspect of affairs changed; obstacles appeared in the way; he became alarmed
lest England should do, what it seems that the
king and some of his advisers probably would

American Peace Commissioners

have liked very well to do, viz., not only patch
up a conciliation with the states, but persuade
them into a union with Great Britain against
France. Thereupon he began to inveigh loudly
against the bad faith of the Americans, and to
employ his usual tactics at Philadelphia to have
them discredited, and their acts repudiated by
Congress. The states, as he truly said, had
bound themselves to make no separate treaty or
peace with England until France and England
should also come to terms of final agreement;
and now they had broken this compact. But
the commissioners defended themselves upon the
facts altogether satisfactorily. They had made
no treaty at all; they had only agreed that,
whenever the treaty between France and England should be signed, then a treaty between
the United States and England should also be
signed, and the exact tenor of this latter treaty
had been agreed upon. This had been done
formally in writing, over signatures, only because the English ministry had agreed to stand
by such a bargain as Mr. Oswald should *sign*,
and any less formal arrangement might be repudiated without actual bad faith. They had
taken care at the outset expressly to provide
that the whole business was strictly preparatory
and could become definitive only when England
and France should ratify their treaty. It is in-

structive to see that neither the French nor the
English ministers felt at all sure that the Americans were honest in this stipulation.　From the
English side they were approached with hints
reaching at least to a conclusive pacification and
treaty, if not even to an alliance with Great
Britain; on the French side they were assailed,
because it was supposed that they might very
probably cherish precisely these designs.　But
these American gentlemen, self-made men repre-
senting a self-made nation, and uneducated in
the aristocratic morals of diplomacy, astonished
the high-bred scions of nobility with whom they
were dealing by behaving with strict integrity, by
actually telling the truth and standing to their
word.　When de Vergennes and Shelburne had
mastered this novel idea of honesty, they went
on with their negotiations, and brought them to
a successful issue.　Preliminaries were signed
by the contending European powers on January
21, 1783; but it was not until September 3
that the definitive treaties were all in shape for
simultaneous execution; on that day the American commissioners had the pleasure of setting
their hands to the most important treaty that
the United States ever has made or is likely
ever to make.

The pride and pleasure which Mr. Jay, Mr.
Adams, and, chiefly by procuration, it must be

said, Dr. Franklin also, were entitled to feel at
this consummation had been slightly dashed by
the receipt of a letter embodying something
very like a rebuke from Robert R. Livingston,
who was now in charge of the foreign affairs
of the United States. Alarmed by the expressions of indignation which came to him from
the Count de Vergennes, that gentleman wrote
to the envoys, not so much praising them for
having done better than they had been bidden,
as blaming them for having done so well without French assistance. The past could not be
undone, most fortunately ; but Mr. Livingston
now wished to apologize, and to propitiate de
Vergennes by informing him of a secret article whereby the southern boundary was made
contingent upon the result of the European negotiations. The commissioners were naturally
incensed at this treatment so precisely opposite
to what they had handsomely merited, and an
elaborate reply was prepared by Mr. Jay, and
inserted in their letter-book. But it was never
sent; it was superfluous. As between Congress
and the commissioners, it was the former body
that was placed upon the defensive, and a very
difficult defensive too. The less said about the
instructions and the deviations from them the
better it was for the members of that over-timid
and blundering legislature. All the honor,

praise, and gratitude which the American people had to bestow belonged solely to the commissioners, and few persons were long so dull or so prejudiced as not to acknowledge this truth, and to give the honor where the honor was due. Yet it was a long while before Mr. Adams's sense of indignation wore away; he said, with excusable acerbity, "that an attack had been made on him by the Count de Vergennes, and Congress had been induced to disgrace him; that he would not bear this disgrace if he could help it," etc. A few days later he wrote : —

"I am weary, disgusted, affronted, and disappointed. . . . I have been injured, and my country has joined in the injury; it has basely prostituted its own honor by sacrificing mine. But the sacrifice of me was not so servile and intolerable as putting us all under guardianship. Congress surrendered their own sovereignty into the hands of a French minister. Blush! blush! ye guilty records! blush and perish! It is glory to have broken such infamous orders. Infamous, I say, for so they will be to all posterity. How can such a stain be washed out? Can we cast a veil over it and forget it ?"

Severe words these, painful and humiliating to read; but perfectly true. Congress, which well merited the lash of bitter rebuke, laid it cruelly upon Adams and Jay, who deserved it not at all. But Mr. Adams, even amid the utterances of his bitter resentment, manfully said : "This state of mind I must alter, and work while the day lasts." Of such sound quality did the substratum of his character always prove to be, whenever events forced their way down to it through the thin upper crusts of egotism and rashness.

The negotiations at the Hague and in Paris, though they take a short time in the telling, had been protracted and tedious; long before they were completed the novelty of European life had worn off, and Mr. Adams was thoroughly, even pitifully homesick. So soon as an agreement had been reached and the execution of a definitive treaty substantially assured, on December 4, 1782, he sent in his resignation of all his foreign employments, and wrote to his wife with much positiveness and a sort of joyful triumph, that he should now soon be on the way home, " in the spring or beginning of summer." If the acceptance of his resignation should not "arrive in a reasonable time," he declared that he would " come home without it." But by May, 1783, he had to say that he could not see " a possibility of embarking before September or October ; " and most heartily he added that he was in the " most disgusting and provoking situation imaginable ; " he was so sincerely anxious to get back that he would

rather be " carting street dust and marsh mud "
than be waiting as he was. These reiterations
of his longing, his resolve to return, his expressions of pleasure in the anticipation, of vexation at the repeated delays, are really pathetic.
Events, however, were too strong for him; the
business already in hand moved in crab-like
fashion; in June he began to talk about the
following spring; then new duties came in sight
faster than old ones could be dispatched. For
in September, 1783, he had the mingled honor
and disappointment of being commissioned, in
conjunction with Dr. Franklin and Mr. Jay, to
negotiate a treaty of commerce with Great Britain. Such a commercial alliance was a matter
which he had long had near at heart, as being
of the first importance to the states; the revocation of his previous commission had profoundly
annoyed him at the time, and had never since
ceased to rankle in his memory; he had opinions
and hopes as to the future relationship of the
two countries, to be carried out through the
ways of commerce, which he had thought out
with infinite care and which he felt that he
could do much to promote. In a word, the
opportunity was a duty, and he must stay abroad
for it. Reluctantly he reached the conclusion,
which was, however, obviously inevitable. But
he made the best possible compromise; he wrote

to his wife urging her to come out with their daughter to join him, indeed scarcely leaving her the option to say no, had she been so minded.

By the autumn, instead of being on the ocean, as he had hoped, he was on a sick-bed. His constitution seems to have been a peculiar mixture of strength and weakness. He lived an active, hard-working life, and survived to a goodly old age; the likenesses of him show us a sturdy and ruddy man, too stout for symmetry, but looking as though the rotund habit were the result of a superabundant vigor of physique; he went through a great amount of open air exposure and even hardship, such for example as his horseback trips between Boston and Philadelphia, his stormy passages across the Atlantic, his long, hard journey from Ferrol to Paris, and many lesser expeditions. These broke at intervals the unwholesome indoor life of the civilian, and, since he bore them well, ought to have added to his robustness. Yet he constantly complains of his health, and at times becomes quite low-spirited about it. That he was not hypochondriacal is sufficiently proved by the attacks of grave illness which he had in the prime of life. Two years before the present time he had suffered from a fever in Holland. Now again, in this autumn of 1783, he was prostrated by another fever of great severity.

He was cared for in Paris by Sir James Jay,
who brought him through it; but he was left
much debilitated, and had to endure the tedium
of a long convalescence. Most of this period
he passed in London, seeing as much as he well
could of the capital city of that " mother country " whose galling yoke he had done so much
to break. He had the rare fortune during this
visit, says his grandson, " to witness the confes-
sion, made to his Parliament and people by
George the Third himself, that he had made a
treaty of peace with the colonies no longer, but
now the independent states of North America."
He was far from fully restored to vigorous
health when he received an unwelcome summons to Amsterdam, to arrange for meeting
" the immense flock of new bills," which the
states were drawing on the Dutch bankers with
happy prodigality and a perfect recklessness as
to the chance or means of payment. A stormy
winter voyage, involving extraordinary and prolonged exposure, was endured more successfully
than could have been hoped by the invalid. Not
less trying, in a different way, was the task
which he had to perform upon his arrival, of
borrowing more money upon the hard terms
made by unwilling lenders with a borrower
bearing, to speak plainly, a very disreputable
character in the financial world. But he achieved

a success beyond explanation, except upon the principle that the banking houses were already so deeply engaged for America that they could not permit her to become insolvent.

Meantime Congress sent out a commission empowering Mr. Adams, Dr. Franklin, and Mr. Jefferson to negotiate treaties of commerce with any foreign powers which should be willing to form such connections. The Prussian cabinet had already been in communication with Adams on the subject, and a new field of labor was thus opened before him. Fortunately, about this time, in the summer of 1784, his wife and daughter arrived; he began housekeeping at Auteuil, close by Paris; and the reëstablishment of a domestic circle, with occupation sufficiently useful and not too laborious, reconciled him to a longer exile. He had several months of a kind of comfort and happiness to which he had long been a stranger, yet upon which he placed a very high value, for he was a man naturally of domestic tastes and strong family affections.

But Congress prepared another interruption for him, by appointing him, February 24, 1785, minister to Great Britain. The position could be looked at from more than one point of view. In the picturesque aspect, it was striking and impressive to appear as the first accredited envoy in the court of that venerable and noble

nation of which his newly created country had
so lately been only a subject part. As the Count
de Vergennes said to him, "It is a mark." It
was indeed a "mark," and a very proud one,
and the responsibility imposed upon the man
appointed to set that mark before the world was
very grave. Mr. Adams was so constituted as
to feel this burden fully; but he was also so
constituted as to bear it well. There was about
him very much of the grandeur of simplicity, a
grandeur which, it must be confessed, scarcely
survived the eighteenth century, and has belonged only to the earliest generation of our
statesmen. He had natural dignity, self-respect,
and independence, and he copied no forms of
social development alien to the training of his
youth. That youth had been provincial, but by
no means of that semi-barbarous and backwoods
character that was afterwards prevalent in the
country. Colonial Boston was a civilized community, wherein a liberal education was to be
had, some broad views to be acquired, and honorable ambitions nourished. One could learn
there, if not much of the technical polish of aristocratic society, at least a gentlemanly bearing
and plain good manners. John Adams had the
good sense not to seek to exchange these qualities for that peculiar finish of high European
society, which certainly he could never have

acquired. Thus in the mere matter of "making an appearance" he was a well-selected representative of the states. Nor was this so petty a point of view as it might seem. Much of real importance could be effected by the demeanor and personal impression made by the American minister. "You will be stared at a great deal," said the Duke of Dorset, preparing Mr. Adams for that peculiar insolence which Englishmen have carried to a point unknown in any other age or among any other people. "I fear they will gaze with evil eyes," said Mr. Adams; the duke assured him, with more of civility than prophecy, that he believed they would not. Mrs. Adams perhaps felt this much more keenly than her husband. She was made very anxious by the thought that she had the social repute of her countrywomen to answer for.

Fortunately the presentation of Mr. Adams to the king was private. The American afterward frankly acknowledged that he felt and displayed some nervousness in his address. He would have been utterly devoid of imagination and emotion, almost, one might say, of intelligence, had he not done so, and his manifestation of excitement is more than pardonable. He had the good fortune, however, to make a remark which has taken its place among the famous sayings of history. The monarch intimated that he was not unaware of Mr. Adams's feelings of imperfect confidence, at least towards the French ministry, and so expressed this as to put Mr. Adams in a position of some delicacy and possible embarrassment. The reply had the happy readiness of an inspiration. The ambassador said a few words, "apparently," says Mr. C. F. Adams, "falling in with the sense of the king's language;" but he closed with the sentence: "I must avow to your majesty that I have no attachment but to my own country." George III. had the good sense and sound feeling to be perfectly pleased with a statement so manly and independent, in spite of certain disagreeable reflections which might easily have been aroused by it, and though it was something nearer to a correction than is often administered to a royal personage.

But if at this interview George III. behaved like a gentleman of liberal mind, he was not equal to the stress of long continuing such behavior. He afterward habitually treated Mr. Adams with marked coldness, he publicly turned his back upon that gentleman and Mr. Jefferson, and he thus set an example which was promptly and heartily followed by the whole court circle, with only a few individual exceptions. This, of course, made Mr. Adams's stay in London far from comfortable. Occupying a position necessarily stimulating all the sensitiveness of his proud nature, living in a strange land lately hostile and still unfriendly, rebuffed in nearly every society by frigid insolence, he maintained as much retirement as was possible. Yet he found some little consolation and moral aid in noting "an awkward timidity in general." "This people," he remarked, "cannot look me in the face; there is conscious guilt and shame in their countenances when they look at me. They feel that they have behaved ill, and that I am sensible of it." Moreover his salary, which had lately been very inopportunely reduced, was too narrow to enable him to keep up a style of living like that of other foreign ministers, and it would have been folly to pretend that, under the peculiar circumstances, this was not a little humiliating. "Some years hence," said his wife, "it may be a pleasure to reside here in the character of American minister, but with the present salary and the present temper of the English no one need envy the embassy." No amount of sound sense or just and spirited reasoning could argue down a sense of irritation at being obliged to make a poverty-stricken showing before the critical, malicious, and hostile eyes of persons of real ability and distinction, yet who, having been bred amid pomp and circumstance, gravely regarded these as matters of profoundest substance. But all this might have been tranquilly endured, had not vastly greater mortifications been chargeable to his own country. He was in duty bound to press for a fufillment of the terms of the treaty of peace on the part of Great Britain ; but so soon as the first words dropped from his mouth, he was met with the query, why his own country did not perform her part in this reciprocal contract. The only reply was that she could not ; that the government was too feeble ; that it was hardly a government at all. Then the Englishmen retorted with insolent truth that in dealing with such a flickering existence they must keep hold of some security. In a word, Adams represented a congress of states, in no proper sense of the word a nation, divided among themselves, almost insolvent, unable to perform their agreements, irresponsible, apparently falling asunder into political chaos and financial ruin. On every side the finger of scorn and contempt was pointed at these feeble creatures, who had tried to join in the stately march of the nations before they could so much as stand up for ever so short a time on their own legs. To all the reproaches and insults, bred of this pitiable display, there could be no reply save in the unsatisfactory way of prophecies. Altogether, there was no denying the truth that this English residence was very disagreeable.

Mr. Adams's courage and independence were never put to a severer test; and though he presented a very fine spectacle, admirable before sensible men then, and before posterity afterward, yet he himself could get scant comfort.

Neither had he the compensating pleasure of feeling that he was accomplishing any service of real value for his country. Even before peace had been actually concluded he had tried to impress upon such Englishmen as he had fallen in with the points of what he regarded as a wise policy to be pursued by Great Britain towards the states. He had given deep and careful reflection to the future relationship of the two countries, which he felt to be of momentous concern to both. He had reached firm convictions upon the subject, which he urged with extreme warmth and earnestness whenever opportunity offered, sometimes indeed in his eager way making opportunities which more diplomatically minded men would have thought it best not to seize. His views were never brought to the test of trial, and of course never received the seal of success. Yet it seems credible that they did not less honor to his head than they certainly did to his heart. He hoped to see England accept the new situation in a frank and not unkindly spirit. Friendship between the two countries seemed to him not

only possible but natural; more especially since
friendship appeared likely to promote the material prosperity of each. As mercantile communities they might be expected to see and to value
the probable results of a good understanding.
Each might forget the past, England condoning
a successful rebellion, the states forgiving years
of oppression and the vast price of freedom.
As friends and allies, commercially at least, the
two might go on to prosperity and greatness far
beyond what would have been possible beneath
the previous conditions. Together they might
gather and divide the wealth of the world.[1] Perhaps there was a little of romance in this horo-
scope; yet it may have been both shrewd and
practicable in a purely business point of view,
so to speak. But in desiring to carry it out Mr.
Adams drew great drafts upon a very scanty
reserve of magnanimity. America's capacity to
forgive and forget was never tried; whether it
would have been so great as he required, cannot
be known. For England, who held the key to
the future by having first to declare her commercial policy, did at once, decisively, and with
manifestations of rancorous ungraciousness, establish a scheme of hostile repression. Her
plans were careful, thorough, merciless. The

<hr>

[1] See, for example, the conversation with Mr. Oswald, December 9, 1782, reported in the diary, *Works*, iii. 344 *et seq.*

states were to be crushed in and driven back upon themselves at every point, to be hampered by every tax, burden, and restriction that ingenious hatred could devise, to be shut out from every port and from every trade that British power could close against them, in a word, to be hopelessly curtailed, impoverished, and ruined, if the great commercial nation of the world could by any means effect this object. Military efforts having failed, civil measures were to be resorted to with no diminution of obstinate and bitter animosity. It was only the field of hostilities which was changed.

Mr. Adams beheld these developments with dismay and cruel disappointment. His generous forecastings, his broad schemes and brilliant hopes, were all brought to nought; his worst dread must be substituted for these fond anticipations. He was not discouraged for his country, nor had he any idea at all that she should give up the game, or that she must in the long run surely be beaten. He only regretted the severe struggle, the needless waste, which were imposed upon her by what he regarded as narrow and revengeful conduct. But he could not help it. He did all in his power; but to no purpose. When at last he became finally convinced of this, when he saw that nothing could be accomplished at London for the states, he made up his mind that it was not worth while for him to do violence to his inclinations by remaining there longer.

Accordingly he sent in his resignation, and on April 20, 1788, set sail for home, bringing with him some very correct notions as to English policy and sentiment towards the states, and yet feeling much less animosity towards that country than might have been looked for even in a man of a less hot disposition than his. A report commendatory of his services in Great Britain, drawn by Jay, was laid before Congress, September 24, 1787. But there was a disposition among some members to think that he had not managed matters with the best skill and discretion, and the report was rejected. A little reflection, however, made evident the unjust severity of this indirect censure, and a few days later the resolutions were easily carried, as they ought to have been in the first instance.

CHAPTER X

THE VICE-PRESIDENCY

THE homeward voyage from Europe breaks
the life of John Adams into two parts, — very
dissimilar in their characteristics. Thus far
he has appeared a great and successful man.
He has owed little or nothing to good fortune.
His achievements have been only the fair results of his hard toil and his personal risk; his
distinction has been won by his ability and his
self-devotion. His fair deserts at the hands of
his countrymen are second only to those of
Washington, and are far beyond those of any
other public servant of the time. He has
appeared honest, able, patriotic, laborious, disinterested, altogether a noble and admirable
character; generally his faults have been in
abeyance; his virtues have stood out in bold
relief. Had his career ended at this point he
would have been less distinguished than he is in
the knowledge and estimation of the multitude
of after generations, but he would have appeared
a greater man than he does to all persons sufficiently familiar with the early history of the

United States to make their opinion and their esteem really valuable. Though he is to reach higher official positions in the future than in the past, yet it is undeniable that the past embodies far the brighter part of his public life. Heretofore the service and advantage of his country have been pursued by him with a single eye; his foolish jealousy towards Washington has been the only important blemish which any fair-minded opponent can urge against his character; and though he has committed slight errors in discretion, yet upon all substantial points, at least, his judgment has been sound. But henceforth, though his patriotism will not to his own consciousness become less pure or a less controlling motive, yet the observer will see that it becomes adulterated with a concern for himself, unintentional indeed and unsuspected by him, but nevertheless unquestionably lowering him perceptibly. His vanity is to make him sometimes ridiculous; his egotism is occasionally to destroy the accuracy of his vision, so that he is to misjudge his own just proportion in comparison with other men, with the great party of which he becomes a member, even with the country which he fancies that he is serving with entire singleness of purpose. Anger will at times destroy his dignity; disappointment will lead him to do what self-respect would condemn. He will be led into more than one unfortunate personal feud, in which, though more wronged than wronging, he will not appear altogether free from blame. In a word, the personal element is henceforth to play much too large a part in the composition, and the politician is to mar the aspect of the statesman. Yet this criticism must not be construed too severely; to the end he remains, so far as he is able to read his own heart and to know himself, a thoroughly honest-minded and devoted servant of his country.

Adams came home to find that new and weighty subjects of popular concernment were absorbing the attention of all persons. Independence had become an historical fact, belonging to the past, a truth established and done with; foreign relationships, treaties, alliances, were for the time being little thought of. These matters had been his department of labor. With the novel and all-engrossing topic which had crowded them out of the people's thought he had no connection; and he stood silently by while men, whose names until lately had been less famous than his own, were filling the general ear with ardent discussions concerning that new constitution which they had lately framed and sent out to the people for acceptance or rejection as the case might be. In the consti-

tutional convention Adams would have been
peculiarly well fitted to play a prominent and
influential part, had he been in the country
during its sessions. His studies and reflections
had been largely in that direction for many
years, and his observations and practical experience abroad gave him advantages over all the
members of that body. But the tardy communication with Europe had prevented his keeping
abreast with these matters; and of course he
could take no active part; indeed, many of the
state conventions were in final session while he
was crossing the ocean, and Massachusetts ratified before his arrival. On the whole he was
well pleased with the document, not regarding
it as perfect, as indeed no one among its friends
did; but in the main believing it to embody
much good, and to involve such possibilities as
to make it an experiment well worth trying.
Certainly he was not among those who dreaded
that it created too strong, too centralized, too
imperial a system of government. He, however,
confined himself to watching with sympathy the
labors of those engaged in promoting its success,
and rejoiced with them in a triumph won without his assistance.

Possibly the fact that Adams had been allied
with neither party in this struggle was in substantial aid of his just deserts from other causes,

when it became necessary to select a candidate for the vice-presidency. If past services only were to be rewarded, it is as certain that he deserved the second place as that Washington deserved the first. He received it, but not in such a handsome way as he had a right to anticipate. That first election, as compared with subsequent ones, was a very crude and clumsy piece of business from the politician's point of view. The Federalists, that is to say, the friends of the new Constitution, ought to have united upon Adams; but they had not time for crystallization. Their opponents, the enemies of the Constitution, were even less able to consolidate. Accordingly the votes for vice-president were disorganized and scattering to a degree which now seems singularly, even ludicrously bungling. Personal and local predilections and enmities were expressed with a freedom never afterwards possible. The result was that out of sixty-nine votes Adams had only thirty-four, a trifle less than a majority, but enough to elect him. He had not been voted for specifically as vice-president, of course, such not being the then constitutional regulation; but this had not the less been the unquestioned meaning of the voting, since Washington's election was tacitly a unanimous understanding. Yet if it could have been explicitly stipulated that the second vote of each elector was given for a vice-president there would undoubtedly have been a larger total for Adams. For several votes which in such case would have been cast for him were now turned from him, in order, as it was plausibly said, to avoid the danger of a unanimous and therefore equal vote for him and Washington. But this argument was disingenuous. There never was the slightest chance of a unanimous vote for Adams, and the withholding of votes from him was really designed only to curtail his personal prestige by keeping him conspicuously in a secondary position. It was the mind and hand of Alexander Hamilton which chiefly arranged and carried out this scheme, not wisely or generously, it must be confessed. It was done not with any hope or even wish to prevent Mr. Adams from alighting on the vice-presidential perch, but only to clip his wings as a precaution against too free subsequent flights. This was the first occasion upon which these two men had been brought into any relationship with each other, and certainly it did not augur well for their future harmony. Unfortunately the worst auspices which could be seen in it were fulfilled. A personal prejudice, improperly called distrust, on the part of Hamilton toward Adams, from this time forth led to doings which Adams, being human, could not but resent; mutual dislike grew into strong ani-

mosity, which in time ripened into bitter vindictiveness. The quarrel had such vitality that it
survived to subsequent generations, so that later
historians in each family have kept the warfare
immortal. The Adams writers represent Hamilton as clandestine, underhanded, substantially
dishonorable. The Hamilton writers represent
Mr. Adams as an obstinate, wrong-headed old
blunderer, whom their distinguished progenitor
in vain strove to keep from working perpetual
serious mischief. In fact, Hamilton, though
constantly carried by his antipathy beyond the
limits of good judgment, did nothing morally
reprehensible; Adams, though committing very
provoking errors as a politician and party leader,
never went far wrong as a statesman and patriot. In the present transaction of this first
election, Hamilton unquestionably overdid matters. Even if it be admitted that his avowed
basis of action was sound, yet he diverted votes
from Adams beyond the need of his purpose,
and exposed himself to imputations which he
would have done better to avoid. But his exertion of influence through letters to his friends
was not blameworthy upon any other ground
than this of indiscretion; he had a perfect right
to use his authority with individuals as he did.
Adams came into office, not so much gratified
at having gained it as embittered at having

been deprived of a free and fair working of his chances, as he expressed it. It was an unfortunate frame of mind in which to start upon a new career.

On April 20 Mr. Adams was introduced to the chair of the Senate, and delivered a brief inaugural address. With an admirably happy choice of language, not without a touch of satire, he spoke of his office as "a respectable situation." It was not a position in which either by nature or by past experience he was fitted to shine; as he correctly said, he had been more accustomed to share in debates than to preside over them. He was always full of interest in whatever was going forward, hot and combative, and ready of speech, so that in many a fray his tongue must have quivered behind his teeth, fiercely impatient to break loose. But he had some unexpected compensation for mere silent "respectability" in an unusual number of opportunities to exercise personal power in important matters. Certainly no other vice-president has ever had the like, and probably no officer of the United States has ever been able to do so much by positive acts of individual authority. This was due to the equal division of parties in the Senate, and his right to give the casting vote.

The chief measures introduced in those early days were constructive, giving permanent form and character to the government. It is true, as has been so often said, that there were at first no parties, strictly so called, that is to say, no political organizations having avowed leaders and defined principles. But there was the raw material, in the shape of two bodies of men holding fundamentally different opinions as to the Constitution, and as to the government to be set up and conducted under it. The Federalists, as they already began to be called, had the advantage of immediate and clearly defined purposes and of able leaders. There were certain things which they wished to have done, a series of acts which they sought to have passed by Congress. Hamilton, an ideal leader for precisely such a campaign, devised the general scheme, got ready the specific measures, furnished the arguments, controlled senators and representatives. But not infrequently it happened that important Federalist measures hung doubtful in an evenly divided Senate, waiting to receive the breath of life from the casting vote of the Vice-President. They always got it from him. He was not in the modern sense of the phrase by any means a party man; he acted beneath no sense of allegiance, in obedience to no bond of political fellowship. He had not been nominated or elected by any party; certainly he had not the hearty or undivided support of any party. Consequently he was perfectly free to vote, and he did vote upon every measure solely with reference to his own opinion of its merits and its effect. He could not be charged by any one with disloyalty or ingratitude, however he might at any time choose to vote. Nevertheless, no less than twenty times during the life of the first Congress he voted for the Federalists.

In fact, Adams was by his moral and mental nature a Federalist. Practical, energetic, self-willed, he believed in authority, which indeed he was resolved for his own part always to have and to exercise. The helplessness of the old so-called government of the states, and their consequent poor standing abroad, had corroborated these instinctive conclusions. High in office, with a chance of rising still higher, even to the pinnacle, he intended that the government of which he was a part should be powerful and respected. When the question was raised as to the President's power to remove his cabinet officers without the advice and consent of the Senate, Adams carried the measure by his casting vote in favor of that authority, and malicious people said that he was dignifying the office because he expected in due time to fill it. But he was no more a democrat than he was an aristocrat; he believed in the masses, not as govern-

ors, but at best only as electors of governors.
His theory of equality between men was limited
to an equality of rights before the law.[1] In
point of fitness to manage the affairs of the
nation, he well knew that, as matter of fact,
there was the greatest inequality; he would have
laughed to scorn the notion that there were many
men who could be set in competition with himself in such functions. He believed that there
was a governing class, and that in it he occupied no insignificant position; he was resolved
to keep that class where it belonged, at the top
of society. But he did not believe that the right
to be in that class was heritable, like houses and
lands; it was appurtenant only to mental and
moral fitness. He was sometimes accused, like
other Federalists, of an undue partiality for the
British form of government. But he scouted
with curt contempt the charge that he had any
"design or desire" to introduce a "king, lords,
and commons, or in other words an hereditary
executive or an hereditary senate, either into the
government of the United States or that of any
individual state." He was therefore no aristocrat in the common sense of the phrase. The
charge of a predilection for kings and lords was
rank absurdity in his case, as in the cases of

1 See, for example, his remarks on equality in a letter of
February 4, 1794; C. F. Adams's *Life of Adams*, oct. ed., p. 462.

most of the other Americans against whom it
was brought; but it was so serviceable and popular a shape of abuse that it was liberally em-
ployed by the anti-Federalists for many years,
and Adams suffered from it as much or more
than any other public man of the times. There
was, however, that certain semblance or very
slight foundation of truth in this allegation of
aristocratic tendencies which is usually to be
found in those general beliefs which nevertheless are substantially false. In 1770, in the
simple provincial days, when he was only thirty-
four years old, he said: " Formalities and ceremonies are an abomination in my sight, — I hate
them in religion, government, science, life." But
there was in him an instinct which he little suspected when he wrote these words in the days
of youthful ardor and simplicity. As he grew
older, saw more of the world, and found himself
among the men happily entitled to receive the
trappings of authority, he grew fond of such
ornamentation. He conceived that high office
should have appropriate surroundings; undoubtedly he carried this notion to excess upon some
occasions. But it was the office and not the
man which he wished to exalt. The trouble was
that people could not draw the distinction, which
seemed fine but was essential. Nor could he
assist them to do so by discretion in his own

conduct. For example, his behavior provoked criticism along a considerable portion of his route from home upon his journey to be inaugurated as vice-president, upon which occasion he rode amid what his detractors chose to call an " escort of horse." The question of titles coming up immediately after the organization of Congress, he was well understood, in spite of his disclaimers, to favor some fine phraseology of this kind. His advice to Washington concerning the proper etiquette to be established by the President savored largely of the same feeling. He talked of dress and undress, of attendants, gentlemen-in-waiting, chamberlains, etc., as if he were arranging the household of a European monarch. But he had seen much of this sort of thing, and had observed that it exerted a real power, whether it ought to or not. The office of president, he said, " has no equal in the world, excepting those only which are held by crowned heads ; nor is the royal authority in all cases to be compared with it. . . . If the state and pomp essential to this great department are not, in a good degree, preserved, it will be in vain for America to hope for consideration with foreign powers."

Such a matter as this seems of small consequence, but it meant very much in those days. Moreover, the opposition wanted some one to abuse, a fact which Adams would have done well to make food for reflection, but did not. For a long while they had to hold Washington sacred; they stood in some awe of Hamilton, whose political principles they could impugn, but whom they could not and indeed dared not try to make ridiculous; Adams alone served their turn as a target for personal vituperation. He had not the art of conciliation; he was growing extravagantly vain; he was dogmatic; without being quarrelsome, yet he had no skill in avoiding quarrels. He was a prominent man, yet had no personal following, no prætorian guard of devoted personal admirers to fight defensive battles in his behalf. Neither was he popular with the principal men of his own party, who cared little how vehemently or even how unjustly he was assaulted by his opponents. He was therefore constantly pricked by many small arrows of malice, none carrying mortal wounds, but all keeping up a constant irritation of the moral system. All this was very hard to bear; yet it did not really mean very much. This was apparent when it came to the time of the second presidential election, when Adams had the pleasure of receiving the full and fair support of his party. He owed this, however, more than he was pleased to acknowledge, to the aid of one whom he did not love. Hamilton, propitiated by the uniform and very valuable support accorded by him, as vice-president, to the Federal measures, now favored his reëlection, and the word of Hamilton was law. But, besides this, parties had at last become well-defined. The anti-Federalists were agreed upon George Clinton as their candidate, and the Federalists were compelled to unite in good earnest. The electoral votes stood, for Adams, 77; for Clinton, 50. He had reason to be pleased; yet he could not be wholly pleased, since he had to see that Washington was the choice of the nation, while he was only the choice of a party. Moreover, in the French Revolution and the excitement which it was creating in the United States he scented coming scenes of trouble. The restlessness of the times was upon him; he longed to take an active part. " My country," he said with impatient vexation, "has in its wisdom contrived for me the most insignificant office that ever the invention of man contrived or his imagination conceived. And as I can do neither good nor evil, I must be borne away by others, and meet the common fate." To be borne away by others never much comported with the character of John Adams.

During the troubled years of his second term little is heard of Adams. The Federalists had gained such a preponderance in the Senate that he had fewer opportunities than before to cast

a deciding vote.   Public attention was absorbed
for the time by the men who could influence
the course of the United States towards France
and England in that epoch of hate and fury.
Adams, in his "insignificant office," enjoying
comparative shelter, saw with honest admiration the steadfastness of Washington's character
amid extreme trial, and witnessed with profound
sympathy the suffering so cruelly inflicted upon
the President by the base calumnies of those
enemies who now at last dared to indulge aloud
in low detraction.   For a time he felt a generous appreciation of that sublime greatness, and
forgot to make envious comparisons.

Monsieur Genet, as every one knows, came
to the United States with the definite purpose
of uniting them with France in the struggle
against England.   The one step essential to
this end was to make the Democratic party
dominant in the national councils, and nothing
seemed to be needed to accomplish this save a
little discretion on the part of the French government, a little tact on the part of the minister.
Fortunately, however, for the young country,
discretion and tact were never more conspicuously absent.   The consequence was that to
France and Monsieur Genet Mr. Adams owed a
gratitude, which it must be acknowledged that
he never showed, for the continued ascendency

of his party and his own accession to the presidency. But the measure of thanks which he might be inclined to return is not to be estimated with confidence. For the distinction came to him in such shape that it brought at best as much irritation as pleasure; and again it was the hand of Hamilton which poured the bitter ingredients into the cup.

When it became necessary for the people a third time to choose a president and vice-president of the United States, it seemed moderately certain that the Federalists would control the election; but they had no such reserve of superfluous votes that they could afford to run any risks or to make any blunders. The first matter to be determined was the selection of candidates. Hamilton was the leader of the party, inasmuch as he led the men to whom the bulk of the party looked for guidance. In its upper stratum he was obeyed with the loyalty of hero-worship; but he was not popular enough with the mass of voters to be an eligible nominee. Eliminating him, there was no one else to compete with Adams, whose public services had been of the first order both in quantity and quality, who seemed officially to stand next in the order of succession, and who was not more unpopular than all the prominent Federalists, none of whom had the art of winning the affection of the multitude. Adams accordingly was agreed upon as one candidate, and then geographical wisdom indicated that the other should be a Southerner. The choice fell upon Thomas Pinckney, an excellent gentleman, of the best character, of high ability, and sufficiently distinguished in the public service. In no department of fitness, however, could any comparison be drawn between Adams and Pinckney which would not show Adams to be unquestionably entitled to the higher position. The matter was not open to a doubt; it was generally understood that Adams was the Federalist candidate for the presidency, and that Pinckney was candidate for the vice-presidency. But, as the Constitution yet stood, the electors could not thus designate them in voting; and whoever should get the highest number of votes would be President.

Hamilton saw in this the opportunity, through his personal influence, to give effect to his personal predilection. He had a deep, instinctive dislike for Mr. Adams; it was very well for him to assert in self-justification that the grounds of his prejudice lay in doubts as to Mr. Adams's fitness for high official position. Possibly he tried really to believe this; yet he certainly did not oppose Mr. Adams with that openness or by those methods which would have naturally resulted from a sense of possessing strong and sound objections to him. The plain truth was, that as matter of fact it was sheer nonsense to deny Adams's fitness. His disqualification was solely his unsubmissive temperament. There was no question that Hamilton was leader of the party; and if it could be fairly agreed that his leadership involved of necessity his right to dictate the general policy, then Adams was not the man for the presidency. But such logic could not be openly proclaimed. Hamilton, if he had worked openly, must have impugned Adams's fitness on some other ground than that he would not fall prone beneath Hamiltonian influence. Such other grounds were not easily discoverable; hence Hamilton had to work in covert personal ways. By private advice and letters he urged strenuously upon the Federalist electors, especially those of New England, to cast all their votes for Adams and Pinckney. There was much danger, he said, that the deflection of a very few Federalist votes from either one, caused by some local or personal predilection, might give the victory to the Democrats, who were a perfectly united body. Every Federalist must vote for Adams and Pinckney, and not a vote must be thrown away. The perfect carrying out of this scheme would give the same number of votes to both these candidates, and practically would only throw into a Federalist Congress the question of ranking them. This was plausible arguing, and the figures of the subsequent election seemed to corroborate it. When the counting showed that Mr. Adams had only one more vote than was necessary to an election, and only three more votes than Mr. Jefferson, who actually secured the vice-presidency to the exclusion of Pinckney, it seemed that Hamilton had been very wise in his monitions.

But the whole story was not apparent in these simple facts. From the beginning it had been almost certain that some Southern Federalists would not vote for Mr. Adams, in order that thus they might give the presidency to Pinckney, provided they could trust the New Englanders to vote equally for both candidates. It was well understood that Hamilton's influence would not be seriously used against a design with which he was more than suspected of sympathizing; and it was apparent that his advice to the New Englanders was not altogether so ingenuous as it seemed. Hence the Federalists went into the colleges in the worst possible condition of mutual suspicion and distrust, with divided purposes, and much too deeply interested in secondary objects. This led

to the throwing away of votes. Some Southerners, who voted for Mr. Pinckney, voted also
for Mr. Jefferson instead of Mr. Adams, and
eighteen New Englanders voted for Mr. Adams
and not for Mr. Pinckney. It was highly improbable that the voting would have gone thus
had it not been known that Hamilton was concerning himself in the election, and that he
preferred Pinckney to Adams. Abstractly considered, his advice was sound, but he well knew
that, if those whom alone he could hope to control should follow it, then others less subject to
him would neglect it, and would bring about
a result which may fairly be called wrong. He
had in fact, though not in form, done what he
could to make Mr. Adams a third time Vice-
President, when the Federalist party intended
to make him President. Mr. Adams did not
at first understand all this. He said that Hamilton and " his connections did not, I believe,
meditate by surprise to bring in Pinckney. I
believe they honestly meant to bring in me;
but they were frightened into a belief that I
should fail, and they in their agony thought it
better to bring in Pinckney than Jefferson. . . .
I believe there were no very dishonest intrigues
in this business. The zeal of some was not
very ardent for me, but I believe none opposed
me." But not many days had elapsed after

these words were written before the whole truth was set before Mr. Adams. Thereupon his feelings underwent a sudden and violent change, and from that time forth he cherished towards Hamilton a resentment and distrust which under all the circumstances were entirely natural and pardonable. He was a good enemy, whole-souled and hearty in his hatreds. Upon the other side Hamilton, generally not so bitter and unforgiving, indulged an exceptional vindictiveness in this quarrel; so that this animosity speedily attained such intensity as to become a potent, almost an omnipotent influence with each of these powerful men, and through them bore powerfully upon the course of national events for many years to come.

It was perhaps a little amusing to see how incensed Mr. Adams was, when he discovered that there had really been a design to deprive him of a place which he seems to have looked upon much as if it were substantially his own property. There is such an opportunity to learn some of his traits from a naïve passage in a letter written by him on March 30, 1797, to Henry Knox, that, though not otherwise valuable, it must be quoted. He says: "But to see such a character as Jefferson, and much more such an unknown being as Pinckney, brought over my head, and trampling on the bellies of hundreds of other men infinitely his superiors in talents, services, and reputation, filled me with apprehensions for the safety of us all. It demonstrated to me that, if the project succeeded, our Constitution could not have lasted four years. We should have been set afloat and landed the Lord knows where. That must be a sordid people indeed — a people destitute of a sense of honor, equity, and character, that could submit to be governed, and see hundreds of its most meritorious public men governed, by a Pinckney, under an elective government. . . . I mean by this no disrespect to Mr. Pinckney. I believe him to be a worthy man. I speak only in comparison with others." Volumes of comment could not tell more than these sentences. The vehemence and extravagance of expression, the notion that his defeat would have destroyed the national existence, the gross depreciation of Pinckney so soon as he became a rival, the vanity involved in the tranquil assumption that in his own hands at least the great republic is perfectly and unquestionably safe, show Mr. Adams's weaknesses in strong relief. His own utter unconsciousness, too, is delightful; he thinks that he is perfectly liberal and just when he frankly says that Pinckney is a "worthy man." In fact Pinckney was very much more, and the interests of the people have more than once since that day been intrusted to presidents much his inferiors in character and ability, and have come safely through the jeopardy.

CHAPTER XI

ADAMS'S victory was none the less a victory because it was narrow. Though he had only seventy-one votes against Jefferson's sixty-eight. he was President of the United States. Vexed as he was, hurt in his vanity, incensed with Hamilton, yet his heart swelled with a not ignoble triumph. If the recognition of his long public service had not come in precisely the shape it should have come, at least he could say to himself that this imperfection was due to the jealous antipathy of an individual. It was Hamilton, rather than his countrymen, who had attenuated his triumph. But the inaugural ceremonies further disturbed his self-satisfaction. Certainly every President may fairly expect to be the grand central point of observation and interest during the hours of his own inauguration. It was exceptionally hard luck for Adams that he undeniably was not so. Washington was present, of course, and toward him all faces seemed to be turned; all were silent, and numbers wept as they gazed at the

great national hero now leaving the public service; when he left the hall the spectators, absorbed only in him, rushed after him in throngs.
A man less sensitive and egotistical than Adams
might have felt that he was unfortunately situated under the peculiar circumstances. He felt
it keenly. He was reminded of the "representation of a tragedy;" he said that he was the
"unbeloved one;" he was surprised, actually
bewildered, at the distance which he saw that
the people had established between himself and
Washington. No one would furnish him any
other solution of the "enigma" of the "stream-
ing eyes," he said, and so he had perforce to
suppose that it was "all grief for the loss of
their beloved." If all this had been designed
by a thoughtful Providence as moral discipline
for an excessively vain man, it could be objected
to solely on the ground that the victim was no
longer young enough to be susceptible of improvement; so the only effect on Mr. Adams
was to exasperate and embitter him.

In this condition of things the Democrats
made an effort to capture Mr. Adams. They
took good care to let him know all that had
been done against him. Pickering, they said,
in his official reports had maliciously kept in
the background his services in connection with
the treaty of 1783; Hamilton and Jay had

meant to keep him only a vice-president, because, fortunately, he was not the man to appear only as the head of a party, and to be led by Hamilton. Jefferson wrote a letter to him, rejoicing that he had not been " cheated out of his succession by a trick worthy the subtlety of his arch-friend of New York, who had been able to make of his real friends tools for defeating their and his just wishes." This letter was indeed never delivered to Mr. Adams ; for Jefferson sent it open to Madison with instructions to deliver it or not, as he should see fit, and, for some reasons not known, Madison did not see fit. But it explained Jefferson's plans. In the letter to Madison he said : " If Mr. Adams could be induced to administer the government on its true principles, quitting his bias for an English constitution, it would be worthy of consideration whether it would not be for the public good to come to a good understanding with him as to his future elections." In pursuance of the same policy the Vice-President, on arriving in Philadelphia, promptly called upon Adams, and also paid him a handsome compliment upon taking the chair of the Senate, and was cordially zealous to establish a friendly relationship. Mrs. Adams, triumphing in the defeat of Hamilton's " Machiavelian policy," expressed pleasure at Jefferson's success, between whom and her husband, she said, there had never been "any public or private animosity." Hamilton had made a mistake, great enough in its real outcome, but which might have borne such fruits as would have seemed to him nothing less than fatal, had they occurred. With many men the anticipations of Jefferson and the Democrats would have proved well-founded. But it was not so with Adams; no one by any subtlety or under any cover could introduce a policy into his brain. He had his own ideas, and did his own thinking. Neither through his wounded self-love, nor his hot resentment, could he be beguiled by Jefferson into the ranks of Democracy. For good or for ill he had no master, open or unsuspected, either in Hamilton or in Jefferson. No writer has ever denied that he was at least an independent President.

To sketch the administration of John Adams with correct lines and in truthful colors is a task of extreme difficulty. The general effect of an accurate picture must be singularly painful and depressing; it must show us great men appearing small, true patriots forgetting their country in anxiety for their party, honest men made purblind by prejudice, and straying perilously near the line of dishonor. The story of these four years, though in them the national emergency was of the gravest, is largely a tale

Abigail Adams

of the most bitter feud in American history. Even the one great act of patriotism which Mr. Adams performed stands like a lighthouse bedimmed in a dense distorting fog of odious personal considerations. The quarrel between him and Hamilton constitutes a chapter which one who admires either of them would like to omit. Each has to stand on the defensive, and the defense is not easy to be made. It was a wretched affair in which heroes became petty, and noble men ceased to inspire respect. The student finds the political literature of the period to be a mass of crimination and recrimination ; amid such acrimony it is not easy for him to hold himself uncontaminated by the temper of the combatants ; nor can he think it pleasant to have as his chief duty the allotment of censure among men at all other times praiseworthy. We have to show Adams pursuing a course substantially of sound statesmanship, but, through hot-headedness, pugnacity, an egotism almost criminal in a republic, and a lack of tact great enough to be accounted a sin, stumbling perpetually and hurting himself sorely upon many obstacles which he ought to have avoided, until finally he emerges from his stony path doing the smallest and most foolish act into which a magnanimous man was ever betrayed; we have to show Hamilton following an object of personal ambition by unworthy machinations, allowing his former prejudice against Mr. Adams to become degraded into a fierce personal resentment, and in pursuance thereof losing sight of patriotism in the effort to destroy his enemy by methods so mean and so unwise that we cannot read of them without a sense of humiliation, which he unfortunately never felt. Neither is it pleasant to see the lesser reputation of Pickering, that brave, faithful, and upright Puritan, and the good name of Wolcott, who always meant to be an honest man, smirched with the blemish of unfairness. Such animosities live forever, even sometimes gaining increased bitterness from the loyalty of the descendants of the original combatants. Thus it has been with these quarrels ; the story has been told many times, never with an approach towards impartiality, till it requires no small courage to tread again upon the " dark and bloody ground."

The wars between England and France, between monarchism and democracy or Jacobinism, or whatever the political principle of the French revolutionists is to be called, were fought over again in the United States, with less of bloodshed indeed, but not with less of rancor than distinguished the real contest. Each party in the country averred that it wished to keep out of the fight, and that its opponents wished to plunge into it. England and France, alike devoid of fear or respect for the United States, were equally resolved, in default of securing her as an ally, at least to get the utmost plunder out of her. England smote her upon one cheek with Orders in Council; France buffeted her upon the other with decrees launched from Berlin and Milan, the conquered capitals of prostrate Europe. England impressed her seamen, France shut up her ships and confiscated her merchandise. Jefferson berated England, Hamilton reviled France. There were abundant reasons for the United States to declare war against each of them; but there was also a controlling reason against any war at all, a reason which none expressed, but to which all submitted; so that the wrath was pretty sure to vent itself only in words, unless the angry partisans should lose command of themselves, and get carried farther than they intended. In a most uncomfortable position between the two factions stood Mr. Adams, on the whole the safest statesman in the country to hold the helm in this crisis. His temperament was that of the English race from which he was descended, and which can never sincerely and permanently appreciate or sympathize with the French temperament; moreover, he had long since made up

his mind that the theory of the states owing any
gratitude to France was little better than sheer
nonsense. But when the Federalists counted
upon these influences to keep him in the so-
called Anglican wing of their party, they forgot
that hostility to England had struck deep root
in his mind through youth and middle age; they
forgot that he had been neglected and insulted
for three years in London, and that he had there
acquired full knowledge of the deliberate design
of England to crush and ruin her ex-colonies.
So, with about equal prejudices against each
combatant, Mr. Adams was undoubtedly the
most even-minded man then in public life in
the states. His eye was single in fact not less
than in intention; he not only fancied himself,
as all the rest fancied themselves, but he really
was, which the rest were not, unbiased, devoid of
friendship and trust towards each country alike.
Caring exclusively for the United States, as he
had so boldly stated to King George, he had
not the slightest doubt that the best policy for
them was to keep out of the war. From the
first days of the Revolutionary Congress he had
always dreaded European alliances; he saw no
reason now for changing the settled opinion
which he had held for upwards of twenty years.
War with either meant, of course, alliance with
the other, and general entanglement in the for-

eign snarl. The resolution to keep the peace, if possible, is the key to his policy throughout his four years. Even Jefferson said of him: "I do not believe Mr. Adams wishes war with France, nor do I believe he will truckle to England as servilely as has been done." Mr. Hildreth, also, who loves him not, says that his "opinions and feelings were precisely such as to free him from all possibility of foreign influence, and to fit him for carrying out with energy and impartiality the system of exact neutrality which Washington had adopted." These estimates of his character and sentiments, from unfriendly quarters, were perfectly correct.

But the grave and very doubtful question was, whether it would be possible to keep the peace. Just at the time of Adams's accession France seemed to be reaching the point of outrage at which the most helpless or the most pusillanimous nation must strike back. Her villainous stealings had been supplemented by even more exasperating insults. The relationship of the two countries was briefly this: Gouverneur Morris, while minister at Paris, had manifested so active an antipathy to the revolution, that the success of that movement made it necessary to recall him. To cure the feelings which he had wounded, Mr. Monroe, of quite an opposite way of thinking, was sent to super-

sede him.   But Monroe was carried away by the
Jacobinical excitement into behavior so extravagantly foolish as seriously to compromise the
national interests.   He was called home, and
General C. C. Pinckney, a moderate Federalist,
was sent as his successor.   Thus matters stood,
so far as was known in the states, when Adams
came to the presidency.   But embarrassing news
soon arrived.   The French Directory, at parting
with Monroe, had given him a grand ovation,
which, under the circumstances, was an intolerable insult to the United States; and further-
more the same reckless body had refused to
receive Mr. Pinckney or to permit him to remain in France, even threatening him with
police interference.   A difficult problem was
already before the new President.

Mr. Adams's natural advisers were the members of his cabinet.   His relations with this
body, soon to become so peculiar and unfortunate, were at first nearly normal and amicable.
He had retained Washington's secretaries, Pickering in the State Department, Wolcott in the
Treasury, and McHenry in the War Department.   The first two were of sufficient ability
for their positions; McHenry was of a lower
grade; but it was then so rare to find men at
once fit for high public positions and willing to
fill them, and Washington had encountered so

much difficulty in reconstructing his cabinet, that Adams very justly conceived it imprudent to make changes. Nor indeed was it through lack of ability that his ministers gave him trouble, but through lack of sympathy with himself and his policy, and later through want of openness and frankness in dealing with him. Under Washington's administration these gentlemen had felt themselves on a different plane from that of the President, who stood far above any personal competition or jealousy. Hamilton had been Washington's most trusted adviser, and had — properly enough under the peculiar circumstances — constantly communicated with and influenced Washington's cabinet. Thus there had grown up a little oligarchy, or clique, consisting of one statesman and three politicians, his subordinates, who had arranged and controlled the policy of the Federal party successfully and agreeably enough beneath the shelter of Washington's prestige, and subject always in the last resort to his sound and supreme judgment. Adams had never been one of this clique; he had not even been regarded with any cordiality by its chief. The pleasantest phase of the relationship between Hamilton and himself, up to this time, had been little better than negative, when at the time of his second candidacy for the vice-presidency Hamilton had accepted him as the least ineligible among possibilities, and had spoken moderately in his praise. But now that he was President, it was a serious question whether the previous comfortable arrangement could be continued. Would he make one of the little governing brotherhood? There was a fundamental condition precedent: he could come into it only as practically subordinate to Hamilton, though he might be spared the humiliation of an avowal or direct recognition of this fact. An instinct told all concerned that he was not the man for this position. But the fatal scission opened slowly. At the outset the ministers were only curious and anxious, not devoid of hope that a little dexterous management might make all go according to their wishes, while Mr. Adams had no idea, or at least no knowledge, that his relationship with them was marked by any exceptional character, or any secret peculiarities unknown to himself. Shortly before his inauguration he had written to Gerry: "Pickering and all his colleagues are as much attached to me as I desire. I have no jealousies from that quarter." It was very slowly that he at last acquired a different opinion. |

At the time of Adams's inauguration rumors had come that Pinckney had not been received. The idea of a new and more impressive mission at once occurred to many persons. On March 3 Adams himself called on Jefferson and broached the topic. He would have liked to nominate the Vice-President; but both had to agree that it would not do for that officer to accept such a post. Nor could Jefferson willingly abandon the direction of his party at this juncture. Then Mr. Adams asked whether Madison would go in conjunction with some prominent Federalist. Jefferson thought that he would not, but said that he would ask his friend. Two days later Fisher Ames, a thoroughgoing Hamiltonian, called on the President, advised a new mission, and even suggested names. Soon the rumors concerning Pinckney were corroborated. Thereupon Adams at once summoned an extra session of Congress for May 15. He heard from Jefferson that Madison would not go to France, but he did not therefore abandon his original plan of a composite mission. He opened the scheme to Wolcott, but got no assistance from him. Wolcott, an extreme " Anglicist," only fell in with the notion slowly and reluctantly, and under the influence subsequently exerted by Hamilton. Perhaps it was fortunate for the success of the President's plan that for once he and Hamilton took the same view of the necessities of the situation.

So soon as the news of the election of Adams

reached Paris, the Directory, greatly incensed that Jefferson had not been chosen, issued a decree more oppressive than any which had preceded against the American commercial marine. This was heard of in the United States before Congress assembled, and aggravated the indignation of the Federalists. The speech of Mr. Adams at the opening of the extra session, in the composition of which he had been aided by his secretaries, was admirable; it was dignified, spirited, and temperate. "The refusal on the part of France to receive our minister," he said, "is the denial of a right; but their refusal to receive him until we have acceded to their demands without discussion and without investigation is to treat us neither as allies, nor as friends, nor as a sovereign state." The "studious indignity" at the leave-taking of Monroe he adverted to in language of natural resentment. Yet, he said, having the sincere desire to preserve peace with all nations, "and believing that neither the honor nor the interest of the United States absolutely forbids the repetition of advances for securing these desirable objects with France, I shall institute a fresh attempt at negotiation." Nevertheless "the depredations on our commerce, the personal injuries to our citizens, and the general complexion of affairs render it my indispensable duty to recommend to your consideration effectual measures of defense." He suggested an increase of the regular artillery and cavalry, possibly also "arrangements for forming a provisional army." Above all he dwelt with especial emphasis upon the need of a navy sufficiently powerful to protect the coast thoroughly. This was a favorite measure with him, which he constantly urged. He believed that the United States easily could be, and certainly ought to be, a great naval power; unquestionably he thought that they should have ample means of naval defense. He had wrought earnestly in the same matter in the Revolutionary war. He now reiterated this advice with all the zeal and persistency in his power, and actually did as much as his authority permitted. In one of his letters to James Lloyd, in 1815, he said that during the four years of his presidency he "hesitated at no expense to purchase navy yards, to collect timber, to build ships, and spared no pains to select officers." But his only reward was extreme unpopularity, even in the seaport towns of New England, with a renewal of the old talk about his desire "to introduce monarchy and aristocracy." He at least cannot be blamed that the American navy never was developed as it should have been, and was left to win its triumphs many years later in spite of utter neglect and discouragement.

The new mission was determined upon, but its composition was not easy to arrange. If Madison would have served, Mr. Adams would have nominated Hamilton as his colleague; at least he afterwards said that this was his purpose. Apparently he was desirous of clinging to the policy, which Washington had tried with imperfect success, of using the best men in both parties. But when Madison would not go, all thought of Hamilton vanished. Mr. Adams then suggested General Pinckney, John Marshall, and Elbridge Gerry. Pinckney and Marshall were Federalists; Gerry had generally been allied with the opposite party; he had opposed the federal Constitution, and had ever since been regarded as an anti-Federalist; lately, indeed, as a presidential elector, he had voted for John Adams, but he had been influenced by an old friendship, and had written to Jefferson a letter of explanation and apology. Adams had a strong personal regard for him, and doubtless now sought to do him a kind turn, though in the end the favor proved rather to be laden with misfortune. The selection now aroused warm opposition on the part of secretaries Pickering and Wolcott. These gentlemen, equally unlike the President, whom they disliked, and Hamilton, whom they revered, were not statesmen; that is to say, they could not upon occasion subordinate the wishes and prejudices, the likings and dislikings, which were items in the creed of their party, to a wise and broad view of national policy. They could not now see that the President's "piebald commission" was a sound measure. After they had yielded with reluctance to Hamilton's approval of any commission at all, they fell back upon the position that at least it should be composed wholly of Federalists. They were submissive to their private leader, but not to their President. Therefore they strenuously objected to Gerry. Adams deferred to them with unusual amiability, gave up his own choice, and named Francis Dana, chief justice of Massachusetts. But Dana declined, and then the President returned decisively to Gerry. The Senate confirmed the nominations, and in midsummer, 1797, the two envoys, Marshall and Gerry, sailed in different vessels to join Mr. Pinckney.

The three met in Paris early in October of the same year and notified M. Talleyrand, then foreign minister, of their readiness to deliver their credentials. What ensued is notorious and may be told briefly. A few days of civility were succeeded by sudden coldness and a complete check in the advancement of business. Then came the famous and infamous proposal, that the envoys should agree to pay large bribes to Talleyrand and to certain members of the Directory. They rejected this proposal with disdain. Thereupon, in January, 1798, a new decree was issued against American commerce. The envoys drew up a very spirited remonstrance against it, which, however, Gerry was not willing to sign. Finally, after some delay, Marshall got his passports on April 16, and Pinckney, after experiencing much discourtesy, was permitted to stay for a time in the south of France with his daughter, who was very ill. Gerry was persuaded by Talleyrand to remain. He was expected to prove more compliant than the others, and might yet be made use of as a conduit to introduce French schemes into American minds.

In October, 1797, Adams expressed his fear that little immediate advantage could be expected from this embassy, unless it should be " quickened by an embargo." On January 24, 1798, he propounded sundry queries to the heads of departments. He had already foreseen as among the possibilities precisely what occurred, viz.: the failure of the mission, and the departure from Paris of two envoys while the third remained abroad. In this case, he asked, what new recommendation should be made ? Should a declaration of war be advised or suggested ? Should an embargo be recommended ? The reply of McHenry is supposed by Mr. C. F. Adams, with probable correctness, to embody the views of Hamilton, Pickering, and Wolcott. It proposed that merchant vessels should be allowed to arm themselves, that the treaties with France should be suspended, that the navy should be increased, that 16,000 men should be raised for the army, with a contingent increase of 20,000 more. In his questions the President had asked what should be done as regarded England; "will it not," he said, showing by the form of his query his own opinion, " be best to remain silent, to await overtures from her, to avoid a connection with her, which might subsequently become embarrassing ? " Pickering would have preferred a close alliance with her, but failed in his attempt to secure Hamilton's approval of the plan, and therefore abandoned it.

Early in March the news came which Mr. Adams had feared, and to some extent had prepared for. On March 5 the President communicated to Congress a dispatch announcing the failure of the mission; and a few days later, having deciphered the accompanying dispatches, he sent a supplementary message, saying that all hope of accommodation was for the present at an end. He therefore advised continuance in the preparations for a war which, though he did not advise declaring it, must yet be

regarded as not unlikely to ensue. Many lukewarm Democrats, disappointed and irritated by
the persistent insolence of the Directory, now
abandoned their political allegiance ; but the
main body of the party, reposing a wise and
perfect trust in Jefferson, that most shrewd,
patient, politic, and constant of leaders, remained unshaken in their sentiments. Whether
the price of friendship with France were greater
or less, they thought that it should be paid and
the inestimable purchase completed. One of
their number introduced into the House of
Representatives a resolution that it was inex-
pedient to resort to war with France. The
Federalists of all shades of opinion united in
opposition to this. A fierce and prolonged
debate ensued, of which the issue was very
doubtful, when it was suddenly cut short by a
motion from the Federalist side, made, as it was
understood, at the instigation of Hamilton, calling on the President for full copies of all the
dispatches. This was carried, of course ; and
the President, well pleased with the demand, at
once sent in the documents, complete in every
respect save that he had substituted the letters
W. X. Y. and Z. for the names of the emissaries engaged in the attempt to arrange the bribes
for Talleyrand and the Directory. Otherwise
the whole story of that infamy was spread out

before Congress and the country, without color-
ing or curtailment.

Amazement and wrath burst forth on every
side. A great wave of indignation against the
venal government, which had offered itself for
sale like a drove of bullocks, swept over the
land, submerging all but the most strong-limbed
Democrats. These sturdy partisans, struggling
in the swirl, confused, enraged, cried out half
in anger, half in despair, for time, only a little
time to breathe, to rally, to reflect. If for a
brief while the country could be held back from
actually committing itself to hostilities, Jefferson
foresaw that the storm would subside. Then
multitudes of his scared followers would drift
back again and would adopt his theory, con-
demning Talleyrand personally, but thinking no
ill of the great French nation. The respite,
however, was uncertain; the times were critical.
Everywhere the black cockade of the anti-Federalists appeared in the streets, provocative of
fights, even of mobs. Crowds sang lustily the
new patriotic ditty of " Hail Columbia." Wherever two or three persons were gathered together
under any name or for any purpose, from state
legislatures down to boys in college, they drew
up an address, full of patriotism and encouragement, and sent it to Mr. Adams. Never was a
President so deafened with declarations of loy-

alty and support. He composed answers to them all, and was doubtless glad to get them, though sometimes tempted to think that the pens of his well-wishers were a trifle over-numerous. Fortunately, amid all the turmoil and excitement he kept his power of cool reflection fairly well. He recognized the facts not only that war would be a national misfortune, but that in the present stage of the quarrel there was no sufficiently powerful war party to justify declaring it, the body of persons who really wished for a war and who could be counted upon long to remain of that mind being, in spite of appearances, not large. He said this many years afterwards, and undoubtedly he judged correctly. He made only one mistake, and that ultimately embarrassed only himself.

In the middle of June, 1798, Marshall arrived at home, bringing with him the latest news and many details. The President at once recalled poor Gerry, now overwhelmed with abuse and unpopularity, and sent a message to Congress communicating that fact, together with all that Marshall had brought to his knowledge. He concluded with the famous and unfortunate sentence: "I will never send another minister to France without assurances that he will be received, respected, and honored, as the representative of a great, free, independent, and powerful nation." This bit of foolish and superfluous rodomontade, characteristically escaping from the too ready lips of Mr. Adams, afterward caused him some annoyance. It can only be said that he was not singular in overleaping the limits of strict discretion in those wild days, when indeed there was no man concerned in public affairs who did not give his detractors some fair opportunity for severe criticism, if he were judged according to the cold standard of perfect wisdom.

The two grand blunders of the Federal party were committed in these same moments of heat and blindness; these were the famous Alien and Sedition Acts. No one has ever been able heartily or successfully to defend these foolish outbursts of ill-considered legislation, which have to be abandoned, by tacit general consent, to condemnation. Every biographer has endeavored to clear the fame of his own hero from any complicity in the sorry business, until it has come to pass that, if all the evidence that has been adduced can be believed, these statutes were foundlings, veritable *filii nullius*, for whom no man was responsible. But Mr. Adams, it must be acknowledged, did not strangle these children of folly; on the contrary, he set his signature upon them; a little later he even expressed a " fear " that the Alien Act would not "upon trial be found adequate to the object intended;" and many years afterward, by which time certainly he ought to have been wiser, he declared, without repentance, that he had believed them to be "constitutional and salutary, if not necessary."

But this summer and autumn of 1798 were signalized by a matter much more unfortunate in its consequences for Adams personally than the rash utterance of an intention which was in itself perfectly proper, or than the signature of some ill-advised enactments. He was obliged to nominate officers for the provisional army, and in doing this he unintentionally and with no fault on his own part stirred up much ill feeling and resentment. Washington, as lieutenant-general, was of course to be commander-in-chief. Of this no one questioned the propriety; neither could fault be found with the concessions by which his acceptance was obtained, to wit: that he should not be called into active service until the need should be imperative, and that he should be permitted to select the general officers who were to serve in the next grade below him. He promptly named Hamilton, C. C. Pinckney, and Knox. Adams accepted the names without demur, and nominated them to the Senate together, in this order. Upon the same day and in the same order the nomina-

tions were ratified. But forthwith there arose
a perplexing question : what was the precedence
between these three major - generals ? The
friends of Hamilton said that it was established
by the order of nomination and of ratification.
Others said that it was determined by the rela-
tive rank of the three in their former service,
that is to say, in the Revolutionary army. The
latter rule seemed to be sustained by precedent ;
but, if adopted, it would make the essential
change of putting Knox first and Hamilton
third. Hamilton, however, had made up his
mind to stand next to Washington, and his
powerful following were resolved upon the same
arrangement. There is not room to give the
details of a competition which evolved infinite
bitterness, and left behind it malignant jealousies and inextinguishable feuds. Adams was decidedly inclined against the pretensions of Hamilton ; he professed respect for the precedents ;
he said that he did not wish to hurt the feelings
of Knox ; he did not say, though doubtless he
could have said with truth, that he did not care
to confer on Hamilton a marked distinction of
very doubtful propriety. But he soon found
that, whether he was willing or unwilling, he
must perforce do this especial favor. Washington expressed his desire to have Hamilton
second to himself, and his wish was conclusive

in the premises.   Adams finally was compelled
to yield, though with no good grace, to a pressure which he could not resist.   He never fully
understood what machinery had been devised
to create that pressure; but the whole story
has since been told.   Admirers of Hamilton
and friends of Adams still wrangle about it.
The former say that Hamilton's preëminent
ability gave him a substantial right to the
place, and that Washington needed not to be
prompted by any one to express emphatically
his genuine preference.   The latter say that
Washington was worked upon by Hamilton
himself, by Pickering and by Wolcott, secretly
and artfully, in a manner at least unbecoming
in the principal, and little short of dishonorable
in the two office-holding assistants.   As usual in
bitter personal quarrels, the truth lies between
the two sides.   Washington undoubtedly had
an independent preference for Hamilton; he
was also probably led to put it in the shape of
a positive *ultimatum* by representations which
ought not to have come privately from the members of the President's cabinet.   As matters
turned out, the affair was unfortunate for all
concerned.   The rank did Hamilton no substantial good, since the army never even got
into camp; but the burning dislike between him
and Adams was blown into a fiercer flame, in

which the good name of each was badly singed. Neither did it bode any good for the Federal party that its chief men were largely concerned with quarrels among themselves, while so watchful, autocratic, and masterly a politician as Jefferson was disciplining the united forces of the Democrats in the opposite camp.

The French government, at this time perfectly unprincipled, and conducting affairs with reckless, hectoring insolence, would gladly have cajoled or terrified the United States into an alliance; failing in this, they intended to give Frenchmen chances to get as much as possible in the way of pickings and stealings from American merchants. But fortunately the Directory had no desire for actual war with a remote people, quite out of the line of European ambition and politics. Thus Talleyrand had held Gerry in Paris as a sort of door for retreat when he should find that he had gone dangerously far. Matters standing thus, the great French minister was astounded and not a little mortified at the publication of his disgrace in the X Y Z dispatches. Of course he denied that he had known anything about the proposals for bribery, but of course also he knew that no one really believed a word of his protestations. In his irritation at his humiliating position, feeling himself an object of ridicule as he stood exposed in his vulgar and disappointed rascality, he berated poor Gerry in a most outrageous manner. But Gerry had spirit and honesty, and retorted. Talleyrand, thus checked, quickly recovered his wonted audacious self-possession, appreciated the exigencies of the situation, and saw the best way out of it. There had been a great mistake, he said, a farrago of lies, an astonishing misunderstanding; the Americans ought not to be so angry; they were under a singular delusion; France felt very kindly towards the United States, only wanted peace and friendship, would receive ministers with pleasure, and in a word was in the very most amiable of humors. He wished to use Gerry as a means of conveying these views to the American government; but Gerry, unpopular and suspected, was likely to be altogether inadequate to this purpose. Another channel, therefore, was found in Monsieur Pichon, French minister at the Hague, who was instructed to make advances to Vans Murray, the American minister. These communications Murray at once repeated in private letters to Mr. Adams. At the beginning of October, 1798, Gerry was back in Boston, and told Mr. Adams, who by the way had not lost confidence in him, what Talleyrand had said to him. A few days later Vans Murray's first letter, mentioning the approaches of Pichon, came to hand.

Beneath these influences, on October 20, the President wrote to Pickering concerning certain "things which deserve to be maturely considered before the meeting of Congress," and upon which Mr. Adams wished "to obtain the advice of the heads of departments." His first query was: Should he recommend a declaration of war? The next: "Whether in the speech the President may not say that, in order to keep open the channels of negotiation, it is his intention to nominate a minister to the French republic, who may be ready to embark for France as soon as he or the President shall receive from the Directory satisfactory assurances that he shall be received and entitled to all the prerogatives and privileges of the general law of nations, and that a minister of equal rank and powers shall be appointed and commissioned to treat with him?" Upon receipt of this very unwelcome suggestion, the cabinet ministers, according to Mr. C. F. Adams, "called together a council of their leading friends, including the military generals happening to be assembled at Philadelphia, Washington,[1] Hamilton, and Pinckney, where they

[1] Mr. Adams says: "There is no evidence yet before the world that General Washington actually took part in the consultation."

matured the language of a draft intended for the use of Mr. Adams in his opening speech." Upon the President's arrival at the end of November this paper was presented to him, as embodying the views of his cabinet in response to his interrogatories. It pleased him so well that he adopted it with the exception of a single clause; but it so happened that in that clause the marrow and chief importance of the whole document lay. For it contained these words: "But the sending another minister to make a new attempt at negotiation would, in my opinion,[1] be an act of humiliation to which the United States ought not to submit without extreme necessity. No such necessity exists. . . . If France shall send a minister to negotiate, he will be received with honor and treated with candor." Now it so happened that "my opinion," thus offered ready-made to Mr. Adams, was far from being held by him. On the contrary, he thought that, under certain circumstances, another minister might be sent without humiliation; should those circumstances come to pass he intended to send a minister; and he was not ready to say that reconciliation could only

---

[1] See this quotation in C. F. Adams's *Life of John Adams*, octavo ed. p. 536; Mr. C. F. Adams says that Gibbs gives it wrongly, by omitting the words " in my opinion." See Gibbs's *Administrations of Washington and Adams*, ii. 171.

be effected if France would take the initiative and herself dispatch the next envoy. So he struck out this passage, which set forth the views of his secretaries, and inserted in its place a long exposition of his own very different notions. His clauses are so framed as not only to express but to explain and vindicate his policy; and, long as they are, they are so important that they must be quoted in full. He said : —

"But in demonstrating by our conduct that we do not fear war in the necessary protection of our rights and honor, we shall give no room to infer that we abandon the desire of peace. An efficient preparation for war can alone insure peace. It is peace that we have uniformly and perseveringly cultivated; and harmony between us and France may be restored at her option. But to send another minister without more determined assurances that he would be received, would be an act of humiliation to which the United States ought not to submit. It must therefore be left to France, if she is indeed desirous of accommodation, to take the requisite steps.

"The United States will steadily observe the maxims by which they have hitherto been governed. They will respect the sacred rights of embassy. And with a sincere disposition on the part of France to desist from hostility, to make reparation for the injuries heretofore inflicted upon our commerce, and to do justice in the future, there will be no obstacle to

the restoration of a friendly intercourse. In making
to you this declaration, I give a pledge to France and
to the world that the executive authority of this country still adheres to the humane and pacific policy
which has invariably governed its proceedings, in con-
formity with the wishes of the other branches of the
government, and of the people of the United States.
But considering the late manifestations of her policy
towards foreign nations, I deem it a duty deliberately
and solemnly to declare my opinion, that, whether we
negotiate with her or not, vigorous preparations for
war will be alike indispensable. These alone will
give us an equal treaty and insure its observance."

These were the outlines of an excellent policy.
For any one who knew the President knew well
that he meant all that he said, that he would
get ready for war thoroughly, and that he would
make it in earnest, when it should become necessary. There was enough spirit, resentment, and
vigor in the message to satisfy any man who
could subordinate his temper to his good sense.
There was much more of real dignity in this
self-control, evidently not growing out of pusillanimity, than there would have been in flying
into a counter-rage against France. In the
comparison between the two governments, the
American certainly appeared entitled to much
more respect for good sense, and to not less for
courage. Mr. Adams showed the happy mixture

of moderation and resolution which indicates the
highest stage of civilization to which mankind
has yet come in international relationship.   But
these traits did not commend themselves at
the time to the Hamiltonian Federalists.   They
wanted what in the present day is called a
"strong policy," so "strong" that it would
almost surely have ended in a war, in which the
country would have been overwhelmed with disaster, in attempting to preserve that crude kind
of honor cherished by knights-errant, duelists,
and pugilists.   Having substantially this aim
in view, though it must be confessed that they
would not have accepted precisely this formula-
tion of it, they were made very angry by Mr.
Adams's message, and by his rejection of the
words which they had so conveniently and con-
siderately got ready for him.   They even fell
into such a frame of mind as to fancy that he
had no political right to do as he had done.
They conceived that in their conference they
had established the policy of the party, and they
did not think that Mr. Adams, simply because
he was President, had a right through his own
sole and individual action to make a fundamental change in that policy.   But Mr. Adams
utterly ignored party discipline.   His own convictions were the sole and immutable law of his
own actions.

During the winter of 1798–99 Mr. Adams received more letters from Vans Murray, which, with some corroborating information, strengthened his faith in the willingness of France to meet any advance on his part towards a renewal of negotiations. At length, apparently early in February, 1799, he received a letter from Murray, inclosing an official dispatch from Talleyrand to Pichon, in which occurred these words: "D'après ces bases, vous avez eu raison d'avancer que tout plénipotentiaire que le gouvernement des Etats Unis enverra en France, pour terminer les différends qui subsistent entre les deux pays, serait incontestablement recu avec les égards dûs au représentant d'une nation libre, indépendente et puissante."

This gave Mr. Adams a sufficient basis for action. More than this, as Mr. C. F. Adams puts the case not unfairly, it imposed upon him a serious responsibility; for it was a semi-official notification to him that France, falling at last into a penitent humor, desired to be addressed again in the way of negotiation. If he, in a distant and haughty temper, should hold aloof before this advance, and if then war should ultimately ensue, he might well feel that he had precipitated a terrible evil from no better motive than an over-strained sense of pride. Moreover, when the facts should become known, as they inevitably must, the Democratic party, even now powerful, would be greatly strengthened by being able to say that French overtures had been rejected. The moderate men who had lately oscillated from Democracy to Federalism would oscillate back again from Federalism to Democracy. What chance would there then be of conducting successfully a war with France, when a large party would be bitterly opposed to it, and another large body, the two together making more than half of the nation, would be at best lukewarm? Mr. Adams felt no need of aid in order to determine upon his course. With a cool independence, unusual then or since upon the part of a president, and not perfectly in accord with the sentiment of the American system of government, though strictly lawful under the Constitution, he dispensed with the form of consulting his cabinet, whose advice he had good reason to feel assured would not accord with his own, and therefore would not be followed. On February 18, 1799, he sent in to the Senate the nomination of Vans Murray to be minister to France, premising, however, that Murray should not present himself in Paris until the French government should give a public and official assurance that they would receive the envoy in character, and would appoint a minister of equal rank to treat with him.

The message fell like lightning from a clear sky among the Federalists. Pickering hastened to send the news to Hamilton. " We have all been shocked and grieved at the nomination of a minister to negotiate with France. . . . I beg you to be assured that it is wholly *his* [the President's] *own act*, without any participation or communication with any of us. . . . The foundation of this fatal nomination of Mr. Murray was laid in the President's speech at the opening of Congress. He peremptorily determined (against our unanimous opinions) to leave open the door for the degrading and mischievous measure of sending another minister to France, even without waiting for *direct* overtures from her."

" I have neither time nor inclination," Sedgwick wrote to Hamilton concerning the message, " to detail all the false and insidious declarations it contains. . . . Had the foulest heart and the ablest head in the world been permitted to select the most embarrassing and ruinous measure, perhaps it would have been precisely the one which has been adopted. In the dilemma to which we are reduced, whether we approve or reject the nomination, evils only, certain, great, but in extent incalculable, present themselves." Angry and astonished, the Hamiltonian wing of the party knew not at first what to do, and then in their confusion did a very strange thing. The committee to whom the nomination was referred, consisting of five Federalists, called on the President to demand reasons and insist on alterations. Sedgwick, the chairman, a thoroughgoing partisan of Hamilton, admitted that this proceeding was an "infraction of correct principles;" Mr. Adams declared that it was unconstitutional, a word perhaps somewhat too powerful for the occasion. It was finally agreed that the interview should be strictly unofficial, and then the gentlemen talked the business over together. Mr. Adams said, according to Sedgwick's statement, "that to defend the Executive from oligarchic influence it was indispensable that he should insist on a decision on the nomination;" that he would "neither withdraw nor modify the nomination;" but, if it should be negatived, he "would propose a commission, two of the members of which should be gentlemen within the United States."

The visitors retired in a bad temper. A meeting of Federalist senators was held; and it was agreed that, whatever they might ultimately be compelled to do, they would at least, in the first instance, enjoy the pleasure of rejecting Vans Murray. Mr. C. F. Adams acknowledges that there were objections against him, "such as senators might legitimately entertain, and as were not without intrinsic weight." But the President stole a second march upon the irritated enemies who were preparing obstacles for his path. At the next meeting of the Senate Sedgwick was asked to hold back his report because the President had another message ready. This was at once delivered; it nominated three persons: Chief Justice Oliver Ellsworth, Patrick Henry, and Vans Murray to be joint commissioners to France. Hamilton, meanwhile, in reply to the news of Vans Murray's nomination, had written to Sedgwick that "the measure must go into effect with the additional idea of a commission of three. The mode must be accommodated with the President." Unwittingly Mr. Adams had come within the advantage of Mr. Hamilton's dictum; and the discontented Federalists, who would readily have encountered the President, yielded at once to their real chief. Sedgwick replied: "This is everything which, under the circumstances, could be done." The nominations were confirmed, and, oddly enough, the confirmation of Murray alone was by a unanimous vote. Henry declined on the score of age and infirmity, and Governor Davie, of North Carolina, was appointed in his stead.

The sole chance now left to the "Anglicist" Federalists was in the possible fruits of delay. The President, feeling that reaction which follows extreme tension, tarried in Philadelphia only long enough to determine the brief and simple *ultimata* of the instructions for the commissioners. Then he went home for rest and vacation at Quincy. On March 6 Pickering wrote to Vans Murray, stating what had been done, and that Ellsworth and Davie would embark immediately upon receipt of the official promise that they should be properly received and admitted to negotiations. Early in May Murray received the dispatch, and communicated its substance to Talleyrand. That minister at once gave the required assurance formally and officially; but, unable altogether to restrain his irritation, he delivered himself also of some insulting criticism to the general purport that the conduct of the Americans had been disingenuous and captious. On July 30 these papers reached Pickering, and he immediately transmitted them to Mr. Adams at Quincy, calling especial attention to the injurious language. But Adams, looking to the substance and not permitting himself to be too greatly incensed by mere impertinence, directed that the instructions should be got ready. Apparently it was nearly five weeks before this order was fulfilled; and when at last the draft reached Mr. Adams, it came inclosed in a letter from Mr. Pickering intimating that in view of

recent political changes in France, including
the resignation of Talleyrand, the cabinet suggested delay. Mr. Adams replied that he was
quite willing to assent to a postponement until
the middle or end of October. By October 10
he was at Trenton, the temporary seat of government.

Matters there were not pleasant. He was ill
and in poor condition for an encounter, yet he
found the opponents of his policy gathered to
resist it. There were assembled his three secretaries, all stubbornly hostile to the mission;
Hamilton soon arrived, and at their invitation
Ellsworth also appeared upon the scene, giving
his influence with much caution and reserve,
but, such as it was, giving it to the opposition.
There came news, too, just at this juncture, of
disasters to the French arms. The Hamiltonians triumphantly foretold that a few days would
bring the glad intelligence that the French king
was enjoying his own again in the royal palaces
of Paris. Mr. Adams listened in an unusually
silent and tranquil temper. On October 15, in
the evening, he summoned a cabinet meeting,
at which he brought up for discussion two or
three points in the instructions, which were
easily settled. He gave no more indication
that he was about to take a decisive step than
he had given before sending in Vans Murray's

nomination. Nevertheless, two of the secretaries " received before breakfast " on the following morning orders that the instructions should be at once put in final shape, and that a frigate should be got in readiness to take the commissioners on board not later than November 1. They actually set sail on November 5.

This French mission was the death-blow of the Federalist party. The political body was rent in twain ; the two parts remained belted together by their common name, but no longer instinct with a common vitality. It had been a very grand party, an organization full of brains and vigor, a brotherhood embracing a remarkable number of able and honest men ; it had achieved deeds so great as to outstrip exaggeration ; it had given form and coherence to the political system, strength and the power of living to the infant nation. A sad spectacle was indeed presented when a party so nobly distinguished lapsed into disintegration and the hopeless ruin of intestine feuds. No wonder that vindictive rage possessed those men who had created it, who had lived in it and for it, who had honestly and zealously served it, and wholly identified themselves with it. Less than half of the party in numbers, but much more than half in influence, ability, and prominence, pointed to Mr. Adams as the parricide who had done this cruel slaying. This assertion, reiterated with furious clamor at the time, has since been adopted as an established fact in American history ; every one thinks that he knows that Mr. Adams destroyed the Federal party by acting counter to its policy. But who had the right to establish the policy of the party ? Hamilton had tacitly arrogated it to himself. When in office, he had created the party, established its principles, formulated its measures, trained and led its forces, and made its victories possible ; since retiring to private life, he had counseled and controlled its leaders. A large proportion of the most influential Federalists, in and out of office, including three members of the cabinet and many of the best speakers of the party in Congress, conceived that revolt against his supremacy was defection from the party. Nevertheless, in no caucus of Federalist members of Congress could these Hamiltonians ever muster a majority against Mr. Adams. Neither does there seem any doubt that upon a simple vote of all the Federalists in the country, taken at any time during his administration, much more than half would have sustained him. War with France never had been, never could be, avowed by the Hamiltonian section as a principle of the party. On the contrary, they professed to desire peace.

Mr. Adams secured peace by a step against which they could urge no graver objection than that it was not sufficiently high-spirited to comport with the national dignity. Then the party divided, and they said that Adams was to blame. Their conclusion does not seem to be fully supported by the facts.

But the allotment of responsibility between Adams and Hamilton and the dispute as to which of them was better entitled to establish the party policy are matters of vastly less importance than the question upon which side right and wisdom lay. This seems to require no discussion beyond the briefest statement of the great facts. War was avoided, by means which no one now thinks of stigmatizing as degrading. The method was devised by Mr. Adams, and the result was won by his persistent adherence to that method. One is inclined to say that, if in all this he ran counter to the policy of his party, it was very discreditable to the party to have such a policy. In fact, pretty much all writers now agree that Adams behaved with courage, patriotism, and sound judgment, and that he placed the country under a great debt of gratitude ; a debt which was never paid in his lifetime, and only since his death has been very tardily and ungraciously acknowledged.

Whether or not Mr. Adams was a parricide as towards his party, he was certainly a suicide as towards himself. The act of Curtius in leaping into the gulf to save Rome was a more picturesque but not a more unquestionable deed of patriotic self-immolation. From that fifth day of November, 1799, Mr. Adams was a doomed man. No effort could now restore harmony among the discordant ranks of the Federalists. For the future all the earnest fighting on their part was done inside their own camp and against each other. It is a melancholy and unprofitable story of personal animosities, which may be briefly told.

That Mr. Adams anticipated the results which followed his action is not probable. There is nothing to indicate that he had any idea that he was disrupting and destroying the Federal party. But to his credit it should also be said that there is no indication that he considered this matter at all. Every particle of evidence — at least all which has been published — goes to show that his mind was wholly occupied with the interests of the nation, to the utter exclusion of any thought of his party or of himself. After the irretrievable ruin which overtook him, amid the execrations of the Federalists, who attributed their utter destruction wholly to him, he never gave a symptom of regret, never said a word except in strenuous support of his action. Beyond question he was too profoundly convinced that he was right to be moved from his opinion by any consequences whatsoever. His unchangeable sentiments were those expressed by him in 1815, in one of his letters to James Lloyd: "I wish not to fatigue you with too long a letter at once, but, sir, I will defend my missions to France as long as I have an eye to direct my hand or a finger to hold my pen. They were the most disinterested and meritorious actions of my life. I reflect upon them with so much satisfaction, that I desire no other inscription over my gravestone than: 'Here lies John Adams, who took upon himself the responsibility of the peace with France in the year 1800.'" Substantially this has been also the verdict of posterity, and a transaction which at the time of its occurrence found hardly any defender, now finds hardly any assailant. Modern writers of all shades of opinion agree that Adams acted boldly, honestly, wisely, and for the best welfare of the country, in a very critical peril.

CHAPTER XII

THE BREAKING UP

Semel insanivimus omnes! In this chapter
the behavior of many wise and illustrious men
is to bear evidence to the truth of this adage.
For madness certainly ruled the closing months
of Adams's administration.

The foregoing pages have given glimpses
rather than a complete picture of the unhappy
relationship existing between the President and
three of his secretaries. Nothing more unfortunate befell any one of them throughout his
career. In the prosecution of the quarrel each
appears at his worst; Mr. Adams's foibles of
hot-headedness and of a vanity almost incredible
in its extravagance stand out in painful relief.
Pickering, Wolcott, and McHenry, honest men
all, do the only ignoble acts of their lives. All
four seem crazed by prejudice and rage. They
are so bereft of all fair intelligence as utterly
to ignore not only the character but the effect
of their own acts, which run counter to sound
judgment even more than to right feeling. By
the time to which our narrative has come the

secretaries absolutely hated the President; they were in such a state of mind that, without appreciating it, they treated him with thoroughly bad faith; they betrayed all official discussions to Hamilton; they sought and followed Hamilton's advice. They did this for the purpose of gaining Hamilton's invaluable aid in their opposition to their proper chief, and they deceived themselves into a belief that in thus conducting themselves they were doing strictly right. Their vindication was that Adams's policy was destructive of their party, and was intrinsically wrong; that therefore it was their duty to counteract it by all the means which even their office as his confidential advisers put in their power. Their ethics were singular and have not generally been accepted as sound. According to received principles, fair dealing to Mr. Adams, even justice to themselves, would have led them to resign, when they so utterly differed from him that their sole aim was to thwart him. But however this may have been, certain it is that any decent sense of propriety, nay, for the word must be used, of honor, would have led them to refrain from communicating cabinet secrets for use against the President by his avowed enemy. Mr. Adams did not know what was going on; he even went down to his grave ignorant of much of this mechanism by

which he had suffered so severely. But without
fully knowing the cause he could dimly per-
ceive where it lay. He wisely concluded that
some changes in the cabinet could be advan-
tageously made.

McHenry was the first to go. He had been
laborious and was in the main a well-meaning
and amiable man, but he was notoriously incom-
petent for his position. His wonderfully ill-
written sketch of his parting interview with Mr.
Adams, the only existing account of a strange
scene, is worth repeating in full. On May 5,
1800, the President sent for him.

"The business appeared to relate to the appointment of a purveyor. . . . This settled, he took up
other subjects; became indecorous and at times outrageous. General Washington had saddled him with
three secretaries, Wolcott, Pickering, and myself. I
had not appointed a gentleman in North Carolina, the
only elector who had given him a vote in that state,
a captain in the army, and afterwards had him appointed a lieutenant, which he refused. I had biased
General Washington to place Hamilton in his list of
major-generals before Knox. I had eulogized General Washington in my report to Congress, and had
attempted in the same report to praise Hamilton. In
short, there was no bounds to his jealousy. I had
done nothing right. I had advised a suspension of
the mission. Everybody blamed me for my official
conduct, and I must resign."

Before such a storm of abuse McHenry went down at once. He "resigned the next morning." This lively picture certainly shows Mr. Adams in one of his worst moods, mingled of anger, egotism, and that one great foolish jealousy of his life, which consumed his heart whenever he heard the praises of Washington. His grandson admits, with nepotal gentleness of phrase, that he was not upon this occasion either considerate or dignified; but says that he appeared to much more advantage soon afterward in ridding himself of Pickering. So he did. Pickering richly deserved unceremonious expulsion; but Mr. Adams courteously offered him the opportunity to resign. It may be admitted that he probably would have been much less considerate had his knowledge of Pickering's behavior been less imperfect. The stiff-backed and opinionated old Puritan, full of fight and immutable in the conviction of his own righteousness, refused to appear to go voluntarily, and was thereupon dismissed. On the whole, it was probably fortunate that Mr. Adams did not know how badly these gentlemen had been behaving towards him, or scenes of awful wrath and appalling violence would have enlivened the biographic page.

The vacancies thus made were filled more easily than might have been expected. Marshall, having declined the position of secretary of war, accepted that of secretary of state, and Samuel Dexter took the war department. Wolcott, who deserved to go quite as much as either of the others, remained; but he only remained to do further injury to his own good name, and to enact a very ungenerous part. He had habitually spoken the President so fair that he was regarded by Mr. Adams as a friendly adviser, though very far from really being so. He now continued for some months longer to combine external civility and deference to the President with the function of cabinet-reporter, so to speak, — and to avoid the word spy, — for Mr. Hamilton. In the following November, amid all the vexations which that ill-starred season brought to Mr. Adams, he sent in his resignation to take effect at the end of the year, thus leaving the President to look for an incumbent who would be willing to hold the office for two months with the certainty, of course, of being superseded immediately upon Jefferson's accession. Yet, strange to say, Adams always felt kindly towards Wolcott, and among the last acts of his administration made him a judge. Never to his dying day did he learn how false Wolcott had played him.

The story went, at the time, that Mr. Adams had turned out Pickering in order to conciliate

Samuel and Robert Smith of Baltimore, and to gain their votes and influence in the electoral college. The malicious calumny was afterward abundantly disproved. Another piece of hostile electioneering gossip was called forth by the pardon of Fries. This man had led the riots, or, as some preferred to say, the rebellion, in eastern Pennsylvania, in 1799. Twice he was convicted of treason and was sentenced to death, which certainly he abundantly deserved. Mr. Adams pardoned him, and was at once reviled as having done so only because it was "a popular act in Pennsylvania." But such attacks as these were the most commonplace features of this presidential campaign of 1800. Never did a political party enter into such a contest in so sorry a condition as that of the Federalists. Harassing as Mr. Adams had found the presidency, he burned with ambition to obtain it again. Before his election, discussing the comparative prospects of Jefferson, Jay, and himself, he had said: "If Jefferson and Jay are President and Vice-President, as is not improbable, the other retires without noise, or cries, or tears to his farm." But circumstances were different now. He had been pitted against bitter opponents in a fierce controversy of great moment, which had divided the country. It was not unnatural that he should desire a popular ratification of his policy. The Hamiltonian section, filled with implacable rage towards him, contemplated the possibility of his success with utter sickness at the heart. Could nothing be done to prevent it? Could no means be devised for setting him aside? Their first plan reflected no credit upon themselves. It was to induce Washington to come out from his retirement and stand as their candidate. It is improbable that any force of personal influence would have sufficed to give success to so unworthy, so cruel a scheme for making a selfish and partisan use of this noble patriot in the days of his old age. If any such danger to him existed, it was indeed an opportune death which rescued him from it. He escaped even the injury of the proposition. After this chance was, it may almost be said fortunately, eliminated, Hamilton traveled through New England to feel the pulse of the party. He was compelled sadly to report, that though " the leaders of the first class " were all right, " the leaders of the second class " were all wrong; he saw plainly that, when it came to scoring votes, Adams was the only Federalist who could bring out the party strength in this section of the country. This fact was undeniable and conclusive; Adams must be the candidate. The old scheme indeed might be resorted to; equal voting for Adams and Pinckney might be urged upon the New England electors, with the secret hope that some faithless Southerner might throw out Mr. Adams and make Mr. Pinckney President; or that in case of real good faith Congress might accomplish the same result. But this poor and exploded device had no virtue in it. Then there was some talk of setting up Pinckney openly to supersede Adams; but this also was mere folly and desperation. The truth had to be faced. Hamilton mournfully told his friends, who could not contradict him, that the fight lay between Adams and Jefferson, and that in such a dilemma they were bound to support Mr. Adams. With wry faces they came up to swallow the nauseous dose.

The Hamiltonian Federalists had for some time past been fond of extending to Mr. Adams such unkind charity as lies in the excuse of madness. He must be insane, they said; and sometimes they seemed more than half in earnest in the remark. But with all his anger, bitterness, and mortification, it soon appeared that there were crazier men than he at work in these acrimonious days. Chief among them was Hamilton himself, who, however, was not without assistants well worthy of the same unpleasant description. Made more vindictive than ever by the necessity of actually aiding the cause of the man whom he hated, Hamil-

ton now determined on the extraordinary step
of writing a public letter containing an arraign-
ment of Mr. Adams in his administration. He
professed that he did not intend to do this by
way of opposition to Adams's reëlection ; on the
contrary, he said that he should close, and finally
he actually did close, this singular document
with the advice that this unfit man should be
again charged with those duties which he had
just been shown to be so incapable of perform-
ing wisely, safely, or honestly. For material for
the criminatory portion of this startling com-
pilation, Hamilton relied in part upon Pickering and McHenry, now out of office and most
willing and vengeful coadjutors ; but chiefly he
depended upon Wolcott, who was still secretary
of the treasury and could give the latest and by
far the most valuable information. It is painful
to know that Hamilton applied to him, and that
he promised to give and did give the disgrace-
ful aid which was demanded. Nay, he did it
readily and with actual pleasure.

This project of Hamilton spread profound
alarm among those of his political friends who
had not been personally engaged in the conflict
with the President, and who therefore retained
their self-possession and coolness of judgment.
They remonstrated against the publication with
as much earnestness as they ever dared to show

in differing from their autocratic commander. But they had scant influence over him. The volcano was full to bursting, and the pent-up fury must find vent. Hamilton was doubtful only on the point of form. He would have liked to seem to write in self-defense. In order to obtain a plausible basis, he addressed a letter to Adams asking an explanation concerning charges of belonging to a British faction, which charges he was pleased to say that the President had preferred against him. This artifice failed; but it was mere matter of detail. Hamilton was, as he admitted, "in a very belligerent humor," and was bent on writing the letter, with an excuse or without it, as might be. He would only promise his alarmed and protesting friends that it should be privately and discreetly distributed, in such a prudent manner that it should not affect the electoral votes. His friends, unconvinced, were still laboring with him, when all choice and discretion in the matter were suddenly taken both from him and from them. The document had already been put in print; no copies had been sent out, but by some covert means Aaron Burr had obtained one. By this accident all possibility of secrecy came to an end. The paper was spread far and wide through the country as the best campaign document of the Democrats, and then at last even Hamilton could no longer deny his blunder.

If before there had been any hope for a Federalist success, this wretched transaction utterly destroyed it. The party went into the elections divided, dispirited, full of internal distrust. New York had already been lost; and the *causa causans* of the loss, as Mr. C. F. Adams explains, had been the machinations of Hamilton intended to bring in Pinckney in place of Adams. It required no gift of prophecy now to see that defeat was inevitable. It came; but Jefferson and Burr, coming in evenly with only seventy-three votes apiece, against sixty-five for Adams and sixty-four for Pinckney,[1] showed that a contest, which under such circumstances was so close, might have had an opposite conclusion had it been more wisely and happily waged by the Federalists. It was a fair conclusion that Mr. Adams would have been re-elected had it not been for the hostility of Mr. Hamilton and his clique.

If Mr. Adams as President had served his country better than he had served his party, at least one of the latest acts of his administration was an equal service to both. Having offered the chief justiceship of the United States to Jay, who declined it, he then nominated John Marshall. The Parthian shot went home. Half

---

[1] An elector from Rhode Island voted for Adams and Jay, instead of for Adams and Pinckney.

of what the Democrats seemed to have done by the election of Jefferson was undone by the appointment of Marshall. By it the Federalists got control of the national judiciary, and interpreted the Constitution in the courts long after they had shrunk to utter insignificance as a political party.

Adams sat signing appointments to office and attending to business till near the close of the last hour of his term. Then, before the people were astir on the morning which ushered in the day of Jefferson's inauguration, he drove out of Washington. He would not wait to see the triumph of his successor. Mr. C. F. Adams seeks to throw a cloak of fine language over this act of childish spite and folly, but to no purpose. It was the worst possible manifestation of all those petty faults which formed such vexatious blemishes in Adams's singularly compounded character.

But it is needlessly cruel in this hour of his bitter mortification to sneer at his silly egotism, to laugh at his ungoverned rage. He was crushed beneath an intense disappointment which he did not deserve, he was humiliated by an unpopularity which he did not merit. For he had done right in great national matters, and had blundered only in little personal ones. Yet he felt and declared himself a " disgraced " man. The word was too strong; yet certainly he was an unfriended, hated, and reviled man. He was retiring full of years but not full of honors. He had been as faithful, as constant, as laborious a patriot as Washington; and, taking his whole career from the beginning, his usefulness to the country had been second only to that of Washington. He had lately done an immense service to his country in saving it from war. Had he not a right to repine and to feel bitter at the reward allotted to him? Certainly he had had very hard luck; everything might have gone so differently had it not been for the antipathy of a single individual towards him. Had it not been for this he might have had real coadjutors in the members of his cabinet; he might have acted with coolness and dignity, having his temper relieved from the multitudinous harassments which he had felt though he could not explain them. He might with a clear mind have moulded and carried out a strong, consistent policy, in an even-handed and dignified manner, which would have made it impossible for the Democrats to defeat him. All this would have been probable enough, if the disturbing influence of Hamilton had been withdrawn. To that one man it seemed due, and perhaps it really was due, that Adams was ending his public life in humiliation and unhappiness.

This volume has grown to such length that a few lines only can be given to Mr. Adams's remaining years. He passed them in his pleasant homestead near the roadside in Quincy, among his family and friends. They were tranquil and uneventful to a degree which must often have seemed tedious to one who had led so stirring a life in busy capitals amid great events. Yet he seems in the main to have been cheerful and contented. The town was full of his kindred and his friends, and he was always met with gratifying kindliness and respect. His wife survived until the autumn of 1818, when she died of typhus fever on October 28. He was then eighty-three years old. His son, John Quincy Adams, could be little at home; but the cause of his absence, in his steady ascent through positions of public trust and honor, must have gone far to prevent regret. The father had the pride and pleasure of witnessing his elevation to the presidency in 1825, and fortunately did not survive to know of the failure and disappointment four years later.

But Adams was too active and too irritable to feel no regret at decadence; at times the gloominess so often accompanying old age seemed to get the better of his courage. It was in such a temper that he wrote to Rufus King, in 1814: "I am left alone. . . . Can there be any deeper damnation in this universe than to be condemned to a long life in danger, toil, and anxiety; to be rewarded only with abuse, insult, and slander; and to die at seventy, leaving to an amiable wife and nine amiable children nothing for an inheritance but the contempt, hatred, and malice of the world? How much prettier a thing it is to be a disinterested patriot like Washington and Franklin, live and die among the hosannas of the multitude, and leave half a million to one child or to no child!" Such moods of repining at their lots, and of dissatisfaction with the rewards meted out for their services, were of frequent occurrence both with John Adams and with his son, John Quincy Adams. The same habit is noticeable, however, as prevailing, though in a less degree, among many of their contemporaries; it was the fashion of the day, and may be considered as the New England form of development of the famous habit of grumbling and fault-finding notoriously belonging to John Bull. At least Mr. Adams's high appreciation of his own preëminent merits and distinguished services remained with him to comfort and console him to the end. His vanity and supreme self-satisfaction passed away only with his passing breath.

He read a great deal during his old age, even

then constantly extending his knowledge and preserving his native thirst for information still unquenched. His interest in affairs was as great as ever, and he kept his mind in activity and vigor. At times he fought the old battles o'er again with not less spirit than in younger days. His first purpose after his retirement was to write a vindicatory reply to Hamilton's tirade against him; but his zeal cooled during the work so that he never finished it. Then he began an autobiography, but this too he left in the shape of a mere fragment. When John Quincy Adams, unable to stomach the increasing British aggressions at the time of the attack by the Leopard upon the Chesapeake, severed his connection with the feeble remnant of the Federal party, John Adams was in full sympathy with him. Pickering published a pamphlet arraigning the administration, and Adams replied to it, actually appearing as the supporter of President Jefferson's policy. This tergiversation, as his enemies chose to regard it, greatly incensed the old Hamiltonians, who now hastened to revamp the charges contained in Hamilton's letter. The spirit of the old fighter was aroused, and he recurred to his design of an elaborate defense. He entered upon it with little appreciation of the extent to which his labors would extend. For after he had once got fairly at the interesting work he could not easily check himself, and his letters to the "Boston Patriot" were continued through a period of nearly three years, and a portion of them, published in book form, constituted an octavo volume of goodly proportions. These letters are not reproduced in Mr. C. F. Adams's edition of the works of John Adams; indeed, the grandson appears inclined to regret that they ever saw the light, at least in the manner and shape in which they did, " scattered through the pages of a newspaper of very limited circulation, during three years, without order in the arrangement, and with most unfortunate typography." It is not surprising to hear that they were marked with " too much asperity towards Mr. Hamilton."

But a much more unfortunate composition was the famous Cunningham correspondence, which also Mr. C. F. Adams declines to republish, and very properly under the peculiar circumstances, which he states. These were written by the ex-President to one of his relatives soon after his return to Quincy. They were "under the seal of the strictest confidence," and contained " the most unreserved expression of his sentiments respecting the chief actors and events in the later portion of his public life." In other words, they were vehement, rancorous,

abusive, and unjust, as was perfectly natural
when it is remembered under what fresh provocation of real wrongs their writer was smarting
at the time.   His vanity and his rage naturally
found free expression as he strove in close confidence to tell to a friend the story of the unfair
treatment of which he had been the victim. Mr.
C. F. Adams says that an heir of the person
to whom these letters were written gave them
to the opponents of John Quincy Adams to be
used against him when he was a candidate in
the presidential campaign; and that this ignominious transaction was rewarded with a post
in the Boston custom-house.   It was of course
a great mistake upon Adams's part that he
wrote them, and it was a grave misfortune for
him that they were, even though dishonorably
and many years afterwards, sent out before the
world.   It was the last and nearly the worst
exhibition of that blind imprudence which at
one time and another in his career had cost him
so dear.   But he could not eliminate or control
the trait; in fact, he never fairly appreciated its
existence; throughout his life he was invariably
convinced that all his own actions were perfectly right and wise; he was always a strenuous and undoubting partisan of himself, so to
speak.

In his declining years he had some flattering

public honors done him by his fellow citizens, of a kind to bring more of pleasure than of labor. He was appointed a presidential elector, and cast his vote for James Monroe at the second election of that gentleman to the presidency. He was also, at the age of eighty-five, chosen the delegate from Braintree to the constitutional convention of Massachusetts, at the time when, Maine being set off, it was deemed advisable to frame a new constitution. The body paid him the compliment of choosing him to preside over its deliberations; but he wisely declined a labor beyond his strength. He took no active part in the debates; but it should be remembered to his honor that he endeavored to procure such a modification of the third article of the bill of rights "as would do away with the recognition of distinct modes of religious faith by the state." It is to the discredit of his fellow delegates that in this good purpose he was unsuccessful. The aged man could only put himself upon record as more liberal, more advanced in wisdom and in a broad humanity, than the men of the younger generation around him.

Before he died nearly all his old animosities had entirely disappeared, or had lost their virulence. Hamilton and Pickering he could never forgive; such magnanimity, it must be admitted, would have been beyond human nature. But he became very friendly with Jefferson. Some advances towards reconciliation, made by his old enemy through Mrs. Adams, he rejected. But later Dr. Rush was successful in bringing the two together, so that a friendly correspondence was carried on between them during their closing years.

His mind remained clear almost to his last hours. He died at sunset on the fourth day of July, 1826, the fiftieth anniversary of American independence. The familiar story goes that his last words were, "Thomas Jefferson still survives." But Jefferson too had passed away a few hours earlier on that day.

INDEX